RETURN TO SWEETHEART LAKE

Also available by Evelyn Jordan

Most Sunny (writing as Jamie Pope)

One Warm Winter (writing as Jamie Pope)

TROPICAL DESTINY SERIES

(writing as Jamie Pope)

Tempted at Twilight

Mine at Midnight

Kissed by Christmas

Surrender at Sunset

THE DRAYSONS: SPRINKLED WITH LOVE SERIES

(writing as Jamie Pope)

Love and a Latte

REDEMPTION SERIES

(writing as Jamie Pope)

Stay Until Dawn

Stay for Me

HOPE & LOVE SERIES

(writing as Jamie Pope)

Love Blooms

Hope Blooms

RETURN TO SWEETHEART LAKE

A Novel

EVELYN JORDAN

This is a work of fiction. All of the names, characters, organizations, places and events portrayed in this novel are either products of the author's imagination or are used fictitiously. Any resemblance to real or actual events, locales, or persons, living or dead, is entirely coincidental.

Published in the United States by Alcove Press, an imprint of The Quick Brown Fox & Company LLC.

Alcove Press and its logo are trademarks of The Quick Brown Fox & Company LLC.

Library of Congress Catalog-in-Publication data available upon request.

ISBN (hardcover): 978-1-64385-782-4
ISBN (ebook): 978-1-64385-783-1

Cover design by Lynn Andreozzi

Printed in the United States.

www.alcovepress.com

Alcove Press
34 West 27th St., 10th Floor
New York, NY 10001

First Edition: November 2021

10 9 8 7 6 5 4 3 2 1

CHAPTER ONE

My weaknesses have always been food and men—in that order.—Dolly Parton

"Calm your hormones."

If Romey Michaels had to pick a place to spend a Saturday afternoon, a crowded airport would not be it. She would rather spend it shopping for funky new never-going-to-be-able-to-walk-in-these shoes, with her nose buried in a book, or in the arms of a nearly naked, hard-bodied man.

Sigh . . .

Okay, so maybe that last one wasn't attainable. But she would rather be any place in the world other than Cargill International Airport.

Like trying on bathing suits after pigging out on ice cream.

Or getting a bikini wax.

Even a root canal seemed like a rocking good time compared to this.

"What are you mumbling about over there?"

"Who me?" Romey asked, startled by the question. "Um . . . nothing."

Busted.

"Uh-huh."

Romey looked over to see her father's girlfriend, Angela, studying her talon-like fire-engine-red nails and Romey at the same time. Angela, along with most of the rest of town, had come back to welcome HIM home in what Romey secretly liked to think of as the Second Coming.

Everybody was there. The *entire* population of Sweetheart Lake, Virginia, with roses and balloons in hand, wearing T-shirts with HIS face plastered all over them.

"I'm not exactly sure why you're here, honey." Angela, finished with inspecting her nails, turned her dark-eyelinered eyes on Romey. "You're no big fan of Gray. You two fought like cats and dogs when you were kids. Hell, long after that."

They'd done more than fight. And that was the problem.

"You know exactly why I'm here." Romey folded her arms under her chest and stared at the terminal HE was supposed to be coming through. "Because if I didn't come, the townsfolk would have branded me with a scarlet B."

"B?"

"Yes. B for bitch. And then the rumors would start. 'There goes Romey Michaels.' " She put on her best Virginian accent. " 'Couldn't even welcome back our hometown hero. I hear she drowns kittens in bleach water for fun. I hear she practices black magic in her bedroom. You know she's got that circus people blood in her? And she's from New Orleans. It's probably why she got herself in that *situation*.' "

Angela raised both her perfectly groomed brows and shook her head. "You should talk to somebody about your problems, honey. And I don't mean me. Like a professional who knows how to deal with people who have full conversations with themselves."

"Oh, I fully realize I am out of my damn mind." Romey nodded, causing her curls to bounce. "The truth is, I'm here pretending to welcome Gray home because I don't want to give him the satisfaction of thinking I cared enough not to."

"What?"

"And," Romey continued, trying to tamp down the nearly hysterical anxiety she was feeling, "he did just spend almost two years in developing nations giving medical treatment to the needy. I really would be a bitch if I couldn't give him an 'attaboy' for that."

And she was here because he was Charlie's best friend.

Charlie would want her to be here. No matter what had happened at the end.

"He really is a good boy, Ramona," Angela said in her thick Long Island accent. "He's a mother's dream."

And a little girl's fantasy.

And the cause of so many of Romey's problems.

Grayson Norton was the definition of golden boy. He had the looks of a Greek god, the body of a fitness model, and a smile that could melt the panties off any woman between the ages of eighteen and eighty-eight. Plus, he was rich.

And his father had been the most beloved mayor in Sweetheart Lake's history.

And he was a doctor.

Dr. Perfect.

He was the boy who'd saved a dog from being hit by a car by throwing himself in front of it. And the teenager who used to volunteer his time reading to the sickly at the hospital. He even helped old ladies cross the street. There was little fault one could find in Gray Norton.

She was surprised they hadn't declared him a saint or erected a statue of him yet. There was already a parade planned in his honor on Founder's Day.

He would hate that.

Romey smiled at his future discomfort.

"You look evil when you smile like that."

Romey blinked at Angela. "Really? Should I stroke my imaginary beard for effect?"

"You're out of your mind today," Angela muttered.

"I am," Romey agreed as she wrapped both her arms around the woman who had practically raised her when her mother had flitted in and out of her life. "But you love me anyway."

She leaned against Angela's shoulder while the older woman smoothed a comforting hand down her back. Romey hated that she needed soothing.

Grayson was coming home after almost two years away. *So what?*

Not a so what, she argued with herself. *A big what. A big, huge what.*

The crowd around them suddenly hushed, and then like an explosion, a chorus of cheers erupted.

Their boy was home.

Romey couldn't help it; her eyes went to him as he walked through the gate carrying a ratty canvas bag. He was as beautiful as he had always been. Maybe a little leaner, a little shaggier. His dark hair was much longer than usual, his face covered with two weeks' worth of growth.

He looked the same and yet totally different.

She had expected to see him smile and nod graciously as he walked through the crowd of excited citizens who had come out just for him.

"Damn it." Her heart lodged itself in her throat, pounding a thousand times a second. She wasn't supposed to be this affected by his arrival. She wasn't supposed to give a damn.

He'd turned his back on her. On Charlie.

But . . .

Grayson was finally home.

And he was coming right toward her.

* * *

There's no place like home.

As Grayson Norton walked through security at the tiny airport that had been named after his maternal grandfather, he wondered who had come up with that saying. Was it even true? It must be.

Sweetheart Lake was like no place he had ever been, and he had now been around the world.

And yet home kept calling him.

He could hear them, the people who'd watched him grow up, waiting for him to make an appearance. He knew by the brief conversation he'd had with his father that the whole town would be here. Waiting for him to return home like he was some damn hero. Nowhere else would he get this kind of greeting. Nowhere else could he walk into a room and feel the pride and expectations of hundreds of people on his shoulders.

He had liked that, being anonymous. He had liked operating in the world without anyone giving a damn about who his family was. Or how much money they had. The only thing that had mattered was what he could do, not who he was from.

There was a dread inside him. It wasn't the feeling he'd expected to have when he landed and saw the familiar sights of his hometown. He had wanted to be here. He had spent so many months in that dark, quiet place desperately wanting to be back home.

But now that he was here, the overwhelming feeling of having to step back into his old self was choking him.

It was almost enough to make him stop walking. To make him turn around and return to El Salvador or wherever the humanitarian organization would send him next.

But he was done running.

He was no hero doctor like they thought he was. He didn't travel to the poorest parts of the world just to do good.

He did it to get away.

Away from this town and its expectations.

Away from his failings.

He opened the double doors to see them, the town, standing there.

A cheer erupted. Their noise hurt his ears. The sight of their smiling faces hurt his eyes.

They all looked so happy to see him.

It made him feel sick.

His face was on their T-shirts.

His father was the first to reach him. His arms extended. His eyes filled with emotion. "Welcome home, son."

The older man embraced him tightly.

Gray barely felt it.

Why the big show, Dad? It's not an election year.

Carey Norton pulled away, searching Gray's face. "How are you, son? I missed you."

Did you? "I'm fine."

"You sure?"

"Yes. Excuse me."

He left his father and headed deeper into his crowd of welcomers. Sandra Adair, the mother of his former fiancée, was standing there. She was smiling, and it surprised him. He had abruptly broken things off with her daughter about a month before he left. But she, like everybody else, thought he was perfect. How wrong she was.

"Gray." She hugged him. "I'm so glad you're back. We all are. Now you can start over."

He didn't miss her subtle message. It was hard to ignore the hope in her eyes. He was supposed to marry Gwen. The whole town thought it was destined to be. Their mothers had been childhood friends. They were from the same wealthy background. Had been educated at the best universities. Raised to be better than everyone else.

She should be furious with him for hurting her daughter, but no anger was there. She probably thought it was a phase. That once he got this do-gooder crap out of his system, he would return home and marry the woman he was supposed to.

She still had no idea that the vision of that perfect life wasn't one he shared. Not a clue that another woman had entered his every thought the entire time he was gone. Hell, it seemed she'd plagued his thoughts his whole damn life.

He gently extracted himself from Sandra and pushed himself deeper into the crowd, not bothering to look back at her or even care what she thought about his silence.

He was numb to the slaps on the back. Deaf to the *welcome home*s and *we missed you*s.

She's not here.

She shouldn't be here.

She was another person he knew he had hurt. And she would be the hardest to face.

And yet he still looked for her.

His heart was pounding so hard and fast that drawing in breath was becoming difficult.

But then he spotted her. One of those wild Michaels kids. Charlie's little sister.

Romey Michaels.

His heart slowed.

Unlike everybody else, she wore black over her curvy body instead of a T-shirt with his face on it. It was like her form of protest. He almost smiled.

It had been a long time since he'd done that.

It had been almost two years since he'd laid eyes on her.

Twenty-one months, to be exact, but he saw her face in his dreams. Same heart-shaped face. Same enormous brown eyes. Same glossy wild black hair.

She was the last person who should be welcoming him back. She knew him too well. Better than his father did. Even better than Charlie had. She knew he wasn't perfect and had made sure she'd told him so.

He finally stopped walking when he reached her.

There's no place like home.

She studied him with those big brown eyes of hers, her arms folded beneath her breasts. He did the same, eating up her image, his eyes unable to move from her face.

"Hello, Romey."

"Hello, Gray. Welcome home." She ran her eyes along his body, and he felt every hair on his skin rise. "You look like shit."

His heart rate returned to normal. This time he did smile. At her. It was the first time he had done so in ages. She was pissed at him and had every right to be.

It appeared he had some making up to do.

CHAPTER TWO

We must have a pie. Stress cannot exist in the presence of a pie.—David Mamet

Romey wasn't sure why her mama had picked Sweetheart Lake to settle down in. Her dancer-artist-traveler mama, who liked action and bright lights and exciting things. It was something Romey thought about as she drove up Main Street to the little pie shop she had opened a little over a year ago.

Sweetheart Lake was the opposite of the French Quarter where they had lived in a tiny crumbling apartment. They could see the Mardi Gras parades from their living room and on any given day be in the thick of tourists and party-goers filling the streets. They ate street food and beignets instead of going to the supermarket. They never went to school. Mama had taught them at home, claiming she could teach them more, teach them better. Romey and Charlie had run wild in the streets with their band of cousins whenever they wanted. A little pack of street urchins, her father had called them. It was crazy and unpredictable. It was a childhood unlike anything anyone else she knew had experienced. But all that had changed when they left for Sweetheart Lake.

They'd exchanged city living for life in a small town with the most beautiful lake at its center.

A place that had a Main Street lined with beautiful old brick buildings. A place so surrounded with flowers and greenery that whenever you stepped out of town, you felt like the world was devoid of color.

New Orleans had been colorful too, but in a different way. There had been a darker side to it. There was poverty and seediness in some parts that couldn't stay hidden to the people who lived there year-round. Her father had wanted to shield them from that.

And so they had come here, where he landed a full-time job working for the richest family in the state.

They moved into a house with a big backyard. Romey and Charlie finally started going to school.

They settled into a normal life. It wasn't the chaotic excitement of their hometown, but it had calmed them down. Romey's mother said it had stolen some of their soul.

She pulled up in front of her pie shop, the Crusty Petal. It was in an old historic building on an old historic street lined with ancient oak trees and wrought-iron streetlights. The front of her shop was decorated with planters filled with flowers. Right now, they were filled with petunias. In the fall she would replace them with mums. She already had an image of how the shop would look in the winter and at Christmastime: evergreen bushes with little pops of silver, white, and red.

Winter was just as beautiful as the summer in Sweetheart Lake, when the air grew icy and the lake froze over. It was one of those greeting-card wonderlands where they skated and had snowball fights.

Of course, the town wasn't perfect. It was just like any town in America, with the same societal problems as less pretty places.

It was filled with its share of nutty people and quirky folks. It also had a big separation between the rich and poor people. Life wasn't idyllic for everyone. It never had been.

She had lived in Chicago for a while, where she'd worked as a pastry chef in some of the best restaurants in the city. She was respected. She made good money. She was in a place where no one cared about who she had come from or what they had done. But it had never felt right being there. It hadn't felt like home.

Home was Sweetheart Lake.

And this morning, being at home meant seeing the police cruiser parked right in front of her shop.

The police chief had come for a visit.

Her stomach sank. Callahan McDaniels was the last person she wanted to see today.

"Well, there you are, girl!" Alice, her only employee, came bustling from behind the counter. "You won't believe what just happened to me. You know that guy I've been dating? The one with the great body? Well, of course you do, honey. I've just been going on and on about him for a month of Sundays. Well, he's inviting me on a little overnight trip to DC. You know he's got family there and his granddaddy was a senator. He wants to take me to the theater. You know how I love the theater. You know how I've been dying to see another show since a former beau took me to see *Hamilton* in New York."

Romey just took in Alice as she rambled on about her upcoming plans. Alice had beautiful white hair cut in a classic bob. She wore pearls around her neck, tailored dresses on her trim body, and high heels that seemed impossible to walk in. In all her days, Romey had never seen someone so classically beautiful or so man crazy.

And since Alice had discovered online dating, there had been more men in her life than had played on the Dallas Cowboys in the last five years.

Good lord, she wished she could be more like Alice.

"So, what you're telling me is that you need tomorrow off?"

"No ma'am! Not all of it, anyway. Just the last two hours or so. I've got an appointment for a facial that I just cannot miss."

"Okay," Romey said, not knowing why Alice even bothered to ask her at all. Alice never cashed her paychecks and worked harder on her nails than she did in the shop, but Romey enjoyed her and she classed up the pie shop a bit.

"And I'm going to need you to watch Beulah for me. I would ask my good-for-nothing son to do it, but he's good for nothing and you are the only one I trust with my baby."

Beulah the cat. Romey held in a sigh as she thought about her. She was toothless, about thirty years old, and weighed as much as a small boulder. "Don't bring any food. I've still got some left over from the last time."

"Such a sweet girl," Alice said as she walked away to answer the ringing phone. "You'll be rewarded in heaven, my dear. You'll be rewarded by the Lord."

Now that Alice was occupied, Romey focused on the tall, black-haired police chief sitting in the back of her shop. She could see only the back of him, but he sat straight up. Stiff as a board. She didn't have to see the front of him to know that his uniform would be perfectly pressed, his hair neatly combed, and his face expressionless.

He took no shit. As upright and moral as they came. Oh, how he had changed in the past twenty years. Criminal turned police chief. Who the hell would have guessed that?

"What's up, cousin?" She went to slide into the seat across from him and noticed that he had a curly-haired baby girl in his lap.

"Is that my baby?" She paused, her heart tugging a bit, the same way it always did when she looked at her unexpected gift. "Why do you have my kid? Hi, baby girl." She kissed both her chubby cheeks.

Lily grinned at her but made no move to leave Callahan's lap.

"I left her with my father." Romey paused and studied her cousin's expressionless face. "Is Daddy okay?"

"I stopped by," Callahan said. "Thought it'd be best if I took Lily for the day."

"Hi." Lily beamed up at her cousin.

"Hello, gorgeous girl." Callahan gently smiled back at her and stroked her cheek. The world thought of him as a tough, humorless bastard, and most of the time he was, but Callahan was sweet to Romey's baby. She knew he wanted to be a daddy, but after his divorce, he seemed in no rush to find someone new. "I want you to put her in day care." He looked back up at her; the smile had dropped from his face.

"What did Daddy do?" She was starting to get nervous. Her father hadn't been the same since Charlie died, but he loved his only grandbaby. He would never do anything to harm her.

"He didn't do anything. I just don't think he's the best caregiver for her."

She had noticed the change in her father's mood the last few weeks. Charlie's birthday had passed, and instead of them celebrating it as a family, the day had gone by with none of them mentioning it at all.

It was hard to deal with a loved one's death under any circumstances, but the way Charlie died had made it all the more difficult for them.

"He's all I got, Cally. It would hurt him if I suddenly took her away."

"She should go," was all he said.

She knew her cousin. He would never say anything against her father, who had taken Callahan in when he was a troubled teenager, after his former sister-in-law had abandoned the boy. Her father loved him like he was his own.

Cally knew something was up, and he wasn't telling her.

"Do you know how expensive some of these day care centers are? I can't afford to send her. Give me one good reason I should, and I'll think about."

"I'll pay," he said, as if that were reason enough.

"No." She shook her head. "Absolutely not. I can take care of her myself."

He raised one of his thick dark brows at her, as if to call her a liar. "You went to see Gray at the airport today?"

"Yes. I noticed you weren't there."

"He's a punk-ass coward. I'll be damned if I go stand in an airport with his face spread across my chest."

"Well, damn, Cally. Tell me how you really feel." He gave her an annoyed look that would have shut up most people, but he was her cousin. She wasn't afraid of him. "Why are you so mad at him? He's done nothing wrong to you."

"Nothing wrong?" Callahan's nostrils flared just a bit, one of the only signs he gave that he was angry. "You may be fooling this whole town, but you can't fool me. I know,

Romey. And even if he doesn't know, he didn't try to find out. Not a single goddamn call, not even a letter. Boy barely sent his own daddy a postcard to let him know he was alive. He threw you away, threw Charlie away, and the rest of us away like the pieces of trash the rest of the town thinks we are."

"That's not true anymore, Cally. It may have started out that way, but it's not as bad as when we were kids."

"If you think for one minute that I would get any respect if I wasn't the police chief, you're dead wrong. I'd just be that trashy boy who got locked up at fifteen and wasn't to be trusted around their daughters. And don't think that just because you're sweet and you own this pie shop people aren't whispering behind your back about who your baby's daddy is."

She knew they had whispered, knew they looked at Lily a little more closely than they should, trying to figure out who in the world her father was. Romey could have made up a lie. She could have said she'd been artificially inseminated. She could have said Lily was conceived by a foreign lover during a fling. But she said nothing at all, and in a small town, saying nothing seemed to stoke the gossip fires more than telling it all.

"You know of a good day care I can send her to?" she asked, changing the subject.

"Did you talk to him?"

"Yes, we had a lovely chat about the weather and whether or not the Electoral College should be abolished right there in the middle of the airport."

"If you weren't going to the airport to talk to him, why did you go?"

It was a good question. One she still had a hard time answering herself. She had needed to see him. She hadn't wanted to see him. She'd needed to. "He was Charlie's best friend."

"He's a hell of a lot more than that." Callahan got up, Lily still in his arms. "You talk to him, you hear?"

She stiffened at his order. "I don't have anything to say."

"You've got a hell of a lot to say. And if he don't act right, you call me. Maybe a nightstick to his pretty little knees will help change his perspective." He grabbed his hat off the table and walked away.

"Hey! You've still got my baby."

"She's mine for the day," he said without turning around. "We've got some things to do."

Yeah, she had some things to do too. Like figure out how she was going to get on with the rest of her life.

* * *

It might have been stupid to buy a house sight unseen, Gray thought as he looked up at the big green monstrosity that was now his. Well, that wasn't entirely true. He had seen this house nearly every day when he was a kid. He had even been inside before.

But he had forgotten how ugly it was.

Last updated in the seventies, the house was home to appliances in the marigold-yellow-and-avocado-green motif. It had carpets so thick that he felt like he was walking through grass when he was in his bare feet. Even the drapes had remained the same after all these years. They were dark green with little pops of yellow and orange and gold. The furniture was slightly newer. Probably made a few years after he was born. Whoever had owned the house before him had rented it out from time to time, praising its lake views and close-to-town location. But Sweetheart Lake had never been a vacationer's hot spot, and so the house had sat empty much more than it was ever full.

The outside of the house didn't look much better. The grass and weeds came up to his waist in some places. The balcony off the master bedroom looked dangerously lopsided. The front step was broken. The color of the house resembled the color of stomach bile. It had probably been a very stupid idea to buy a house that no one had been inside for the past five years.

But this house had to be his.

It was on the poor side of the lake, as some of the older locals called it. He had grown up on the other side—except that wasn't strictly true. He was born on the other side of the lake, but his formative years had been spent here, with the middle-class folks who actually kept the town running. His parents owned the biggest house in town. Although *house* wasn't the right word. *Mansion* didn't fit either. It was a lakeside estate. As a child he had been able to walk out his back door and be in the water in a few minutes. The estate came with a boat dock and a boat that his grandfather had liked to take him out in on the weekends when he was a child.

It was one of those houses that had two sweeping staircases. He remembered his mother descending them in one of her designer gowns whenever they had an event there. Events, not parties. Caviar and Cornish game hens. Trays and trays of champagne served by uniformed waiters to guests who had more money than most of the people in the state put together.

It was a life people dreamed of but he rejected, much preferring to eat hot dogs and frozen pizzas, sleep on the floor in his best friend's room, play card games that somehow turned into screaming matches. He preferred being with a family instead of servants who were there only because his parents had paid them to be.

"Beulah? Beulah?" he heard in the distance.

He turned around to look for the voice, but he didn't see anyone at first. His house was far away from those of most of his neighbors. He had an acre of land surrounding it, and the only other house he saw was the one behind him.

The place was slightly isolated.

The doctor they'd made him see after he left his last assignment had told him it would be good for him to surround himself with people, to interact with the world, but he didn't think he could take living in town. It was too much. They were all so damn nice to him. He wasn't sure what he had done to earn their favor except be born into the right family.

He could have stayed with his father in the big house or even in the guest house where he had lived after he came back from working in DC.

But he couldn't take staying with his father right now. They were practically strangers. His father had been gone his entire childhood, building his reputation as one of the most revered defense attorneys in the country.

"Beulah?" a woman's voice called again. "Where are you, you old fat thing? Come here right now, or I'll put your food out for the strays that live in the alley behind the shop."

Sure enough, Gray heard a rustling in the tall grass to his left where he had yet to mow. Out came the biggest, oldest, most funny-looking Maine coon cat he had ever seen. "Beulah, I presume?" he asked.

The cat looked up at him, almost nodding, as if confirming her identity.

"I think there might be somebody looking for you, girl." She lumbered toward him with the most unfeline movements he had ever seen in a cat and stopped right at his feet, then proceeded to rub her blobbish, gray-and-white calico self all over his legs.

"Well, damn, Gray. I knew the ladies liked you, but I didn't think it extended to the animal kingdom."

Romey Michaels with her lightly Creole-flavored accent was standing before him.

She was a sight for sore eyes in her tight blue jeans, white tank top, and bare feet.

He had been away from her for almost two years. He'd hoped that time and distance would give him some kind of clarity. That the space would make him more enlightened.

But it hadn't.

It was still there. That feeling that went buzzing all through his body, the feeling that made his skin hot and his brain mush. None of the intense attraction he felt for her had died.

It hadn't even diminished. It was louder now, more insistent. His body felt like a running car that needed to be driven.

He stooped down to pick up the heavy cat, who curled close to him and sank like putty in his arms. He rubbed his face against her soft fur. "I don't know about all women, but this girl seems to find me tolerable."

"I guess there's no accounting for taste, is there?" She stood stiffly, her arms crossed over her generous chest, her eyes taking him in with that little spark of heat that always drove him wild. She had beautiful high cheekbones and dark dramatic eyebrows that she'd inherited from her mother. There was something extraordinary about her, and she might have been an intimidating beauty if it weren't for that head of big bouncy ringlets that made her sexy and adorable all at the same time.

"You mad at me?" he asked. He stepped closer to her.

So many people had wanted to hug him yesterday, had tried to be close to him, but he didn't want the attention of any of them. He wanted hers, but she had left as soon as she saw him. It was like she was there just to make sure he was real, that it was really him who had come home after too much time away.

But the man she'd seen yesterday, the man who stood before her now, certainly wasn't the same man who'd left her.

That selfish asshole had died a year ago in Syria.

"Am I mad at you? Do birds fly? Do fish swim? Did you get stung on your naked ass when we were fooling around in the grass over there when I was eighteen?"

She remembered.

The connection he had to this house, the connection they had to this place. He wondered if they were going to bring it up right away or dance around it, ignore it like they had done for years. She was the last girl in the world who wanted to be with him but the only girl he had lost his mind for.

And now he was home to get her back.

* * *

Romey had never in her life harmed an animal, but right now she wanted to smack Alice's cat. Not only had it escaped the house, causing her to go on a trek through high, probably tick-infested grass toward the old green house, but it had caused her to run into Gray. He was the last person she wanted to see. And now the spoiled cat had the nerve to be sprawled in Gray's arms, looking like the feline version of Cleopatra, purring and looking up at Gray as if he were catnip and she had a serious craving.

She almost didn't blame the old girl for rubbing herself against him like a horny inmate after a long prison sentence. Beulah was Alice's cat. And Alice loved herself a good-looking man. And Gray was good-looking.

She hated to admit it. She'd kind of hoped he'd come back missing some teeth or some hair, or with a big fat pot-belly and a lazy eye. But no.

He wasn't the cute, clean-cut doctor who'd hightailed it out of here anymore. He was deeply tanned, bronzed, really, his straight, dark-brown hair overly long. His clothing was dark and ratty. His body was harder and leaner than it used to be. She didn't have to touch it to know that. She could see the muscles beneath his shirt, see the way his biceps bulged as he held the cat like a baby.

Part of her wished she were that cat, snuggled against his hard chest, getting petted and stroked. She also wished she had the cat's claws so she could scratch his eyes out afterward.

She was really pissed, she realized.

She wasn't supposed to care.

But it had been almost two damn years without a word. Without even a good-bye. He hadn't come to Charlie's funeral. For that, she didn't want to forgive him, but she could understand. Saying good-bye to her brother was the hardest thing she'd ever had to do.

It was Gray's silence that had killed her. As if she wasn't good enough for an explanation.

"I guess what you are saying is, 'Yes, Grayson, I'm madder than a wet hen at you.' " He put Beulah down and stepped closer to her, not stopping until he was right in front of her, his big hot hands reaching for her arms.

She wanted to step back, but she couldn't. It was like her feet had up and sprung roots. She'd always had a thing for his hands, especially the way he touched her. He'd never failed to make warmth spread through her core, never failed to get her out of her clothes.

But she was older now. Wiser.

Pissed off.

She still shouldn't feel the heat, the extreme attraction.

Callahan was right. He'd thrown her away. She was pissed at herself too, because she had allowed herself to be thrown away by letting their relationship go on in secret for so long.

"You back for good? Or are you going to disappear in the middle of the night again?" She peeled her gaze off him and focused on the monstrosity of a house behind him. Of all the pretty houses in town, he had to be at this one. On her side of the lake.

"I'm back." He slid his hands down her arms. "You look good, Romey. Better than when I left."

"I gained some weight." She thought about her baby. "I'm totally undesirable to some in these parts. You sure Gwen isn't more what you're looking for? She's Little Miss Perfect. Still single. Honors her parents. I heard she even started teaching that Sunday school class."

"I don't want to be with her. You know that."

"You don't? Well, maybe you'll change your mind later. She was always your standby girl. The one you kept hanging in the background just in case. Oh, wait. That was me, wasn't it?"

"Damn it, Romey," he growled.

"Damn it is right." She was feeling angry and sad. Her throat was starting to burn with all those tears she'd refused to shed over the last two years, but she was still so drawn to him. She still wanted to push her body against his and hold on tight. She had missed him. She hated herself for it, but she had missed him so damn much. "You've got this ugly-ass house on your hands now. I had heard someone had bought it. I thought it was a developer that was going to tear it down and put up something that was worth looking at. But you're the unlucky bastard that has to deal with it. Or maybe I'm wrong again. Maybe you're just the hired help to clean away the weeds."

"Romey," he warned, and she knew she was pushing him, but he needed to be pushed. To be poked and prodded and feel a tiny ounce of what she had felt for so long.

"That would be some poetic justice, wouldn't it? Mr. Perfect, Mr. Beloved. The town's son reduced to cleaning up somebody else's mess. You would actually know how it felt to be in the Michaels clan, like my daddy who spent years cleaning up after folks. Like the people your family didn't want your precious ass hanging out with."

"That's not true. They never stopped me from being with your family."

"No, that was you alone, wasn't it? You stopped being our friend because we weren't good enough for you. Charlie and his problem—"

"Enough!" he barked at her. She saw rage in his eyes, and she swallowed because she knew she had finally pushed him too far. He yanked her closer to him, not giving her a second to inhale before his mouth came down hard on hers. It was a painful, almost brutal kiss. Not just on his end but on hers too. It was like she hadn't eaten for weeks and he was the nourishment she couldn't get enough of. She grabbed on to him, digging her fingers into his hard back, pushing herself closer to him. It was like she wanted to be inside him, like she couldn't get enough of him. She knew it was the same way for him. His hand slid up her shirt. She could feel his erection digging into her thigh. It was always like this with them, maybe a little more intense now. But the connection, the heat, the need to be near each other even when they knew it was disastrous, was always there. And that's why they were in this mess in the first place.

"I'm sorry." He broke the frenzied kiss and slid his lips along her cheek. "I'm sorry, Romey. I'm so damn sorry." He took her mouth again. This time the kiss was slower, deeper, bone melting. It reminded her of the first time. It reminded her of why nobody else had ever come close to him in her heart.

It reminded her that she couldn't get sucked into him again. Especially not now. Especially when it wasn't just her heart on the line.

She broke the kiss and backed away, because she knew the temptation to reach out and touch him was too much. "We just can't do this, Gray."

"Why?" He looked at her mouth, the heat still in his eyes. "We're so good at it."

She wanted to nod, but she kept her head still. "There's something you should know. There's something I've got to tell you."

CHAPTER THREE

When life throws you lemons, make lemon meringue pie.—Unknown

"Romey!" She heard her name being called from across the field and regained all the sense that had fled from her mind. "Where are you?"

It was Angela. They were supposed to be making dinner together tonight. It was something they did together once a week. It had started after Charlie died. A small way to keep their family feeling like a family after such a heavy loss.

"I have to go." She started to turn away from him.

"Wait," he said, placing his hand on her arm. "You were going to tell me something."

"It was nothing," she lied. Now wasn't the right time. She wasn't sure why it wasn't the right time. It should be like ripping off a Band-Aid.

The quicker the better.

But she couldn't bring herself to tell him right now. He was messing her up her plans. She wasn't supposed to be seeing him twice today. Just a quick trip to the airport so he would realize that she didn't care enough to stay away. He sure as hell wasn't supposed to have bought the house right behind hers.

"It *wasn't* nothing."

"I hate you. That's what I was going to tell you. Are you happy now? You made me forget the whole damn reason I came out here." She looked around her. "I need to give Beulah her meds."

"She couldn't have gotten that far," Gray said, looking around him. "She doesn't look fast."

"Looks can be deceiving. I mean, you are a prime example of that."

"If you are looking for me to defend myself, I'm not." He walked into the high grass he hadn't cut yet.

"Why? You think you're too good to argue with me?"

"There's nothing I can say to defend myself." He disappeared for a moment, only to return with Beulah in his arms. He walked over to her, handing her the very naughty cat. "When can I see you again?"

The question surprised her.

"Why do you want to see me, Gray? We aren't just going to pick up where we left off. I'm not going to be the one who you screw around with when you're bored. I respect myself too much for that shit."

"Romey . . ."

"You can't deny it. Can you?"

"It was never like that." He shook his head.

"Save your lame excuses for someone who gives a damn. I gave my last one away two years ago."

She turned around and walked back toward the home she shared with her father, holding the extremely heavy cat in her arms.

He would be near her. All the time. Not halfway across the world. No cities separating them. There wasn't even the lake between them anymore. He now lived right behind her. He had moved into her mind long ago, and he had no right to move into her neighborhood.

Screw him.

By the time she got back to the house, she was completely breathless, and the twenty-five-pound cat she was carrying had little to do with it.

He was the only one who could stir up so much inside her. She hated that he had that kind of power over her.

"Oh, there you are. I was wondering where you wandered off to."

"This cat . . ." was all she offered.

Angela had been in her life for so long, but she didn't know about her and Gray. She only knew what they had projected to the world. That to Gray she was just Charlie's little sister. She felt bad for keeping it from her, but she also felt strongly about not telling anyone who the father of her child was until the father himself knew.

"Did your father leave the sliding door open again?" She shook her head. "He's been so spacey lately."

"Since Charlie's birthday." She thought about her baby, whom Callahan still had with him. "You think it's anything we need to worry about?"

"I don't know." Angela shook her head. "He's gone through a lot of changes these past couple of years. Losing Charlie was hard enough for him, but I think retiring from the school really messed with his head. He's not used to being still. I think he's adjusting."

"Okay," Romey said, willing to put the issue to the back of her mind for the moment. "I guess Miss Beulah here wanted to do a little exploring. I wouldn't mind so much, because lord knows, she needs some exercise. But she needs to get her meds. Alice would have three strokes and two heart attacks if something happened to her cat."

"Alice needs a good knock on her ass. That cat is more yours than hers at this point. She dumps her over here every five minutes. What kind of owner is that?"

"If we are making a list of people to knock on their asses, Alice wouldn't be at the top of mine." She set Beulah down and went about the process of giving the cat her evening medicine.

"She drives me crazy," Angela said. "I worked in New York City. Women from New York are some of the most demanding, exacting clients in the world. But none of them compare to a divorced former debutante. You know she had the nerve to take out a ruler and measure the length to see if it was the same on both sides?"

"Damn." Romey blinked. "Well, was it?"

"Of course it was! I've been doing hair for twenty years. I know what I'm doing."

"Well, that's why she won't go to anyone else in town. You should have messed up her hair. Gave her a mullet. Or a reverse mohawk. Something that will make her wear a hat for six months straight."

"I could never do that. A mullet?" She shuddered. "Not even to my worst enemy."

"I've got a soft spot for Alice and she's good for business. She doesn't cash her paychecks and makes all her friends buy pies from me. So I'll take care of her cat if it helps bring people in."

"You make the best pies in the entire state. They would come to your shop regardless."

"Maybe, but she gets them in the door the first time, and I hook them with all the sugar and fat."

"That reminds me. Can you put aside a strawberry cream pie for me tomorrow? I'll come get it in the afternoon. We're having a little party at the shop the day after tomorrow. It's Sissy's birthday."

"I'll make you a fresh one the day of the party."

"But you only make strawberry cream pies on Tuesdays. Wednesday is your cherry-almond mousse pie day."

"Yes, thank you for knowing my pie-of-the-day menu as well as I do. But it's no trouble. I know the boss. She's kind of a bitch, but she lets me do what I want."

"You're a sweet girl, Romey." Angela gave her a quick squeeze and a kiss on her cheek. "Even if you don't want anyone to know it."

Angela had been there for her more than her mother these past fifteen years. A steady and loving figure in her life when she needed one the most. Romey wasn't necessarily on bad terms with her mother. She had learned long ago not to expect her to act like a mother or be there when it really mattered.

Luna Michaels wasn't one of those people who were happy staying still. She was from a family of circus folk, the ones who traveled from town to town putting on a show for whoever would come out to watch. They were misfits and freaks to the world, but mostly just misunderstood. Most of them didn't know how to live normal lives. It was in their blood. But Luna had tried to be normal. For a little while, at least. When she was nineteen, she had fallen in love with Romey's father, Cyrus. They were married five days after they met in New Orleans, where he was working as a barback.

They had made their home there for a while. The city was exciting enough to keep her busy. She could perform in different bars and clubs around town. There were enough creative people there to stimulate her mind. Enough culture to keep her enriched. But once the children came along, the romance of their bohemian life wore thin on her husband. He told her he wanted to move, to settle down, to give his kids a normal life.

And that's why they had ended up here. Her mother said her family's circus had performed in this town. It had left an impact on her. There must have been hundreds of pretty towns her mother had been to, but this one spoke to her.

This was the place she also got tired of, and when Romey was twelve, she took off. The first time, it was for three months; the next time, it was a year. The last time . . . it didn't matter how long. Her father hadn't let her come back. He said they weren't a rest stop on her way to her next adventure.

The last time Romey had spoken to her mother, she had been in Paris. She'd finally found a man who could afford to take her there. She promised Romey she would come see her baby one day soon. But Romey wasn't counting on it. There were so few people she could count on. Angela was one of them.

"There's your mama." Callahan walked into the kitchen at that moment with her daughter in his arms. Callahan was the other person she could count on. He looked out for her when she didn't need to be looked after. He had done so much for Charlie when he came home. Even when Charlie's sickness made it impossible for him to be around.

He looked so natural with a baby. He should be a father now. He wanted to break the cycle of their family. He wanted to give a child a home with two parents who lived in one place and didn't run across the country on a whim. But fatherhood hadn't happened for him, and his marriage had ended in a divorce.

She wanted him to start dating again, but she knew better than to bring it up. Cally did what he wanted when he wanted.

"How's my baby today?" She reached for daughter and kissed her chubby face a half dozen times. "Mama missed you. Were you a good girl for Uncle Cally?" She buried her nose in her baby's curls and inhaled. Sometimes she hated Gray so much, but he had given her this baby. She couldn't hate him for that.

"She was perfect. Everyone at the station requested that I bring her in every day. They say I'm much more pleasant when the baby is around, but that's a lie. I'm pleasant all the time."

Romey frowned at him. "Cally, I've known you my whole damn life, and I would never call you pleasant. I would say you are always either pissed off or less pissed off."

"I'm a goddamn ray of sunshine," he said without a hint of a smile and walked over to the refrigerator to take out a beer that was kept there just for him. "What's for dinner?"

"Your father asked for spaghetti," Angela said. "I'm going to make my famous meat sauce, and Romey's on salad and garlic bread duty."

"Where is Uncle Cyrus?" Callahan asked.

"Last time I saw him, he was wandering around the house looking for his wallet."

Callahan made a small noise but said nothing more.

Romey put her daughter in her high chair and started on her part of the dinner while Angela worked on hers.

Callahan sat at the table, entertaining Lily. There was a comfortable silence that came with being with your family.

It was what she needed right now, after her run-in with Gray.

"Has anyone seen my wallet?" Her father walked into the kitchen. He had been a groundskeeper for years at Gray's family home before he left to take a job as the head custodian at the high school. Even though he worked with his hands, he was always well kept. His face clean-shaven. His hair neatly trimmed. But now . . . She hadn't noticed that the father she knew, the steady parent in her life, had been slipping away little by little. But Callahan had brought it to her attention today. Maybe she had noticed. Maybe she just didn't want to admit it to herself.

He'd stopped tucking in his shirts. Stopped going to the barber every week. Most days he barely moved from his recliner.

"You mean the wallet that is sitting here on the table in the fruit bowl?" Callahan said, without looking away from Lily.

"I looked there! More than once." He picked up his wallet and shoved it in his pocket. "Why are you back here?" he asked Callahan.

"What do you mean, why is he back here?" Angela asked, turning away from the stove. "You know we all have dinner together tonight."

"Callahan thinks I can't take care of my own grandchild. I raised him. He would have been in prison if it weren't for me, and he has the nerve to take the baby away from me today."

Angela looked at Callahan and back to Cyrus. She knew as well as Romey that Callahan didn't overreact. He wasn't prone to hysterics. He was the most level-headed person they knew. "Why would Callahan take Lily from you?"

"You didn't tell them?" He looked at Callahan.

"No, sir. I told Romey that I thought it was best that she stay with me for the day. Uncle Cy, you've raised enough kids. Maybe you should enjoy your retirement. It might be time for Lily to go to day care."

"I just went outside for a moment, Callahan," her father said, with an edge to his voice. "She would have been fine. You overreacted."

"The back door was wide open. The pot of water you were heating had boiled over. Lily was on the floor in the kitchen. Anything could have happened."

Romey looked at her father and then back at Callahan. He hadn't given details this morning, careful to not air family business in public, but now that she knew why he had taken her, that little hard pit of anxiety in her stomach grew.

Callahan had been there at the right time. What if he hadn't?

"Daddy . . ." Romey started, not knowing how to continue. "You seem tired lately. I know you were only helping me because I was in a bind. But I can afford to send Lily to day care now."

"You don't trust me?" her father asked her, and she found his question painful.

"I do. But Lily's almost one, and she's moving around and getting into stuff. It might be good for someone else to watch her."

There was pain in his eyes, a quick flash of it before it morphed into anger. "I never thought I would live to see the day my kids would turn against me."

He walked out of the room then, and the tense silence hung thick in the air for a long moment.

"You did the right thing, Callahan," Angela said, giving his shoulder a squeeze. "I'm going to go talk to him. Maybe I can be here more."

She left them alone, and Romey sank into the chair across from Callahan.

"Well, shit," she said. "That was awful."

"It had to be done. You shouldn't feel bad."

"Then why do I feel like the devil incarnate? I know there's some people in town that think we've got devil's blood in us because we were born in New Orleans and our mamas were circus folk, but I didn't believe it until this very moment. Maybe I do need to start going to church like the ladies who come into my shop suggest."

"Those old bags are full of shit. Can't stand fake religious folk. One of the deacons down at First Baptist was popped three times in DC for solicitation. Next time his wife comes in, ask her if her husband has been to DC lately, and that will shut her the hell up."

"Damn, Cally. You were holding out on the good gossip."

"People in these kind of nice small towns like to think they're better than everybody, but they've all got their secrets. Don't ever let them make you feel bad. They've all got something they don't want anyone to know about."

His words hit her particularly hard. She knew all about secrets. She had too many of her own.

"What are we going to do about Daddy?"

"Nothing." He shook his head. "His feelings hurt now, but it wouldn't compare to the guilt he would feel if something happened to Lily."

"His son is gone. How can I take away his only grandchild without feeling like a monster?"

"I'm tired of tiptoeing around the Charlie issue with him. He never wanted to admit Charlie had an issue when he was alive, and now that he's dead, he's got us pretending like there wasn't one either."

"What good will it do to make him face facts? Charlie will still be dead."

"Yeah. He will be, but us acting like Charlie just died of a heart problem is a lie. The way he died isn't shameful. It happens to millions of Americans who go to their doctors seeking treatment and come out with a bottleful of pills stronger than heroin. The lying is the shameful part."

Romey shut her eyes for a moment and rubbed her temples. This had been a day. The mother of all days. She wished she could go to sleep and that when she woke up again, everything would be fine. No heartache over the brother she'd lost. No worry about her father. No anger over Gray.

She had tried to remain numb for the last couple of years. For survival. But with Gray back, numbness was no longer an option.

"Have I thanked you, Cally?" she asked him.

"You don't have to. Lily is my family."

"I'm not thanking you for that. I'm thanking you for everything. For being the sane one. Every family needs one person who has their shit together, and you are it."

"Me having a job with benefits and a pension makes me the sane one?"

"Cally, we are from circus people. That's years of inherited weirdness, and here you are—normal. They put you in charge. They let you carry a gun. And you managed not to shoot any unarmed people. I'm impressed."

"Normal, huh?" He gifted her with a little grin. "Can't believe I worked this damn hard just to be normal."

"You know my mama cried when I told her you were going into the police academy. Almost as hard as she cried when she found out that Charlie was joining the Marines. Said you both were going to become hired killers for the state."

Cally rolled his eyes, unable to hide his exasperation. "Your mama is the most dramatic woman on the planet. She wasn't thrilled when I went to college either."

"She doesn't believe in the idea of paying for an education. My years of student loan debt agree with her."

"But you paid it off. You opened your own business. The people in town like you. You're doing all right for yourself."

"They would like me more if I weren't an unwed mother whose child's father is a mystery."

"Guess it won't be a mystery much longer."

She looked at her cousin for a long moment. "Nobody knows except for you. You knew the moment I told you I was pregnant. How did you know who the father was?"

"It was the way he looked at you. It started when you were sixteen and hasn't stopped."

"We didn't think anyone knew," she said quietly.

"Anyone paying attention would have known."

"But no one here paid attention, and they never would have suspected that Gray would be interested in me that way. He was supposed to marry Gwen, or if not her, someone like her."

"Never would have worked out."

"I want you to know that I was never with Gray when he was with anyone else. I would never do that."

"I know. But even if you were, it's none of my business."

"My business will soon be out there. This town is going to be shook."

"Maybe not. I heard that when he got off the plane this morning, he came right to you. Barely said hello to anyone else and disappeared right after you left. Gray definitely wasn't trying to hide who he was there to see."

She sat up a little straighter. "Who told you that?"

"Does it matter?" He shrugged. "Word travels fast in this town. Especially when its favorite son is involved."

"I doubt anyone read into it. They knew Gray and Charlie were friends. They probably thought he was committing an act of kindness for acknowledging me." She glanced at her daughter, who very much looked like her, but there was some of Gray there too. His perfect nose. The dimple in his left cheek. "He hated the reception he got. I'm sure him leaving so soon had nothing to do with me. The last thing I would want to do after I got off a long flight from another continent is to be social with a hundred people."

"That would be my worst nightmare."

"He looks exhausted, Cally." She thought back to the new image of him that was burned into her mind. He was barely recognizable as the man she had fallen for so many years ago. "He's thinner too. Wherever he was was no luxury vacation. I expected him to go home to the other side of the lake and let his father's servants take care of him. Color me shocked when I discovered him standing by a push mower at the old green house back there."

"What?" Cally shook his head, but she knew he'd heard her.

"He bought the green house." She motioned toward the yard that separated them. "I learned this about a half hour ago when I went looking for Beulah."

"You didn't tell him?"

"No. He took me by surprise. I couldn't think straight, so I called him names, let him kiss the sense out of me, and told him I hated him before I ran back here with the cat." She ran her fingers through her curls, needing to do something with her hands as her anxiety rose a little higher.

"Have you thought about how you're going to tell him?"

"No. Part of me doesn't want to."

"You have to tell him," he said firmly. "Lily has the right to know who her father is. I never knew who my father was. My mother refused to tell me, and it made me resent her."

"I'm going to tell him, but I'm scared. What if he calls me a liar? Or accuses me of trying to trap him? What if he doesn't want anything to do with her at all?"

"Then I'll break his kneecaps."

"Could we set his ugly house on fire?"

He nodded. "And I'll bring the marshmallows to toast while we watch it burn."

"I love you, Cally."

"Don't go getting mushy on me. I don't like it." He stood up. "Let's go get some pizza. I don't think anyone feels like cooking tonight."

CHAPTER FOUR

Life is uncertain. Eat dessert first.—Ernestine Ulmer

Gray glanced at his watch for the third time that evening.

Another half hour.

He wondered if it had been smart to stay up all night instead of getting a few hours of sleep before his long journey home. But he wanted to be awake when the call came from his driver. He was leaving after too many months. He never should have been here in the first place. But when he'd seen the pictures of devastation coming out of this place, he'd known he had to come.

He'd had to do it in secret. There was a civil war here, too complicated and multisided for him to begin to comprehend. Americans were not welcome. So much so that the organization he was working for had refused to send him here. At first.

But then paperwork had been changed. Identification had been altered. His identity as a U.S. citizen had been stripped away. While he was here, he was Canadian. A doctor from Montreal. He'd used his twelve years of private lessons and

French classes that his mother had made him take to help him in his lie.

So far, none of the others he had worked with on this assignment had questioned him. They were from all around the world. New Zealand. Japan. Argentina. Not that he was worried that they would out him. They were all here for the same reason: to serve.

Gray had gotten slightly nervous only when one of the doctor's girlfriends came to visit. She was from America, and her blonde hair, bright-blue eyes, and wholesome midwestern air made her look like a walking advertisement for their country. She worked for another humanitarian agency. Her father was an executive for a telecom company in Chicago. She, like him, had been brought up with everything. And she, like him, grappled with the guilt of knowing that things had been handed to her when so many people died for basic rights. Like clean water and medical care.

He suspected that Rachel had guessed his secret. They had gone to the same university—a few years apart, but he knew things only a person who had gone there could know. She never said anything, only asking him to have a couple of hot dogs and beers in her honor when he returned home.

Her presence had made him miss being home.

He was anxious about returning. That's why he didn't bother to go to bed. He knew sleep wouldn't come.

He had disappeared.

He'd boarded an overnight flight to Europe out of DC without a word to anyone, filling his father in a few days later because he didn't want anyone to search for him. He'd also sent a letter to his practice, resigning his position as a physician there.

But there hadn't been a word to anyone else.

Nothing to Romey, whom he had broken his engagement for. Nothing to Callahan, whom he had become much closer to over the years.

And it was all because he couldn't face them after what had happened with him and Charlie.

He had never considered himself violent. But that night he had been driven to it. He would never forget the image of the blood running down his best friend's face. Or the look of betrayal when he broke the promise he had made to him so many years ago.

His phone rang. He answered quickly so as not to disturb his housemates. A man with a deep voice told him he was there to pick him up.

Gray scooped up his bag and slung it over his shoulders. In forty-eight hours he would be home. In forty-eight hours he would have to face the mistakes he had made and the people he had hurt most.

He walked outside. It was dark. No light but the glow from the moon. He saw a black truck first and then some sort of dark-colored sedan. He paused for a moment, confused. Only one car was supposed to be there for him. He walked closer, and that's when he saw the driver with his hands in the air. There was another man behind him with a gun, shoving it into the first man's back.

And then everything happened so quickly. Men came from seemingly nowhere. Their faces covered, their hands filled with guns.

"Where is the girl?" one of them asked him.

He said nothing.

Rachel . . .

He knew what was going to happen next. A girl from the States with wealthy parents was valuable to them.

The man who had addressed him stepped closer.

"Where is the girl?"

Gray shook his head, saying nothing.

He wouldn't be able to stop what was going to happen, but he sure as hell wouldn't contribute to it.

"You will learn." The man's weapon came out with a flash, the side of his gun slamming into Gray's face. Everything went black.

* * *

The sun streamed in from the sliding glass doors in Gray's bedroom the next morning. He sat up, knowing it would be impossible to get back to sleep. The sun was too bright. His mind was too full. The dreams about that time in his life didn't happen with the same frequency as they used to, but they were still there.

He stood up, staring outside at his personal view of the lake. It was oddly soothing. His childhood home was directly on the lake. Never once had he stopped to appreciate the views. When he was a kid, it had been just another ordinary sight to him. One he had taken for granted.

He opened the doors and stepped out on the deck, testing it to see if it could hold his weight before he stepped out further. He'd had an inspector come and check for structural issues. According to the report, this deck was fine. Overall, the house was in decent shape. There were a few big-ticket items that needed to be fixed by a contractor, but most of the work was cosmetic. He was going to do that work himself. That was his only plan for now. He had some more figuring out to do.

When his assignment ended in Central America, he had become officially unemployed. He needed to figure out what his next career move would be.

But more importantly, he needed to figure out what to do about Romey.

He had been just as surprised to see her as she had to see him yesterday. When he left, she'd been living in a little apartment downtown. She must have moved home. He wanted to ask why, but he knew he had no right to question her.

He had no idea of the kind of life she'd led since he'd been gone. Or how she had been coping with Charlie's death.

The three of them—her, Callahan, and him—had never openly discussed Charlie's struggles together. How he'd been changing into a nearly unrecognizable person. How he had become so difficult to be around that it was easier to avoid him.

He and Callahan had gone over once, only to be greeted with denials and anger. It was hard to help someone who didn't want to help himself. But Romey and Callahan had kept trying, while Gray had washed his hands of the situation. That was his biggest regret. Not the fight that had led to the end of their friendship but the fact that he had stopped being Charlie's friend long before it came to that.

He took in a deep breath, filling his lungs with the still-cool morning air. He was going to have to leave this house today. Leave his relative isolation and solitude and venture out into the town of people who were so very fond of him.

He'd never understood why they praised him as excellent when he was only mediocre. Every opportunity he had, everything he had become, was all because it had been given to him. He had never been the golden boy they made him out to be.

Just a boy.

He got dressed, not bothering to shave. Not bothering to even look at himself in the mirror as he brushed his teeth. He had promised his father he would come see him today.

He hadn't gone home with him like the man had requested, not wanting to stay in the big empty house that was the symbol of his old life. The therapist he'd seen after his release had told him that now was the time to make a fresh start. So he had come to the home he had purchased right after leaving the airport.

She had also told him he couldn't avoid his past.

Gray hopped into the used car he'd had delivered to his house before he came back to the States. There was a luxury car waiting for him at his parents' house, but he didn't want any part of the gift his mother had bestowed on him when he finished medical school. His mother, much more than his father, was prone to giving him lavish gifts to show him she was pleased with him.

She had been gone nearly three years now. She was his mother, and while part of him had loved her and still missed her, he couldn't say they had been close, or even that he'd known her at all. She was all about appearances. Her son was never supposed to be a doctor; instead, he would go into the family business and be some kind of executive at the oil company that had been in her family for over a hundred years.

Still, she ate up the fact that her friends were impressed with his chosen career path. The truth was, he couldn't just get by in medical school. He didn't have his family money or connections to get him through. If he made a mistake, someone could die. It was the first time he actually knew what he was capable of. For years he had been afraid that he wasn't smart and the world was hiding it from him.

After parking his car on a side street, he walked into city hall. He had been stopped a few times as he made his way to the mayor's office. People welcoming him home. Praising him for spending so much time overseas. He'd thanked them but felt no pleasure from these encounters.

He made his way upstairs to his father's office. When his father had first told him he was running for mayor, Gray had thought it odd. He was one of the most high-profile attorneys in the country and had spent all of Gray's childhood building his practice. It seemed strange to put it all aside to be the mayor of a small town.

"Well, look what the cat dragged in," an older woman said to him with a smile. "Come over here and give me a hug." Mrs. Jefferson, his father's secretary, had been with his father for years. She had run the local branch of his law office. Gray was positive that over the last thirty years his father had spent more time with Mrs. Jefferson than he ever had with his wife.

"Hello, Mrs. Jefferson." He hugged the older woman, feeling a rush of affection for her. "How are you?"

"I'm doing just fine. You, however, are skinny. Weren't they feeding you right wherever you were?"

"Why do you think I came back home? They don't have your macaroni and cheese down there. It was all I could think about these past few months."

"Are you dropping hints?" She grinned at him. "I guess I could make you a pan. Oh, and we have some leftover honey-baked ham from Sunday dinner. And some pineapple upside-down cake I could bring you."

"I want to tell you not to go out of your way for me, but just hearing you talk about food is making me want to cry."

She smiled brightly at him. "I'll drop it off at your house. I heard you were the one who bought that great big green monstrosity. I never thought it would sell. You know I live just a few streets over. I hope you got a good deal on it."

"I did." He nodded. "I'm planning to fix it up."

"And change the color, I hope. It's not that I'm opposed to a green house, but that color green . . ." She shook her head. "Have you considered sand? Or maybe a cheery yellow? I'm fond of blue houses myself. A good old-fashioned coat of white paint never did anyone any harm either."

He had forgotten how much the Mrs. Jefferson could talk. And boy was she good at it. "I haven't picked the color out yet, ma'am. I think I'll need to take a vote."

"Yes. Sounds like a plan." She nodded as if it were normal for people to take votes on what color they painted their house. But this was Sweetheart Lake, and everyone seemed to want to know everything about everybody. "I've got a grandson to lend you if you ever need help with anything. And I mean anything. Scrubbing toilets. Picking up dog mess. School is almost out, and that boy will not be laying on his behind playing video games all summer."

"Thank you, ma'am," he said, feeling amused. "I will let you know if I need him."

"Great! You don't even have to pay him. Just feed him. Do you know that boy ate a whole rotisserie chicken? As a snack! Bought it with his own money too. He walked to the market and got it himself. Have you ever heard of such a thing?" She stood up. "Carey," she yelled into the office behind her.

"For god's sakes, Emma Jean," he yelled back. "Use the phone if you need to call me."

"Why would I do that when this is faster? Your son is here."

"Well, send him in!"

"I am! You think I'm going to keep him out here all day? I'm going to lunch."

"You're leaving for lunch at nine thirty? Where are you eating? New York?"

"New Jersey, actually. I've been wanting to see that Atlantic City I've heard so much about."

"Well, bring me back something."

"I'm going to fix Gray some macaroni and cheese. The boy looks skinny."

"Bring back some of that!"

"I'll bring you back a salad. He's skinny. You aren't." She looked back at Gray and gave him a sweet smile. "Go on in, honey. He isn't doing anything in there."

Gray grinned and shook his head as he walked into his father's office. Carey Norton looked every inch a small-town southern mayor sitting behind his big mahogany desk. He was a large man. Tall, wide shouldered. He had one of those friendly faces that seemed inviting. Gray had looked more like his mother, but he got his dark hair and eyes from his father.

"That Emma Jean is something, isn't she?" his father asked him.

"I have always liked Mrs. Jefferson," he responded quietly.

"I told her she needs to retire, but she said I wouldn't know what the days of the week were without her, and she's kind of right." He smiled. "I'm surprised to see you here, son. I thought you would have come to the house to see me."

"It seemed weird to me to return to a lakeside estate after spending almost two years in emerging countries." He gave a half shrug. "The house always kind of felt like a museum."

"It's a completely ridiculous place to live. Always thought so."

Gray blinked for a moment, not sure he had heard his father correctly. "You don't like the house?"

"It's too damn much. My family had done pretty well for themselves, but we never had the kind of money your mother's family had. I was a young lawyer when we got married. The most I could have given her was a nice colonial with a two-car garage. That wouldn't do for your mother, the princess of Culpeper County. She told her father she wanted a place she could entertain. Next thing I know, he's handing me the keys to a massive house I couldn't afford to upkeep."

"I guess saying no wasn't an option."

"You've met your mother. How did saying no to her work out for you?"

"I don't think I ever did tell her no."

"Me either. It was best to let your mother do what she wanted. I knew when I married her that I wasn't getting one of those girls who only ever dreamed of being a housewife."

"A woman like that would have bored you," he said, understanding his father a little more than he'd realized.

He nodded. "I would love to sell the house, but we have four full-time people that have been working there for years. I can't in good conscience leave them without employment. Still, I've started to look at apartments in town."

"You could rent it out as a vacation property. I'm sure you would have interest. You could keep the staff on and generate income at the same time."

His father looked at him as if he were seeing him for the first time. "That's a good idea. I'm mad I didn't come up with it myself. I've been trying to think of ways to grow our community. The young people are going off to college, and they aren't coming back. New people aren't coming in. We need some new blood here."

"Really?" Again his father had surprised him. "I thought you were of the same mind-set as some of the older people here who want to keep things the exact way they were fifty years ago."

"People who don't want change are people who are afraid to grow. Communities like this one need new people and new ideas, or they grow stagnant and start to die. I refuse to let this place die."

"You sound like a politician."

"You think I'm bullshitting you? I don't want or need to impress you. You didn't even vote for me."

"To be fair, I didn't vote at all."

"It's your civic duty. You should have. Also, I'm your goddamn father. A little support would have been nice from my only son."

"Everyone likes you. You got over eighty percent of the vote. Why would my support matter either way?"

"It matters because I am your father and you are my son, and right now we are all we have left in this world."

He hadn't expected the conversation with his father to go like this. His father was gregarious, popular, and insanely intelligent, but the one thing Gray never would have described him as was fatherly.

"I don't know how to respond to that."

"Yes you do. You want to call me an asshole for not being around. You think I don't know anything about you because I was always so busy? It's why you hightailed it to the Michaels' house every chance you got. You wanted to feel like you belonged to an actual family. Before, I would have said it didn't matter that I worked all the time because you turned out fine, but when you ran to the other side of the world for twenty-one months, I started to think maybe you weren't as well adjusted as I thought."

And there it was . . .

He'd wondered how long it would take his father to question him about why he'd left.

"You think I ran away?"

"Hell yeah, I think you ran away. You broke off your engagement to a very lovely woman. Your best friend dies. You were unhappy with your job. You ran away thinking when you came back here, you would know yourself better."

He wanted to deny it, but he couldn't. There was no point. "Do you blame me?"

"Yes," he said bluntly. "Not for everything, but you should have gone to that funeral. You owed it to the Michaels family to be there. They did a lot for you."

"I know." He looked down at his hands. His father had rarely shown disappointment in him. He was thirty-three years old, and seeing his father that way made him shrivel up inside. It made him feel like he was five years old again and caught in a dumb lie. "I couldn't see him that way," he said, and barely recognized his voice. "I couldn't see Charlie dead."

"It was a closed casket. You wouldn't have had to."

He looked up, surprised by what he heard. "You went to the funeral?"

"What kind of question is that? Of course I went. Cyrus worked for our family for over ten years. You boys went to school together. He had you in his home every day. He treated you with kindness and showed you what it was to work hard for something. You and I might not be close, but you should know me better than that. Our families are intertwined. Of course I was there."

"Things got very complicated with Charlie at the end. I handled so many things wrong."

"I guess you handled them the only way you knew how. There's no book on what to do when your life falls apart." His father wiped his hand over his face. "Where exactly were you all of that time? I only got a few messages from you. And one of them was to tell me that I wouldn't be hearing from you for a while."

"Yemen. Syria. Then Central America after that. I helped set up hospitals."

"You were in Syria?" His father frowned. "That was incredibly dangerous."

"It was why I couldn't communicate with anyone for so long. I wasn't exactly supposed to be there," he said, not telling his father the full truth.

It was over. He was fine. No need to worry the man.

"I called the organization when I hadn't heard from you for a few months. All they would tell me was that you were alive and still on assignment."

Gray nodded. "They had to keep my assignment quiet for safety reasons." It was their secretiveness about his background that had kept him alive in the end.

"Have you gotten the chance to speak to Romey?" his father asked. "I saw her at the airport. She didn't stay too long."

"I hurt her," he admitted. "She doesn't want to speak to me right now."

"After what she's been through, I would imagine not. I'm surprised she didn't slap the taste out of your mouth as soon as she saw you."

"How has Romey been, Dad? She moved back in with her father. Is everything okay with her?"

"I think that's a question you need to ask her."

"She hates me, remember? I may deserve to get slapped, but I'm not really trying to get hit."

His father laughed softly. "She's Romey. She always seems to find a way to make things work. Callahan is there for her. He was made chief of police about a year after you left. He's very good at his job."

"She opened her pie shop?"

"Yes. Some unexpected things came up, but she got it opened. You really need to speak with her. It's not my place to tell you her business."

"Please, Dad. I'm not expecting you to know a lot. I need to know how her life is going."

"I can tell you about her pie shop. She calls it the Crusty Petal. It's a cute little place. She and her family did all the work themselves. That girl makes an incredible pie. I'm not even a pie guy, but she gave me a piece and I took one bite and I was hooked. The crust, son. You can't believe how damn good that crust is. I stop in every morning for breakfast for a slice of her home-fry pie. It's got potatoes and maple sausage and three kinds of cheese. I dream about it."

Gray laughed at his father's description. "That's a ringing endorsement if I ever heard one. Are people coming to her shop?"

"They are. She refuses to take my money, though. She's a good girl, but that's bad for business. She could easily be making hundreds of dollars off of me."

"She should charge you double. You're rich."

"She's sweet, Gray. You really need to have a conversation with her. It's important that you do. Don't waste any more time with her."

"I tried to speak to her yesterday. She told me she hates me."

"Hate is a strong word, but it sure as hell is better than her being indifferent. You are going to have to try harder."

He stared at his father for a moment, curious as to why he was pushing so hard for him to talk to Romey. Could he know how Gray felt about her? "I will."

"Good," his father said. "Let me know how it goes."

"Yes, sir." He got up this time, ready to leave.

"Gray?"

"Yes."

"I'm glad you're home."

"I'm glad to be home."

"Don't you ever disappear on me again."

CHAPTER FIVE

Food is like sex: When you abstain, even the worst stuff begins to look good.—Beth McCollister

"Romey, come over and look at this guy's profile."

Romey wanted to say no, to tell Alice that it was unprofessional for her to be out on her phone while she sat behind the register, but she didn't. The shop was empty. It was their quiet time of the day. The time when the breakfast crowd was already at work and before the afternoon crowd rushed in to pick up pies for the evening's dinner.

Despite the lack of customers now, Romey was generally happy with how things were going. She wasn't planning on making a profit this year. The business was new in town. It wasn't a regular bakery or coffee shop. She didn't have money for advertising or promotions. All she had was her skill and a dream.

People were coming in. Not in droves, but each week she was seeing more and more of them. She knew Gray's father had something to do with that. He sent pies as gifts.

For staff birthdays. As get-well presents. He bought them for dinner parties. He paid for them online and had someone from his office pick them up. He knew that if he came in person, she wouldn't take his money.

He had been so kind to her. Especially after Charlie died. She knew Gray had never been close to Carey. To either of his parents. But she had always found him to be a nice man, and if he'd had a problem with his son hanging out with kids whose mother "free schooled" them until they were in fourth and fifth grade, he never let on. Gray's mother, however, had barely been able to hide her distaste for her, Charlie, and especially Callahan. But even she never stopped Gray from spending days at a time at their house when they were kids.

She walked over to Alice and peeked at her phone. There was a guy in a tuxedo with a wide toothy smile staring back at her. "I haven't seen a man wearing a tux with tails in a long time, but he looks like he has a nice face."

"Read his profile."

" 'I'm a man who enjoys the finer things in life,' " she read aloud. " 'I take care of myself and you should too. I firmly believe that women shouldn't weigh over a hundred and fifty pounds. I like my women in heels and will gladly rub your feet after a long day. Prefers blondes but will date the right brunette. Please be shorter than five foot six. Message me and learn what it's like to be with a real man.' " She looked up at Alice. "Is he supposed to be attracting women with this profile? Because it seems to me this would repel them."

"What happened to men who wooed you? Who romanced you? Nowadays they put a list of wants into a little box and act like we are supposed to be flocking toward them. This one isn't even the worst of them."

"They get worse than that?"

"Romey, I can't believe you have never been on a dating app. You've got to join one. You're gorgeous. You would get so many matches."

"I can't, Alice. I've got a baby at home. And I'm not exactly looking for a relationship. I've been burned before. In fact, I'm going to get a tattoo that says 'men are trash' right in the middle of my forehead to scare away anyone who might hit on me."

"You don't have to be in a relationship. You could just meet a friend. You know, someone to take you out and tell you you're pretty." She wiggled her eyebrows. "Someone who can take care of your *needs*."

"There are things you can buy off the internet to take care of your *needs*, and they're a lot less trouble than a man."

"You really got burned, didn't you, sugar? I was that way for a little while after my divorce. It took me two years to get myself back together. You'll want to see someone again."

The little bell over her door sounded, alerting them to a customer. She looked up to see Gray Norton walk in the door. She had been hoping she didn't have to see him today. She was still all kinds of agitated from her unexpected run-in with him yesterday. She needed more time to think about how she was going to tell him about Lily. But she couldn't think when he was around her.

"What are you doing here?" she blurted out.

"Romey!" Alice scolded. "That's not how you greet a customer. Especially the mayor's son."

"I knew him long before he was the mayor's son. And it's my shop; I'll be rude to him if I want."

"It's okay, Mrs. Cooper. I've known Romey for over twenty years. She doesn't have to be nice to me. How's your family? I heard your youngest son moved to New York."

"Everyone is fine. Thank you for asking. And yes, my Bobby did move to New York. Brooklyn. He's one of those . . . what do you call them? Hipsters? Makes beer for fun."

"We all need a hobby," he said, smiling at her.

This was why people loved Gray. He was polite. He always remembered little details about people. He was welcoming. He was like his father in a lot of ways. He would hate to hear that.

It made Romey want to tell him.

He walked over to her display case and took a long look at everything she had to offer. She met him on the other side, watching him as he took in her goods.

"I'm here for pie." He looked up at her. "I heard it was very good. In fact, someone told me they dream about it at night." He pointed at one. "What is this? There's only one piece left."

"It's a bacon, egg, and cheese pie. It has smoked bacon from Glasson's farm as well as a cheddar-Gruyère cheese blend."

"And your famous buttery crust." He looked into her eyes. "I'll take a piece, please."

"Go sit down. I'll heat it up for you."

"Promise me you won't poison it."

"Last time I checked, spit wasn't poisonous."

"Romey!" Alice scolded. "You can't say things like that."

"I'm joking, Alice. We're neighbors. If I was going to mess with him, I would do something to his house like leave a flaming bag of dog mess on his steps."

Alice rolled her eyes and shook her head. "I guess I'll never understand this generation's humor."

He walked away and sat at the table in the back corner. He was the first one she had told about her dream to open this place. He had seen her shop only when it was an empty space, a former insurance broker's office. With the help of mostly her father and Callahan, they had transformed the sterile-looking space into a whimsical, sugar-scented dream. All of the tables and chairs were vintage—or just old, as her father had called them—and had been sanded and stripped and refinished in cream colors. Her display counter was gorgeous, a light mint green with curved glass. Callahan had found it and surprised her with it for her birthday. There were flowers on every table, delivered fresh every morning by the farmer who supplied her with her fruit.

She loved this little shop more than she loved anything in the world except Lily. And as she walked over to him with his pie, she wondered what he thought of it. She hated that she still even cared at all about his opinion, but her brain couldn't stop the thought.

"Here." She set the plate and fork down hard in front of him.

"Thank you." He nodded as he picked up his fork and started to eat. He took a huge bite and then moaned. She walked away then, back behind the counter.

She returned just as he was finishing his last bite. She placed another piece of pie and a bottle of cranberry juice in front of him. "This is my home-fry pie."

"My father told me about this one. Thank you." She watched him devour his second piece. He was eating like she had never seen him eat before. He was eating like he had been a man without food.

She couldn't get over how thin he was. She thought his face was a little more chiseled, but it was covered in facial hair that could be hiding its gauntness. She walked away again, this time cutting him a large slice of her apple-cherry pie. She set it in front of him, preparing to leave him alone to eat, but he grabbed her hand.

His touch felt familiar. The tingles invaded her hand. It was annoying to be so affected. "Sit with me, Ramona."

She should have flipped him off and walked away, but she sat. Her arms folder across her chest, as if that would protect her. "You're skinny," she said.

"Am I?" He looked right into her eyes again, knocking her even more off center.

"I don't like it."

"I'll work on that."

"Why are you skinny? Please tell me that you got some sort of intestine-eating parasite from drinking unclean water."

He gave her a little grin. "Yeah, something like that."

"You're eating like a starving man. Your mother would be appalled."

"She would."

"Did you eat last night? I expected you to go home with your father, but you didn't."

"No. That place isn't my home."

"But the big green ugly house is?"

"Yes."

"You didn't answer my question," she said, knowing she hadn't let him. "Did you eat last night?"

"I ate some overpriced trail mix and a bag of chips I bought at the airport."

"That's not food."

"I feel like it's a uniquely southern thing for women to care if a man has gotten enough to eat."

"I don't care if you had enough to eat. I was just asking. Go to the supermarket today, dummy."

"You couldn't pay me enough to walk into a supermarket in the middle of the day."

She knew why. He didn't have to explain. "People are happy that you're home, Gray."

"Are you?"

It was a fair question, one she didn't know the answer to. "If you're looking for me to throw you a parade, you'd better look elsewhere. I'd sooner run you over with my car."

"That's my girl," he said, smiling again.

She didn't want him to smile at her. He didn't smile at her the way he smiled at strangers. He smiled at her the way a man smiles at a woman he knows intimately. It was alluring and alienating at the same time. She got to her feet.

"Meet me at the counter when you're done. I'll wrap up something for you to take home."

She made herself busy behind the counter, boxing up all the leftover pieces of breakfast pies she had. She was aware of Alice, but she refused to look at her, fearing it would give away how out of sorts she was.

He walked up just as she finished, and she walked around the counter to hand him his bag.

"There's a piece of chocolate cream pie in there. Put it in the refrigerator until you're ready to eat it."

He nodded and took a bill out of his pocket.

"Don't you dare give me your money, Grayson Norton," she warned. "I will not have it."

He took the bag from her and set it on the counter before he surprised her by sweeping her into a hug. "Romey." He put his lips to her ear. "You're going to go out of business if you keep giving everything away for free." She felt his hand slide down her back and his fingers slide something into her back pocket. He kissed the side of her face. "Thank you."

He let her go, said good-bye to Alice, and then walked out of her shop. Romey stood there for a few moments, her heart beating too fast.

"I'm either having a hot flash or that man just turned up the heat in this place."

Romey looked at Alice, who was fanning herself.

"I don't know what's wrong with him," she said, trying to shake the experience off.

"You're what's wrong with him, girl. Romey! Gray Norton has a thing for you, and he certainly isn't trying to hide it."

He wasn't. And she didn't know how to feel about it.

* * *

Gray walked out of Romey's shop and around the corner to where he had parked his car. He smiled, shaking his head at the memory of the look on her face right after he released her from his hug. Her eyes were wide, her lips slightly parted. There was anger and confusion and familiarity all there at once. He had gone to the shop to talk to her. But he couldn't.

He was in awe of how she had transformed the place. He had been there at the beginning of the process as she painstakingly budgeted the opening. He had offered her money. A loan, he'd told her. A silent investment that he didn't want back. He had a trust fund that his mother had gifted him with when he turned twenty-five. It was all sitting there unused, the product of somebody's hard work, that hadn't come from him or his family.

She'd refused.

He'd known she would.

She would never take anything from him. Even now. She had refused his money today, even though it wasn't a gift. Her stubborn streak drove him crazy. But it also fascinated him.

"Gray?" He looked up at the sound of his name, not really feeling like making conversation. But when he saw who it was, he knew he couldn't brush her off.

"Gwen." The woman he had asked to marry. The woman his mother had wanted him to be with.

"Hello," she said softly. "I heard you were back in town."

"Did they announce it in the paper? Or maybe on the local news?"

She smiled at his dumb joke. "I believe a flyer was sent to everyone's house. There was going to be a parade, but I think your father put a stop to that."

He sighed. "It's unfortunate that all those people went out of their way to come to the airport. I'm sure they had better things to do."

"They were glad to see you come home. You mean a lot to everyone in this town."

"I wish there was the same turnout when Charlie came home." He shouldn't have said that to her. It wasn't her fault or doing. Charlie had signed up for the Marines when he was eighteen years old, after the prospects of a college football career had died and his father had no way of paying for him to go to college. He hadn't wanted to be burdened with loans for more schooling he didn't want to attend, so when the recruiter came to town and told him he would have a good career, with benefits, that he could be proud of, Charlie had jumped at the chance.

Eighteen. It seemed so young to sign up to be willing to die for your country over reasons that no one could fully comprehend. Gray had been sent off to the same prestigious college his grandfather had attended. He had gone to frat parties, gotten drunk, dated girls. He'd had the freedom to do what he wanted. Charlie never had that. And then an explosion almost killed him and robbed him of the good career with benefits he had been promised. It wasn't fair.

"I'm sorry about Charlie. You two were close."

"I shouldn't have brought it up. Being back here reminds me of him." He shook his head. "I should be asking you how you are. You look beautiful, by the way."

She was beautiful in the most classic way. He had never heard her raise her voice. A curse word had never slipped from her lips. She was always poised and perfect. They had been together for a year, and he had never seen her slip.

She would have been the perfect doctor's wife. A perfect addition to their family, his mother had told him. He liked Gwen, but he wasn't sure he had ever known her. And when she came into his life, Romey had pulled away from him.

He'd thought he could live with never sleeping with Romey again. But when he chose Gwen, he had started to realize it had never been about sex with him and Romey. He needed her friendship. Her thoughts. Her humor. Her honesty.

He needed *her*. And when Gwen had brought up asking Romey to make their wedding cake, he was sure he couldn't marry her.

"I've been well, Gray."

He studied her for a moment. She was tall and thin but shapely. Her clothing was stylish and immaculate. Her hair was cut into a simple but modern style. She was elegantly beautiful, but he had never felt a rush when he saw her smile. He'd never felt the driving need to be with her.

She deserved someone who needed to be with her.

"Please tell me you have found someone better than me to love you."

She let out a quiet gasp. He had surprised her with his words. "And here I thought we were just going to make awkward small talk when I saw you."

"You always had better manners than I did. How is your life now?"

"I am enjoying being single."

"I didn't know what I wanted out of life. I wasn't sure who I was or what I wanted from my career. I know some people think it a bullshit excuse when someone says 'it's me and not you.' But this time it really was me. I wouldn't have been a good husband for you."

"I'm not angry with you, Gray," she told him. "When you spent two years in some of the poorest countries on earth, I figured you were searching for something greater than yourself."

"I was."

"Did you find it?"

He shook his head. "I still don't know."

They were quiet for a moment. "I won't keep you, Gray. I just wanted to say hello."

"It was good seeing you again," he said.

"It was good seeing you too." She left then, and Gray felt guilty as he watched her go.

He hoped she would find someone to make her happy.

CHAPTER SIX

Sour, sweet, bitter, pungent—all must be tasted.
—Chinese proverb

"Listen to me, baby girl," Romey said to her daughter as she walked through her backyard and toward Gray's. "You're going to be meeting your daddy tonight."

Lily looked up at her with her huge round eyes, as if she were listening intently.

"I'm not sure how it's going to go. Your daddy doesn't know about you. We made you, and then he went away to another country. But now he's back. And he needs to know about you. I'm surprised no one told him yet. He's been home more than twenty-four hours now, and no one in this town can keep a secret."

Lily made a little noise as if she were agreeing with her.

"No one knows he's your daddy. They would never expect it. Not in a million years. Your daddy is from fancy people. The rich kind. Mama's side of the family is working class. Poor people. Usually rich and poor people don't mingle. But your daddy was friends with my brother and thought I was cute."

Lily let out some more indeterminate baby babble, which encouraged Romey to continue.

"And don't go getting excited about having a rich side of the family, because you aren't going to be spoiled. I'll let him get you a car when you're sixteen, but it won't be a new or fancy one. And college, he can pay for your college, but you will not grow up expecting the world to be handed to you. You are getting a job and working for your pocket money just like everyone else. Your mama worked in a fast-food place. Came home smelling so much like hamburger grease the neighborhood dogs used to follow me around."

She was fully aware that she was babbling to her baby, but she was nervous. It wasn't every day she told a man he was the father of her child.

It was evening now. The day was starting to get a little cooler. She stood outside Gray's front door, not lifting her hand to knock. She needed to get her nerves under control. She had tried for so long not to think about him, about them, about all the memories they had with this house.

They had been inside before. Dozens of times. Not once as invited guests, but they had never been caught. No one had ever seemed to live here long.

This was the house where she'd had her first drink. This was the house where Gray had kissed her for the first time. This was the house she'd lost her virginity in.

He'd bought it. There were so many nicer, newer houses in town, and yet he had bought this one.

Why did he buy it?

What the hell was he trying to do to her?

"I love you, Lily," she told her daughter. "So much. No matter what."

She finally raised her hand and knocked on the door. It was silent for a moment, but then she heard footsteps. And then there he was on the other side of the door. He smiled when he saw it was her, and then he noticed Lily.

"Hi," Lily said to her father.

"Hi," he said back. But his smile had dropped, and he looked at Romey, then back to Lily. "Romey Michaels. Did you make me a daddy?"

* * *

Gray looked at the little girl in Romey's arms. It was her daughter; there was no denying it. She had Romey's eyes, her cheeks, her curls. But there was some of him there too. Not a tremendous amount, but enough that he could recognize it.

He had a daughter.

Well, holy shit.

There was a little piece of himself staring up at him.

He took the baby from her and brought her close to him. She had tiny hands. Cute little chubby fingers, which he stared at in awe before he brought them to his lips to kiss.

"I'm a daddy," he said to himself.

"You're happy about this," Romey said, sounding shocked.

He was. His gut reaction was happiness.

"We have a baby," he said. "What's her name?"

"Lily."

"Hi, Lily." He smiled at his daughter, and she smiled back. "I'm your daddy."

"Hi," she said again, smiling at him. She had two little perfect teeth in the front of her mouth.

"She's beautiful, Romey."

"You aren't going to question me? Or ask for a DNA test?" She seemed horrified.

He frowned at her. "Why would I do that?"

"Uh. I don't know. You left without a word, causing me to spend my entire pregnancy and nearly the first year of her life alone. If I didn't know any better, I would think you were avoiding me."

A heavy flash of guilt struck him, but instead of pushing it away, he let it settle. He had gotten her pregnant and disappeared.

He was a world-class asshole. He couldn't defend himself.

He took her hand and tugged her forward. "Come inside."

Once inside, she looked around, her arms wrapped around herself as if she were cold, but he knew she wasn't.

"Damn. It's like stepping into a time machine," she said.

He remembered all the times they had sneaked in here, but this time was different. There was no rushing. No sneaking about. No fear that someone might discover them.

"It never crossed my mind not to believe you."

She shook her head. "I don't want you thinking that I was trying to trap you. Because I'm not. I never would. I don't want anything from you. I just thought you should know."

"Trap me?" He was genuinely surprised by her statement. "Romey, I'm the one who has been going after you my entire life."

"Go after? You say it like I didn't have a choice. I did what I wanted to."

"I know. But it was me who couldn't stay away from you. I always knew you would be fine without me, but I could never be fine without you."

She shut her eyes, turning her head away from him. His guilt spreading a little more into his chest. "I can't hear this right now."

"It's the truth."

"If it's true, then why did you stay away so long?"

It was a damn good question. One he wasn't prepared to answer. "I was in Syria. They are in the middle of a civil war. My team couldn't get out of there safely for a long time. We were cut off from communication for a few months."

She was quiet for a while. He hadn't told her the entire truth. She didn't need to know it. It didn't matter anyway. "Syria? Americans can't just go traipsing in there. Are you insane? You could have been killed. There was an American humanitarian aid worker captured there. Her parents were on TV. Our government couldn't do anything to get her back."

He was shocked into silence for a moment. She knew so much more than he'd expected. He hadn't been sure how much of the story had reached home. All the other doctors he'd been with were from all over the world, and American news channels wouldn't have picked up on foreign doctors being held captive. "We should talk about Lily," he said, switching back to the more important topic.

"Yes. Let's. Are you going to publicly acknowledge her?"

"What do you mean?"

"You know what I mean. I won't have you treating her like your dirty little secret. If you're only going to play daddy in private, then don't bother playing daddy at all." She reached her hands out toward Lily. "Give me my baby."

"Hold up. I know I hurt you, and you don't have to forgive me for that, but you will not charge me with something I'm not guilty of. We made a baby. She's ours. I would never keep her a secret. I never would have left if I had known you were pregnant. It would have changed everything."

She shut her eyes and rubbed her temples. "Would it?"

"It knocked me on my ass when Charlie died. I . . ." He needed to be careful with his words. He didn't want to hurt her any more than he already had. "It was too many things at once. My mother died, and then I broke up with Gwen. And Charlie . . . we had our own issues."

"I know he asked you to write him a prescription."

Her statement shook him. "I never did. Not once."

"I know. You figured out he was addicted to his meds long before anyone else did. Cally told me you tried to intervene before things got worse."

He had offered to send him to rehab, only to be greeted with a big *fuck you*. Charlie didn't think he had a problem. He thought it was all under control. Until he didn't.

"I don't want to talk about this anymore. Not in front of Lily." They had never talked about Charlie's addiction. Maybe they should have. If they'd all confronted him with it, they could have saved him.

Lily had been quiet in his arms for the past few minutes, just staring at the two of them, probably wondering what the hell was going on.

"I'm sorry, princess." He kissed her smooth round cheek. She had that indescribable smell that some babies had. He pressed his nose into her curls and just inhaled.

"I wash her clothes in special detergent," Romey explained, seeming to read his mind. "I sniff her too."

He leaned over and kissed Romey as well. "You smell good too, Mommy."

"Don't kiss me," she said, but didn't move away. He wrapped his free arm around her and pulled her close. She seemed more than tired. She was weary. These past couple of years must have been so hard on her. She'd had to carry all of her burden alone.

"We need to show Lily that we like each other."

"But I don't like you." The bite was gone from her voice. She leaned against him. Her head rested on his chest.

"We are going to pretend like you do for the baby's sake."

"You're catching me in a bad moment. I'm so damn tired." He kissed the top of her head. "I'll hate you later."

"I would like her to have my last name. When can we change that?"

"My baby will not have a different last name than me."

"We can make it so all three of us have the same last name."

"You're going to change your name to Michaels? I'm not sure your daddy would like that, but it's fine with me."

"You could marry me. It's a little old-fashioned, but it could be fun."

"Don't say stupid stuff to me right now, Gray." She thought he was joking. But there was nothing funny about him wanting to her to be his wife. "I'm not in the mood for it." She gave a sleepy sigh. "You had better be glad you're acting right about me telling you about Lily."

"What would you do if this had gone wrong?"

"For starters, Cally said he was going to break your knees. I think I suggested burning down your house and roasting marshmallows with the flames."

"Damn. You Michaels kids are bloodthirsty."

"Life has taught us that sometimes we have to be."

CHAPTER SEVEN

Dinner is better when we eat together.—Unknown

"You know, we don't have to have a family dinner every week," Callahan said to her the next evening as he stood beside the grill. "We could have let it go this week."

She could have let it go. There would always be next week, but that wasn't necessarily true. No one knew what tomorrow would bring. Her life had changed so quickly in the past couple of years. She liked their weekly dinners. She needed to feel some kind of normalcy in a world that was anything but normal.

"Do you not want to be here? You got plans I don't know about? A whole fun-filled exciting evening of sitting on your couch eating whatever sad single-man dinner you scraped together?"

He turned to face her. "Has anyone ever told you that your mouth is going to write a check your ass can't cash?"

"Is that a threat?" She put her hands on her hips. "I'm not scared of you, Callahan. Everyone thinks you're so big and tough, but I know you're scared of spiders and you scream like a little punk when you see one."

"First of all, that spider was the size of my damn hand. And I did not scream. I was . . . surprised to see it is all."

"We had to call the thirteen-year-old neighbor girl to come and get it because you were a chickenshit."

"You'd better watch who you are calling a chickenshit, Ramona."

"And if I don't?"

Callahan stuck his hand into the cup he was carrying and pulled out some cubes of ice. He looked at his hand and then at her before he took off toward her. She ran away screaming, but he was a man with long legs at the height of his prime, and he caught up with her in seconds. She was rewarded for her smart mouth with a handful of ice down the back of her shirt.

"Damn you, Cally." She tried to smack his arm but missed. She lunged toward him again, but he quickly avoided her strike.

"Hey! Children! You're supposed to be starting the grill, not trying to murder each other."

They both paused and looked at Angela, who was holding Lily. "We were just playing, Angela," he said, sounding like he had when they were kids.

"Well, quit it. You're going to have the whole neighborhood thinking someone is getting killed over here."

"Romey started it," Callahan said. and playfully pushed her head as he walked back over to the grill.

"I did start it," she admitted with a shrug. "I don't want Cally thinking he's above messing with. People don't say boo to him anymore. He might start getting a big head."

"It's impossible to get a big head with you all as my family." He returned to the grill and fired it up.

Callahan, despite his wild youth, was a calming force for her. Just teasing him made her feel better. It reminded her of when they were the kids and life wasn't so damn complicated. She had been feeling out of sorts all day. Unable to concentrate at her shop this morning. Unable to exchange more than just the most basic courtesies with her customers.

She had noticed that Gray's father hadn't come into the shop this morning for his daily slice of pie. She wondered if Gray had told him yet. He must have. Probably called as soon as she left last night. Carey Norton had always been kind to her, but how did he feel about Gray having a child with her? The daughter of one of his former employees?

She wouldn't be surprised if he was unhappy. The people who were kindest to your face were often the most brutal behind your back.

"Are you being a good girl for Nana?" Romey asked Lily as she walked over and touched her cheek. She tried to push the possible ugliness of Lily not being accepted out of her mind.

There was enough love in this house for her.

Lily grinned in response. Romey had been gifted with such a sweet baby. She had seemed to warm to Gray right away. Could she sense he was someone more than just a stranger?

It was probably because of the way Gray had smiled at her when he realized Lily was his. Romey had spent hours thinking about how she would tell him. She had gone through every possible scenario in her head. She had been prepared for anger, disbelief, disappointment, and at best simple acceptance.

She had never expected him to be happy.

She didn't know how to take it.

"Of course she is being a good girl," said Angela. "We had a very nice morning here with Pa."

"Thank you for being here," Romey said softly. Angela had spent the past two mornings here with her baby and father before going to work. She'd dropped Lily off at the shop, where Alice kept her entertained in the afternoons. It was a compromise of sorts. Angela had volunteered to be there, thinking it would be a much softer blow if they didn't immediately remove Lily from her father's care.

It wasn't the ideal situation. She couldn't keep Lily in the office of her shop forever. And she couldn't expect Angela to babysit forever. The woman Callahan had said could watch Lily during the day ran a small daycare out of her home. She had a spot opening up next week. Still, Romey hesitated about calling the woman. Even though Callahan had recommended her, she didn't feel comfortable sending her baby off to a woman she had never met.

"Don't thank me. Your father is my problem too. We've been together fifteen years. You're my family."

"Can't you marry him?" Romey asked.

"We talked about it couple of years ago, but things change."

Cyrus had changed. She didn't say that, but Romey knew.

They had all taken Charlie's death so differently. Her father had withdrawn inside himself, in denial about how bad Charlie had been just before he died. She and Callahan had been hurt, but they weren't surprised by his passing. Gray had fallen apart. She had learned last night that his guilt over distancing himself from Charlie had driven him away.

But what choice had he had? What choice had any of them had? It was impossible to save someone who didn't want saving.

"Romey, you want cheese on your burger?"

"Yes, please."

"Can you go ask Uncle Cy what he wants?"

Her father wasn't speaking to Callahan either. When Callahan had tried to greet him this afternoon, he hadn't even responded. It was a shitty thing for her father to do, but she hadn't said anything.

She went in the house and found him sitting at the kitchen table instead of in his usual place in his recliner in the den. "Callahan wants to know if you want cheese on your burger."

He looked up at her. "I do. Can you ask Angela to bring it in here when it's done?"

"No. I will not do that. You want to eat inside? You can get off your behind and carry your food in the house yourself."

"Excuse me," he said, in that same tone he'd used when she was twelve and being fresh. "Just because you are over thirty doesn't mean I'm not your father."

"You haven't been acting like my father. You have been acting like a moody, sullen teenager. Lily is my baby. I would die for her. I would kill for her. What would you have done in our situation?"

"I wouldn't hurt my granddaughter."

"No. Not on purpose." She bent closer to him to look into his eyes. "But things happen. Callahan sees those things that happen when well-intentioned people aren't paying attention for even a moment. You can sit here and be mad and not speak to us, or you can think about what we're trying to say. You haven't been yourself, Daddy. And that's the truth, and as the days have gone by, you have been slipping farther and farther away from us. I know Charlie was your favorite and I know how much you miss him, but me and Cally are here, and we want our father back." She stood up straight again. "So either you come outside and eat dinner with your family or you sit in here and starve, but I'll be damned if I ask Angela to bring you a hamburger just because you want to hurt us."

He sat there silent for a moment. Romey, done with the conversation, turned away from him. "Charlie wasn't my favorite," he said. "I don't have favorites."

She walked out, not knowing if he'd gotten anything out of what she had said.

"Well?" Callahan asked.

"Just put cheese on all of them. I don't trust people who don't like cheese on their burgers," she huffed.

"Well, okay then." Callahan shook his head and turned back to the grill.

Romey went over to the sides she had made earlier today and needlessly gave them all a stir.

"You okay?" Angela asked, coming over to place her hand on Romey's back.

She wasn't. "I'm fine," she lied. The past few days had been a roller coaster for her. So many damn emotions pummeling her.

The sliding door opened, and her father walked out, shutting it behind him. He took a seat at the patio table.

"I hope you didn't smash the burgers when you were cooking them," Cyrus said. "All that does is squeeze the juices out of them."

Callahan looked at him for a long moment.

"No, sir. I just flipped them once, like you taught me," he said after a while.

Her father nodded. "Potato salad looks good."

That was his apology. It was all they were going to get.

It was good enough for them.

A few minutes later, they all sat down to eat. They ate without speaking for a little while, all of them seemingly lost in their thoughts.

"I took Lily to meet her father last night," Romey said, breaking the silence.

They all stopped eating and looked up at her. Her father and Angela had matching expressions of shock on their faces.

"Who's her father?" Cyrus asked. "He's in town?"

"Come on! You really don't know who her father is?" she asked. She was grateful that neither one of them had asked, but she figured they must have known.

"I have no damn clue," her father said, raising his voice. "You didn't tell me, and I didn't ask."

"It's Grayson Norton, Daddy."

"Gray? He's back in town?" he asked, seeming surprised.

"Oh, Cy," Angela groaned. "Even people on Jupiter know Gray Norton came home. You really haven't been paying attention to anything."

Callahan's expression was tense as he looked at her. "How did he react when you told him? Do I need to pay him a visit?"

"He can keep his knees." She looked down at Lily, who was sitting on her lap. "I didn't have to tell him. He looked at her and knew. I've never seen him so happy."

"I'm having a hard time understanding this." Her father frowned at her. "Gray Norton is back in town, and he's Lily's father?"

"Yes, sir."

"Did he know you were pregnant?"

"No. He was long gone by the time I found out. I had no way to contact him."

"He made himself hard to contact," Callahan said. "It's completely ridiculous." He was nowhere near forgiving Gray.

The fact that he had been in Syria was troubling her. Of all the places in the world to go, he'd had to pick the one that was in the middle of a multifaction civil war. He could have died. It was astounding that he had come out of there alive.

"Well, isn't that something." Cyrus grinned. "My granddaughter is a Norton." He looked at Lily. "You are officially one of them. Nothing can hold you back now."

"Nothing held her back before," Romey said hotly. "It doesn't matter who her father is."

"We all know that's not true. Money buys you access. Money buys you opportunity. Let's not pretend we believe the pipe dream that if we just work hard enough, all of our dreams will come true. I know plenty of people who have worked damn hard all their lives and ended up nothing but dead. The American dream for people like us is a myth. Gray Norton, now, that boy is the real American dream."

She wanted to disagree with her father's harsh outlook on life. But the truth was that nearly everyone she knew was living paycheck to paycheck. They worked hard. They were good people who were just one emergency away from financial ruin. It depressed the hell out of her to think about it.

"So you're just glad that I got knocked up by a rich man?" Romey asked, trying to keep the lightness in her voice.

"No. I'm glad it's Gray. He was here so much, I was starting to think he was one of my kids."

"Uncle Cy," Callahan started. His jaw was clenched. "I'm not sure how you can be so calm about this. He didn't come to Charlie's funeral. He took off, leaving Romey to have their baby alone. You should want to kill him."

"For what? Not putting on a black suit and being sad in the same room as us for a few hours? He went to the hospital as soon as you called, didn't he? Paid for the entire service out of his own pocket."

"What?" Romey said, truly surprised. "I didn't know that." Her father had told her everything was taken care of when she asked.

"People who don't think they're going to die don't take out life insurance." He looked at Callahan. "You can't blame other people for how they grieve. And you shouldn't blame them for their past decisions. Lord knows, I didn't blame you for yours. Everyone thought I was crazy for taking my ex-wife's juvenile delinquent of a nephew in. But I knew you had some good in you, and I knew you made the decisions that you made because you didn't know any better."

Callahan didn't argue the point. "He'd better be glad he took the news the right way," he huffed, looking down into his plate. "I won't tolerate him mistreating Romey or Lily."

"What do you think about this, Angela?" Romey asked. "You have been awful quiet."

"I never thought it would be Gray. But so many things make sense, now that I know it's him. The way he looked at you at the airport . . . he couldn't hide his feelings." She exhaled and shook her head. "What the hell are you going to do now?"

* * *

A waiter dressed in a formal uniform walked up to Gray, tray in hand, offering him a glass of the champagne his mother had flown in from France for the occasion. She was throwing one of her charity balls, her way of giving back to the world, but Gray knew these sorts of events were never about the needy people they were supposed to be helping. His mother needed to see and be seen. She lived to entertain, and tonight she had pulled out all the stops. She had brought in acrobats from around the country to be this evening's entertainment and hired some fancy celebrity chef to prepare all the food. Not only were there waiters with trays walking around to serve her guests, but she had three bartenders stationed around the event, mixing up the most elaborate drinks.

There were politicians there, not just those local to the area but some from around the country, as well as a few CEOs. Most everyone there had enormous wealth.

He was a doctor. He made a good living, but he was poor compared to these people. He was supposed to be one of them. Or so his mother had said, but he felt very uncomfortable in spaces like these, and so he hadn't come to one of her events in a while. But this time she had guilted him into coming. Not overtly. Her recent diagnosis had made him realize that doing little things like this to make her happy wasn't hardship. It was one evening out of his life.

He'd asked her if he could invite his friends. She'd immediately agreed, but when she asked where to have the invitations sent, she seemed surprised that he wanted Romey, Callahan, and Charlie to come.

"Is there a problem with my guests?" he asked her.

"No," she said, her voice unnaturally high. "I trust your judgment."

"My judgment?" he challenged her. "Callahan just became the deputy chief of police. Romey is the executive pastry chef for one of the best restaurants in the country, and Charlie is a Marine. You act like I want to invite escaped convicts here. They are—"

"I haven't said a word against them," she said, cutting him off. "I just didn't realize you were still close to Cyrus' children."

She had walked away after that, ending the conversation. The invitations had been sent. All three of them had declined to come. And that had made him want them to be there even more. He'd practically begged them.

He spotted Romey first. She was hard to miss in her emerald-green dress. It fit her curvy hips like a glove and then flared out at the bottom. Her signature ringlets were gone. Her hair had been sleekly styled and pulled back with a few wispy tendrils brushing her face. Just seeing her jump-started that feeling in his body. He had tried to stop being attracted to her. They were supposed to be just friends now. She had been dating someone for a while. He had just made things official with Gwen.

But the feelings were still there, and it was hard for him to be with someone else and not compare them to her. He walked over. She was standing at one of the bar tables outside, looking over to the lake, which was perfectly lit by the moonlight tonight.

"You better be glad you came," he said to her as he approached. "If you didn't, I was going to find you, throw you over my shoulder, and bring you here myself."

"You can't put me over your shoulder. The weight in my ass alone will take you down."

He grinned at her. "What a way to go down."

She looked around at everything. "It's very beautiful. All of it. I've worked events like this, but from the other side. I never thought I'd be out here." She looked back at him, and he saw vulnerability in her eyes. "Do I look okay? Was I supposed to wear black? Almost every woman here is wearing a black dress. Did I read the invitation wrong?"

He put his glass down on the table and impulsively hugged her close to him. "You are the most beautiful woman here," he whispered to her. "Thank you for coming."

He knew he should let her go immediately, but it had been a while since he'd seen her, their lives taking them in opposite directions. They stayed in contact, but he had missed her. Feeling her pressed against him reminded him just how much.

"What are you doing to my sister?" He heard Charlie's voice from behind him.

"He's giving me a hug, dummy," Romey shot back. "What does it look like?"

He let her go and looked at Charlie to see if there was any trace of humor in his face. There wasn't. Charlie was vehemently against Gray being anything other than friends with Romey. It had been over ten years since Gray had made that dumb promise to his friend. The one he'd broken almost immediately after.

Romey was a grown woman. He didn't know why Charlie would care. But things had been weird between them lately. Every time Charlie had come home on leave, he had been a little more distant. And then he'd gotten injured. Shrapnel in his spine from an explosion. He'd had surgery to remove it, but the surgeons hadn't been able to get it all, as doing so would have caused more damage. Charlie was labeled unfit for duty and medically retired.

It had been life changing for him, of course. Charlie was angry about it, as he should be. But as Gray tried to be there for his friend, Charlie wanted less and less to do with him.

He didn't know how to fix it. And he sure as hell wasn't about to make it worse by trying to be with Romey.

"I'm glad you're here, Charlie. You look good in a tux."

"I looked better in my dress uniform. If I could have walked in here with my dress uniform on, these people would be falling all over me, going out of their way to thank me for my service, when in reality they don't give a shit about sending poor kids off to foreign countries to die."

"Charlie." Callahan appeared with a glass of amber liquid in his hand. "You're at a goddamn party. What normal people do is thank the host for inviting us." He looked at Gray. "I'm pretty sure you had to convince your mama to let us come."

"I didn't have to convince her," he told them, feeling like he was lying though in reality he wasn't. "I wanted you guys here so I would have someone to hang out with. You know I never liked these things."

"Your father doesn't seem to like them either. He cornered me as soon as I walked in and invited me to his office. He's got some damn good bourbon. Kept refilling my glass. Your mother is the one who found us and made him come out of hiding. We had been in there almost forty minutes."

Callahan's story surprised him. His father was the friendliest man in town. It was probably why he'd won his mayoral election by a landslide. But Gray also understood that his father had worked defending some of these people in court. He might not want to socialize with them. "You guys hungry? The formal meal won't start for another hour or so, but there's a lot hors d'oeuvres. I can have a little bit of everything brought over."

"I'm starving," Romey admitted. "Is this one of those things people eat at? I've been to events where we spent hours preparing and no one eats. They just drink, acting like carbs will ruin their entire lives."

"I don't care what other people are doing," Gray said to her as he signaled a waiter. "We're eating. Besides, I was kind of hoping we could sneak away before the charity auction starts. Maybe go out on the boat? We haven't done that since we were kids."

"One of us has to stay sober to drive the boat. I'm already out of the running. Your father filled my glass twice in that short time," Callahan said.

"I've only had half a glass," Gray said. "I can drive."

"What if I want to drive the boat?" Romey asked. "Nobody ever lets me drive the boat."

Gray grinned at her. "You can drive for a little while, Ramona."

A little while later they had a tableful of food. It was like old times—just the four of them talking and relaxing, no cares, no tension. Gray had missed this. He had made other friends in his life. He saw them socially. He enjoyed their company, but there was no type of comfort like the comfort you got from being with people who had known you your entire life.

"Excuse me, Gray?"

Gray turned around to see one of his father's former clients, currently a senator, standing behind him with a woman he had never seen before.

"Senator." He extended his hand. "It's nice to see you again. I hope you're planning to get a flu shot this year. We don't want to see you back in the office unless it's for your annual visit."

"I will. Don't you worry, son. I have never been so sick in my entire life. My future missus here will make sure I do," he said, gesturing toward the woman. "I wanted to introduce you to my fiancée, Katherine."

"It's nice to meet you." Gray shook her hand.

"You as well," Katherine replied. "I hear you are a very good physician."

"I try to be. Thank you, ma'am."

"Katherine is an attorney. I went searching for a new one and found the woman I'm going to marry instead."

"Congratulations," Gray said, and turned back to the table. "Let me introduce you to my friends. This is Callahan, Romey, and Charlie. We grew up together."

"It's not important who we are," Charlie said. "We're the poor people he invited to bring some diversity to the event."

Both the senator and his fiancée looked uncomfortable with Charlie's words.

"Excuse my brother, Senator," Romey said. "That's his idea of a joke. It's nice to see you again. We've met before. I'm the executive pastry chef for Ami Bistro. We catered your Christmas party last year."

"You're the one who sent over that box of pastries to my office when my assistant told you we were considering another place. The little chocolate thing you made was enough to get me to go down to the restaurant myself and book you. Cost me twenty percent more, but I didn't care."

Romey had beautifully defused the situation, but Gray could barely focus because he could only think about Charlie.

He gently grabbed his friend's arm and led him away from the group. "What the hell was that?" he asked.

"What?" There was hostility in Charlie's eyes. "It was a joke."

"It wasn't funny."

"Did I embarrass you in front of your important friends?"

"They aren't my friends, but you are. Why would you say that?"

"Let's not pretend like we belong here. You know it and we know it. That's why none of us wanted to come."

"You belong here because you're my friends."

"Whatever, man. It was a joke." Charlie shook his head. "You don't invite the servant's kids to the boss's party. Leave us off the guest list next time. Then you won't have to worry about us embarrassing you." He walked away.

They didn't speak for three weeks after that.

* * *

Gray sat in his car, in the same place he used to park when he lived at his childhood home. Dozens of memories flooded him. Not much had changed since he'd left. The landscaping wasn't as ornate as when his mother was alive, but that was about it. Though there hadn't been any more balls or parties since she died either. The grand house, his mother's dream home, sat nearly empty, with only his father, who had never liked the house, left living there.

It seemed like a lonely place to be. His father hadn't seemed lonely when he last saw him, but maybe Gray didn't know his father enough to tell.

Gray had certainly been lonely here. His mother was always somewhere, not the type to stay home and dote on a child. His father had been building his practice. But Gray was never alone. He had a nanny, a housekeeper, and two maintenance men in the house daily.

It was one of them, Mr. Michaels, who brought his son over one day.

There had rarely been other children in his home. Gray went to a private school forty-five minutes outside of town.

Most of his classmates lived in the wealthy suburbs of DC. There weren't many playdates.

He sat outside and watched as Charlie helped his father prune the weeds and clean up discarded trimmings. He was always fascinated by seeing people working with their hands. Sometimes he followed Mr. Michaels around, watching as he worked. The man never sent him away. Sometimes he told him stories about his children.

And now one of them was here.

Noticing that Gray had been watching for a while, Charlie walked up to him. "Hey. Are you just going to sit on your butt and watch me all day, or are you going to help?"

Cyrus stopped what he was doing and came over to his son. "You aren't supposed to ask him to help. His parents own this house."

"So?" Charlie said. "He's got two hands. There's nothing stopping him from helping to clean up his own yard. He's no king."

"I can help," Gray said. He walked over to Charlie and took the bag he was holding from him. "What do you want me to do?"

"It's easy. You see something on the ground. You pick it up."

Cyrus brought Charlie to work with him every day that summer, and by the time autumn came, Gray had not only learned to mow grass but informed his parents that he didn't want to go back to his stuffy private school.

His mother had been horrified. His father, who also had gone to public school here, had agreed.

Shaking himself free of his memories, Gray walked up to the front door, prepared to ring the bell, but Anna, the housekeeper who had been with the family since he was a small boy, opened the door.

"Dr. Gray!" Her smile was wide. She looked happy to see him. "I'm so glad you're home. You've gotten so skinny."

"Hello, Anna." He hugged the smaller woman. It was good to see her. She used to make him chocolate-chip cookies every day. They would be sitting on a plate on the desk in his room, a snack for him to have while he was doing his homework. "I've missed you. How have you been?"

"Bored! There's no one here for me to cook for. Your father won't let me do much for him."

"I'm sure my father wouldn't mind some cookies every day."

"He's been on a pie kick lately. He eats a whole apple pie by himself every week. Your mother would have a fit if she were alive, god bless her soul."

"She was always on him to watch his diet. It's ironic that she's the one who ended up with the heart disease."

"Sometimes you can't overcome genetics no matter how hard you try. I used to think you took after her, but now you're looking more and more like your father."

"You think so?"

"I know it." She smiled at him again. "Now come on in. Your father is waiting on the patio. We were so excited to hear you were coming here for lunch. I made all the things you loved as a kid."

"You mean the stuff my mother never wanted me to eat."

"Yes," she answered, as she led him to the back of the house. "Her biggest fear in life was that she was going to be fat. I'm fat and I couldn't be happier. She should have just eaten the damn fried chicken." She looked back at him. "Maybe I shouldn't have said that. I got too comfortable. Please forgive me, Dr. Gray."

"I won't forgive you because you have nothing to be sorry for. I agree. She should have just eaten the damn chicken."

They grinned at each other, and soon he was being presented to his father.

His father was gazing out at the lake. It was a beautiful view, clear rippling water and lush greenery as far as the eye could see. Gray's new home had a view of the lake, but it wasn't as perfect as this. The irony of the fact that he had spent more time at the town beach than here didn't escape him. The Michaels kids had never felt comfortable here. That didn't change when they became adults.

"Hello, son." His father stood up and greeted him. "I was surprised you asked to have lunch here today. I thought it would at least be two or three more weeks of you avoiding me before I wore you down."

"I'm not avoiding you," he replied.

His father raised one brow and looked at him. There was no smile on his face. He wasn't playing the role of the jovial mayor right now. He had been a defense attorney for over thirty years, defending huge corporations, politicians, even high-profile murderers in some cases. He had the reputation of being ruthless. Of being a winner. But his firm also took on more pro bono cases than anyone in the state. It was hard for him to merge both sides of his father into one man.

He didn't know who he really was. If someone had asked him to describe his father when he was a child, the only word that would have come to mind was *busy.*

"I'm really not avoiding you," Gray told him. "I'm just not sure what you expect from me."

"I don't know either, Gray." He shook his head. "Have a seat, son. I do love this view. I never spent enough time here looking at it. It's a shame. We have all of this and no one here to enjoy it."

Gray sat across from his father at the table. "Did it ever bother you that I spent so much time with the Michaels and not here?"

"Not at all. I wasn't here to know that you weren't here."

"You always knew where I was, didn't you?"

"Of course I did, son. I could dig up dirt on a saint if you gave me enough time. The truth is, I thought Cyrus Michaels was a good influence on you. Your mother wanted me to fire him when she saw you mowing the lawn, but I thought it was good for you. Character building. And I sure as hell didn't want you growing up like her brother. I can't stand his spoiled, entitled pompous ass. He's one of those assholes who is always telling people to pull themselves up by their bootstraps when he hasn't done a hard day's work in his life. I wish people could see how damn stupid he is. I know kindergartners who could outthink him."

Gray couldn't help but smile at his father's little rant. "I didn't know you felt that way about Uncle Julian."

"Your mother was a princess, but she was smart. She's the one they should have put on the board of directors."

Anna returned with a huge platter of food. Chicken, roasted corn, potato salad, fresh-made biscuits. It was clearly too much for the two of them. He knew he would be taking some home with him.

"Anna, you have outdone yourself," Carey Norton told her. "I can tell just by the smell that I'm going to have to give you a raise."

"Oh, Mr. Norton." The older woman blushed. "Don't be ridiculous. You never let me do enough. I'll be right back with your drinks."

"You told her I was skinny, didn't you?"

"I might have mentioned it. She won't fry anything for me. I don't pay the woman to be concerned about my health."

"She said you wouldn't let her make you cookies."

"That's because she made them without butter. Used applesauce instead. Do I look like a man who eats applesauce cookies? Give me the butter, damn it! Nothing tastes better than butter."

"So that's why you've been eating so much pie lately. Romey isn't watching your diet."

"That pie is damn good. That girl isn't afraid of some full-fat butter."

"It's funny, me and Anna were just talking about how Mom would never allow this kind of food to be cooked when she was around. She was always hounding you to watch your diet. I'm having a hard time understanding your relationship. You two led very separate lives."

His parents had rarely been together unless there was a function. Even when they were both home, they stayed in separate parts of the house. He hadn't realized that married people slept in the same bed until he went to his first sleepover at the Michaels house.

"We cared for each other. She was someone I could talk to about anything. And the woman was fantastic at a party."

There was no mention of love there, Gray had noticed.

Anna returned with their drinks—two tall glasses of fresh, ice-cold lemonade. They both thanked her and waited for her to leave to resume their conversation. "Sounds like the same reasons I had for proposing to Gwen."

"Yeah. The same reasons you ended up not marrying her. Honestly, I was surprised when you proposed to her. I know your mother was pushing for you to be with her, but I didn't think you were the society marriage type."

"I guess I wanted to make Mom happy. Especially after we found out she was sick."

"Your mother loved you. It didn't matter who you married. She was always going to love you."

But would she have loved his choice in a wife?

"Did you know that I'm the father of Romey's baby?"

His father was quiet for a moment. "I'm glad it's finally out there."

"You knew, then?"

"I suspected. She sure as hell didn't drop any hints."

"I wish you would have given me a hint when you knew how to get in contact with me. I wouldn't have done that second assignment in Central America. I would have come home sooner."

"It wasn't my place to tell you. I also wasn't sure. I knew you and Romey had been chasing after each other for years."

"How? No one knew. We were careful."

"I saw the way you looked at her, Gray. It happened to be at your engagement party, which was when I knew you and Gwen wouldn't last. She also spent the entire night trying to avoid you and left as soon as humanly possible."

"You noticed all that?"

"Dirt on a saint. Remember? But if that didn't clue me in, the trips to wherever she was living before she came back home did. I mean, who the hell goes to Hyde Park, New York, for fun?"

"FDR had a home there. It was very educational." He thought for a moment. "I never told you I went there. I never told anyone."

"I'm your father and had access to all your bank accounts until you were twenty-five."

"You think Mom would have ever accepted her?"

"That's hard to say. Your mother could be a terrible snob at times. She really disliked Luna Michaels. Maybe she thought Romey would take after her."

"I wondered how Cyrus could have been married to her." They were polar opposites. He had been so steady and dependable. She had been so carefree and lighthearted. Nothing was a big deal to her. Rules didn't matter. Her entire life had been about freedom.

"She was gorgeous and fun. She's the type of woman who keeps your heart pumping and your blood racing. And she was a dancer. I imagine he had been hypnotized by her moves more than once."

"You seem to know a lot about her."

"No." He shook his head. "I knew someone just like her a long time ago. Those types of women are fun, but they don't make good wives."

"I can understand that." He looked out across the lake, to the other side of town. "I came back home for Romey."

"I know, son."

"She's not going to make it easy."

"It shouldn't be easy. She should make you suffer a bit. You've not told me how you feel about being a father."

"I'm in love," he said honestly. "With her smile and her cheeks and her curls. She looks so much like Romey."

"I've only seen her a few times in person, but Romey shows me pictures."

"I would like for you to publicly acknowledge her as your grandchild."

His father stiffened. "Do you think that's a request you really need to make? I've seen Romey Michaels almost every day you have been gone. I went to the hospital when your daughter was born. I've sent gifts. I've done everything a grandfather can do who is not supposed to know he's a grandfather. Of course I will acknowledge my grandchild. I've been waiting for you to come home so I can."

He really had thought his father had been indifferent to him all those years, but his anger was showing Gray that that simply wasn't true. "I'm sorry, Dad." He shook his head. "Romey said the same thing to me. She said if I wasn't going to publicly acknowledge Lily, then she'd rather me not be in her life. I thought maybe she was worried that you wouldn't accept Lily."

"I would hope she knows me well enough to know that I would never deny my grandchild. I always wanted to be a grandfather. I think I would be good at it. Better than I was at being a father."

"She seemed so shocked that I was happy about it. It bothers me that she thinks I would be ashamed of my own child."

"You kept your relationship a secret. You ever wonder how it made her feel to have to hide it?"

"She can't think I'm embarrassed of her. That's ridiculous. It was only supposed to be a fling that ended when I went away to college. If she ever told me she wanted more, I would have given it to her. There were two of us in it."

"Why did you need for her to tell you, son? If you wanted to be with her, why not just make it happen? No woman should have to guess if you love them."

"Charlie . . ."

"Ah." His father nodded. "That makes sense. I broke my friend's nose when I caught him kissing my little sister, but that guy was a dog. I knew because I hung out with him."

"He made me promise when we were seventeen. A week later I broke my word. I couldn't stay away from her."

"Gray, you haven't been seventeen for a long time. You should have just told Charlie."

"I did. Right after I broke up with Gwen. It got nasty. Our friendship ended for good that night because I couldn't stay away from his sister."

"Your friendship ended because Charlie died. And he died because he was addicted to medication that is too damn strong to ever do any good. You would have worked things out if he had lived. Especially if you treated his sister well." His father sat back in his chair and studied his face for a long moment. "Gray, sometimes you have to put yourself first. You let a promise you made to your friend when you were a kid affect your happiness for far too long. This is one of those times that if you want something, you need to go and get it, everyone else's feelings be damned."

He let his father's words sink in.

He was right.

Gray had to find a way to finally get what he wanted.

CHAPTER EIGHT

Cooking is the art of adjustment.—Jacques Pépin

It was two minutes till closing when Romey heard the bell over her shop's door ring. She looked up, expecting to see a hurried customer wanting to buy a pie for dessert just before she closed, but it was Gray who walked in instead.

He wore a black T-shirt with spots of paint splattered on it. His hair was messy, as if he had been running his fingers through it all day. His chin was shadowed with stubble. There were no traces of the preppy doctor she used to know. She would never have called him vain, but before he left, he had been very careful to keep up his image.

To be the man everyone wished was their son.

She wondered if he even bothered to look in the mirror anymore.

But damn . . .

She still found him attractive. Maybe more now than before.

He had been back for a few days. She'd have thought he would have shaved and gotten a haircut by now. That he would have morphed back into the image of the man who walked away from his life nearly two years ago.

"You're looking at me like you want to snatch my eyeballs out of my head."

"I do," she said softly.

She wondered when the complicated mix of emotions she felt whenever she looked at him would die down.

There were no signs of them even slowing down.

The anger was there just below the surface. Simmering. She needed to keep it there, because if that got stripped away, she knew what she would be left with.

Those feelings that she didn't want to feel.

"What would you use?" he asked her, coming close to her. The cash register separated them, but she could still feel his nearness, his heat.

It made her want to back away.

"What would I use to what?" She stayed rooted to her spot and looked into his eyes.

"To rip my eyeballs out with. A fork? A spoon? A sharp stick would be effective."

"I would use my fingers. Duh."

He grinned at her. It wasn't the polite smile he gave to everyone else. It wasn't the mask she was used to seeing him slip on and off when others were around. It was the smile he saved for those who knew him in a way the world didn't.

"Don't smile at me, Gray." She looked away from him and his stupid perfect teeth. "Did you come for more pie? I don't have any of the savory ones left. But you can take home whatever's here."

He looked at her for a long moment, taking her in. She was still looking away, but she could feel his eyes on her. "I came for you, Romey. But I'm thinking you aren't going to allow me to wrap you up and take you home with me."

Ugh. He was flirting with her. It shouldn't have any effect on her. But she felt that stupid flutter in her stomach.

Butterflies.

She needed an entire bottle of insect killer.

"Damn, Gray. Where the hell did you pull that corny-ass line from?"

"I got it from a book called *How to Seduce your Local Baker*. It's pretty good. I'm on chapter ten. It's called 'Butter Them Up.' "

He had gotten her with that one, and a smile unwillingly spread across her face.

"There she is." He stood there staring at her, still drinking her in. "Your smile is what got me the first time. You were sixteen, and we were hanging out in your backyard. Just me and you. Charlie and Callahan had disappeared somewhere together. It was the summertime, ones of those days that sent people running for the air conditioning. You wore cutoff shorts and a tank top printed with yellow flowers on it. Your hair was piled high on your head. Curls springing out of the bun you tried to contain it in. I had just come back from a visit with my mother's family and told you how my great uncle had moved that twenty-five-year-old ripped guy from Brazil into his house. He was claiming to be his mentor, and no one in the family called him out on it."

She remembered that day. She remembered what it had felt like being alone with him. How he had spoken to her like an equal instead of like the annoying little sister of his friend.

"You smiled at me, Romey, and I thought, holy shit, I'm done."

"Stop it, Gray."

She didn't want to think back. She didn't want to remember that time in her life and those feelings. It would be like poking an open wound. "Why did you come here?"

"To talk to you."

"You could have called. Or texted. You don't have to slum it in here with me."

"Don't do that," he said, very seriously. "I didn't like it when Charlie did it, and I sure as hell don't want to hear it from you."

She was taken aback by the sharpness of his tone, but she knew how hurt he had been when Charlie said it to him. It had ended up ruining their friendship.

"I would apologize to you, but I think I get to do two thousand more mean things to you before I have to."

He nodded. "That's fair. Are you going to let me apologize to you?"

"I don't need an apology. It doesn't change the past."

"No. It won't. I can live with you not forgiving me, but I can't live without you understanding how sorry I am."

Sorry for what? she wanted to ask, but she didn't. She wasn't ready to go down that road with him. She wasn't sure she wanted to hear his answer.

"What did you want to talk about?" She felt awkward around him. It was so easy to go from only wanting to be in his presence to almost physically hurting from being in the same room with him.

"I want to see Lily regularly. We should work out some times."

"We don't have to. You can see her every day. I was thinking you could have dinner with her every night."

"I would like that very much. Do you want me to pick her up?"

"I can bring her over around five, but you won't have to wait to see her today. She's here."

His eyes widened. "Lily's here?"

She nodded. "My father used to watch her, but he's been really depressed since Charlie's birthday passed a few weeks ago. Callahan doesn't think he should watch her anymore because of how distracted he is."

"What do you think?"

"I think what Callahan thinks. He doesn't overreact. He even offered to pay for her day care because he knows I can't afford it. But I can't let him spend over twelve hundred dollars a month on a day care center. One of his officers has a family member who watches children in her home. She's cheaper, but I'm still not sure about sending Lily there. Right now, Angela stays with her and my father in the morning, and then she drops Lily off here before she goes into her shop."

"That's very kind of her."

"I know. I feel so damn guilty about it too. I have to figure out something soon. Can you lock my door and flip the sign? I'll take you to Lily. She's just about to wake up from her nap."

She led him to her office, which was just off the kitchen. She had tried to make it as homey as possible.

There was a playpen set up in the corner next to the love seat. She spent so much time here—planning out menus, doing the bookkeeping. When she found this place, she'd been so excited that she was going to be her own boss. She was finally going to be in control of her destiny. But then her brother died, and Gray left, and she found out she was pregnant.

Destiny had laughed in her damn face.

Gray walked over and looked down at Lily, who was still sleeping. His face changed when he looked at her. His features softened; his lips almost curled into a smile. Romey studied him hard to see if there was any regret, any shame in his newfound fatherhood. She tried to find any sign that he would reject Lily and her again by extension. But there was no trace of anything. Except maybe amazement and wonder.

It appeared that he wanted to be her little girl's father.

"Let me take care of Lily during the day."

"What?" He had taken her off guard again. "You can't babysit for her."

"It's not babysitting." He gave her an incredulous look. "She's my daughter. It's called raising her."

Well, damn.

He had said exactly the right thing.

Still, she couldn't agree to it.

"But you've never watched a baby before. I just can't give her to you all day."

"I think I can handle it. I am a doctor. They literally let me cut people open."

"Serial killers also cut people open. Nobody gives their babies to them."

"I've treated a lot of children when I was away. I find them much more tolerable than adults."

She wanted to make a smart remark, but her curiosity got the better of her. "What exactly did you do while you were away?"

"We provided access to health care where there was none. We have ten different kinds of doctors in this town alone. Where I was, there were no doctors around for hundreds of miles. A simple cut on a finger could lead to an amputated hand. A lack of a vaccine could decimate entire villages. I spent most of my times running mobile clinics for people who were displaced by fighting between terrorist groups. After spending a few years giving out prescriptions for erectile dysfunction pills and telling rich old men to not eat at the steak house so frequently, I finally felt like I was practicing medicine. I can tell you right now without a doubt that everyone deserves health care. Money shouldn't ever be a prerequisite for maintaining health."

She was quiet for a long time, taking in what he'd said, trying not to be impressed by his words.

"What are you going to do about being a doctor?" she asked, feeling that nervous energy bubble up inside her. He had walked away from her. She shouldn't admire what he had done while he was gone. She didn't want to respect it. "I've heard a few ladies wishing you would open up your own family practice. They think you're real cute. Said they wouldn't mind you being the one to give them their yearly full-body checkup."

He frowned at her. "No they didn't."

"Yes they did. Although I'm not sure they would be so eager to undress in front of you if they saw how you looked right now."

"Do you really hate how I look now?"

"No," she said honestly. "But I've always been drawn to the dirty-backpacker look."

"That's true. I remember that guy you were with. What was his name? Marshall?"

"Marcel," she corrected.

"He always walked around with his guitar, acting like he was some kind of tortured artist."

She thought back and smiled at the memory of the man she had dated in her early twenties. "But he had the prettiest long black hair. And the most gorgeous deeply tanned skin."

"I hated that guy."

"Hey, I've never said anything about the uptight broads you brought back here over the years."

"They all hated you," he said, and she was surprised and a little stung by his admission.

"Were you even raised right? That's the kind of thing you say behind someone's back, not to their face."

"What woman gets introduced to her boyfriend's sexy lifelong friend and is happy about it?"

"They were jealous?" She rolled her eyes. "I'm not even sexy. I'm too cranky for that shit. There was nothing for them to worry about."

"There wasn't?" He glanced at Lily. "I think our daughter shows that there was. I could never just be your friend. They knew that. It took me too many years to figure that out."

She thought back to those times. How she had met those women and knew they were never going to last. They were cookie-cutter versions of each other. No spice. Nothing there to keep his interest.

But when he brought Gwen to meet her, it had been different.

Romey had liked her. She had tried to find something wrong with her, but there was nothing.

She was the perfect match for the son of Sweetheart Lake.

When he had broken up with her out of the blue and showed up on Romey's doorstep, it had shocked her.

And when he left Romey without a word, she'd thought that maybe Gray regretted leaving Gwen.

That he had just wanted one more fling with her before settling down.

But now he was back here, dropping not-so-subtle hints that he wanted to be with her.

"Have you seen Gwen?" she asked, not able to help herself.

"I ran into her the other day when I was leaving here." He gave her a curious look. "Why?"

"Did seeing her bring up any old feelings?" she asked in a rush. "She's a sweet person. I think she might be understanding about you having a baby with another woman while you two were broken up."

Anger flashed in his eyes. "Why do you do that? Why do you always twist and turn and change the conversation? You know I don't want to be with her. Lord knows she would be a hell of a lot easier to be with than you, but apparently I don't want easy. I want you, damn it."

They fell quiet for a moment. Only the sounds of their breathing could be heard. Romey didn't know what to say to that. How to react.

He'd left her.

He'd left when Charlie died.

He'd left her pregnant and scared.

He'd left her for almost two years.

How the hell could that mean that he wanted her?

"Mama?" they heard a little voice call.

Gray's anger immediately faded. He walked back over to the playpen with a big smile on his face. "She's awake!" He lifted her up and kissed both her cheeks. "Daddy's been thinking about you nonstop."

Lily looked up at her father, studying his face, in her way trying to figure out who he was in her life.

"Your daddy came to see you, Lily." Romey walked over to them. "Say hi to Daddy, baby."

"Hi," Lily said softly. She looked at Romey and then back to Gray. They were her parents. It was still hard for Romey to wrap her head around it.

They were going to have to coparent. The thought was so incredibly overwhelming to her that it had robbed her of sleep the last few nights. She wanted Lily to love Gray. She had to trust that he would be a good father to her. She had to trust him not to walk away again.

But could she?

She felt ridiculously close to tears.

"I'm going to take you and Mama out to dinner," Gray told Lily. "And then we are going to buy you another car seat for my car and a new crib for my house and all the toys you want."

Romey shook her head. "Gray, I don't want you spoiling her. Just be there."

"I will be there. Buying furniture and a car seat is not spoiling her."

"Two sets of everything seems so unnecessary."

"Fine. Then move all of your stuff into my house and live with me. We won't need two sets of everything."

She rolled her eyes at him. "Can you say things that aren't completely ridiculous?"

"It's not ridiculous." He looked back to Lily and softened his voice. "Mamas and daddies should live together, don't you think, gorgeous? Wouldn't you like to see me and Mama living together?"

"Oh, sweetie, don't listen to your daddy. You know Mama wouldn't like to explain to Uncle Cally why she smothered your daddy with a pillow while he was sleeping."

"Vicious," he said, right before he bent his head to kiss Romey's cheek. "Come on, Mama. It's time to go shopping."

* * *

Gray sat across from Romey at the fifties-style diner a few miles outside Sweetheart Lake. Their daughter was sitting in a high chair next to them, chewing on a french fry.

Their daughter.

He still couldn't believe it.

He would have made it back in time to see Lily born if everything has gone according to his plan. After six months in the Middle East, he had been ready to be back home. He had seen some of what Charlie had seen. He had helped people he otherwise never would have met. He had tried to assuage his guilt by working in some of the most depressed parts of the world. He had tried to make up for being a bad friend to Charlie. But nothing had gone to plan. And instead of heading out of Syria the next day, he and six of his colleagues had been captured and held.

He was one of the lucky ones. He had finally made it back home.

He reached out and touched one of Lily's curls. He was glad he wouldn't be missing her entire life.

"When is her birthday?" he asked Romey.

"June thirtieth."

"Can I come to her party?"

"You have to be there. You're paying for it."

"You didn't want me buying a bedroom set for her, but you'll allow me to pay for her party?"

She took a sip of her milk shake and looked up at him. "I guess I like giving you a hard time, Gray."

"You always have."

"I was thinking we would just have a cake. Maybe we could take her to the zoo. I'll invite your father if he would like to come. He knows about Lily, right?"

"I think he knew before I did."

"I suspected. He's okay with it?"

"He likes you, Romey. You know that."

"I like him too. I should thank him. He was kind to me. He came to the hospital to see me and the baby. He bought me a stroller. And I know he's the one who put new tires on my car."

"Tires?"

She nodded. "He overheard me asking who had the best prices in town one morning when I was in my shop. When I went to my car in the afternoon, I had brand-new shiny tires. I'm pretty sure he broke several laws to do that. He won't admit it, but I know it was him."

"People really do like him, don't they?"

"He's on his fifth term. I would think they did."

"It's not an act."

"No. I know he wasn't around a lot when you were a kid, but it doesn't mean he's not a nice person."

"Don't be on the opposite side of him in a court case. He was ferocious. His work consumed him."

"You didn't want to be like him."

"I tried extremely hard not to be like him. But I'm no better than him." He bent down and kissed Lily's forehead. His father had at least been there when he was born.

"Eat your cheeseburger, Gray," she said, as she lifted a bite of pancake to her lips.

His eating had become irregular. It wasn't that his body didn't crave food, but it was as if his brain had stopped responding to his hunger. He had to make himself eat now.

He had been so preoccupied with working on the house today that he couldn't remember the last thing he ate. It was probably coffee and a leftover piece of cold fried chicken his father made sure was sent home with him.

"I will." He took a big bite of it. It was good. Greasy. Still warm. The bacon coated his mouth with a salty flavor he had missed. "Why did you choose this place? I would have taken you anywhere you wanted to go."

"I wanted to go here. Where else can you get two pancakes, two eggs, two strips of bacon, home fries, and toast for five ninety-nine? It's a damn good deal."

"The queen of the bargain." He smiled at her. "I get to pick next time," he said, taking another bite. "We need to go for some barbecue. Brisket, corn bread, baked beans with those little bits of smoked meat inside of it."

She was quiet for a long moment.

"How did you lose so much weight, Gray?"

"It's not that much. I'm surprised everyone is making such a big deal about it."

"It's at least twenty pounds, which is a lot for someone who wasn't overweight to begin with."

"I'm fine." He reached across the table and took her hand in his. He thought she would pull it back right away, but she didn't. "I'm glad you still care."

"Yes, I care. If you die of some terrible disease and leave me alone with this baby again, I'll have you brought back to life just so I can kill you myself."

"I'm not sick, Romey. I promise."

"Did you go grocery shopping yet?"

He shook his head. "I've got food in the house, though. Anna made sure she sent me home with the leftovers from the lunch I had with my father."

"We thought you were dead." Her voice was so soft that he almost didn't hear what she said. "So many months with no word, Gray. Your father tried to have an investigator find you."

He sat up straighter. "He mentioned he had called to see where I was. He never told me about an investigator."

"I don't think he wants you to know how worried he was."

"I didn't think it would matter that I was gone."

"How the hell can you say that?" She removed her hand from his. "You are loved in Sweetheart Lake. You saw all those people who came to the airport when you came back."

"Those people don't know me. How can you love someone you don't know?"

"Your father loves you. What about him?"

He shook his head. "We were never close. I just didn't think it mattered where I was."

"It mattered. To him. To me. To Cally. How could you be so thoughtless?"

That he couldn't deny. He was quiet for a moment, trying to think of the right thing to say, but only the words *I'm sorry* resonated in his head. Their waitress came over, interrupting the tense moment.

"How y'all doing over here? Can I get you anything else?"

"Yes, please," Romey answered. "He would like a chocolate milk shake."

"I'll get that going for you," she said, and gave them a smile.

"I didn't want a milk shake."

"Too bad. You're drinking it."

"Charlie and I got into a very big fight right before he died," he told her in one breath. He wasn't sure he'd ever wanted her to know.

"Charlie argued with everyone then. He was at his worst. He threw me and Callahan out of his apartment. I didn't speak to him for over a week."

"No, Romey. It wasn't an argument. It was a fight."

She froze, a realization coming over her. "That's how you got that big bruise on your cheek, isn't it?"

He nodded. "We weren't friends when he died."

"What was the fight about?"

You.

"Does it matter?"

"I don't know. Maybe."

"It wasn't about one thing. Fights like that never are."

"He asked you for money, didn't he?"

He shook his head. "It wasn't about that."

"He resented you. To him your life was perfect, and nothing had ever gone right in his."

Charlie had had reason to resent him. Gray had been given so much, while Charlie had worked so damn hard and ended up with nothing. "I'm sorry I brought it up." He lifted Lily out of her high chair and placed her in his lap. "I need to be paying more attention to this girl." He buried his face in her curls and inhaled her soft baby scent. "Do you think your father would be okay with me visiting him?"

"Yes. He was glad that it was you who turned out to be her father."

He looked up at Romey. "He didn't know?"

"No one knew. Except Cally, but he guessed, and I never denied it. I wanted you to be the first to know."

That made him somehow feel worse.

"How do you think Callahan would react if I visited him?"

She shrugged. "You thought Charlie hit hard; Callahan has three inches and twenty pounds on him, and right now you're too skinny to take that kind of blow."

"I'll wear a helmet. Better yet, I'll bring the baby with me. He won't hit me while I'm holding her."

"Smart."

"Since you don't want me to take care of her all day, I'm going to pay for her day care."

She opened her mouth to protest, but he gave her such a hard look that she shut her mouth.

"You'd better not say a damn thing about it," he warned. "I'm her father. I don't want to hear your independent-woman bullshit right now."

"Misogynist," she said softly.

He reached into his pocket and pulled out a card with her name on it.

"I know you don't want to talk about child support, but this is for you and Lily. I had an account set up for you. It should cover any expenses you had for the past year. If Lily ever needs anything, I would like you to use this card."

"Gray . . ."

"No arguments, Romey. Not tonight. I need to do this."

She took the card from him and slipped it into her pocket. There would be no fight about this. They were getting somewhere.

CHAPTER NINE

What my mother believed about cooking is that if you worked hard and prospered, someone else would do it for you.—Nora Ephron

"I guess you wanted to be fashionably late," Callahan said to Romey as she walked up to him. They were in the swankiest restaurant in Sweetheart Lake. The one she had been past a thousand times but never set foot in. She was sure that restaurant existed just for the people who lived on the other side of the lake. The rest of them couldn't afford to drop forty bucks on a pasta dish they could make at home for a fraction of the cost.

"Am I late?" She knew she was. She'd been hoping to slip in unnoticed. "I thought only nerds arrived to parties right on time."

Callahan just looked at her. He was the type to arrive everywhere on time. It didn't matter what the occasion was.

"You want a drink?" he asked. "There's an open bar. They've got a signature cocktail to celebrate the happy couple."

"What's in it?" she asked him.

"Grapefruit juice and champagne."

She shook her head, imagining the too-tart taste of the drink. "I'd rather drink sweat. I need something with whiskey in it."

"I know what you like. I'll be right back."

"No." She grabbed her cousin's arm. "Don't leave me alone. I'll go with you."

"If you didn't want to be alone, then why did you insist taking your own car?"

"I can't stay long. I'm working tomorrow. I need to be at the restaurant early. Tomorrow will be the first day of our new menu." It wasn't a lie—the restaurant she worked for was *starting a new menu tomorrow—but that wasn't why she needed to leave early. She needed to leave early because it was too hard to be here.*

When she had gotten the invitation to the engagement party, she'd put it in a drawer and out of her mind. It was hard to look at. There was a picture of them on it. Taken by a professional photographer outside Gray's childhood home, the lake serving as a backdrop. Of course, they looked beautiful. Like two rich kids coming together to create another generation of wealthy preppy kids.

It was how it was supposed to be.

"Why don't you go say hello to Gray and Gwen while I get you a drink? You won't be alone with them."

They were the people she least wanted to see. It wasn't the wealthy members of their community that she didn't want to be left with. It was Gray.

"I don't want to bother them. It's their night."

Callahan looked at her, and she knew her excuse was lame. "This party is supposed to be for that purpose. Stop being silly and go."

Callahan gave her a tiny push in their direction. He had no idea of her and Gray's history. Of how they'd secretly seen each other for years. The last time had been not long before she moved back here. He had surprised her in front of her apartment in Chicago. It was the middle of December and bitterly cold. He'd told he was there to give her her Christmas present. It was a mug the said Virginia is for Lovers.

She kissed him right in the middle of the sidewalk, not giving a damn who saw. He stayed with her for a week, and then he went back to DC, where he was living at the time. There was no talk of a future together. It was the pattern they had fallen into. They lived far apart; both of them had busy careers. They were just supposed to enjoy each other.

She hadn't ever thought that would be their last time together. But he had started dating Gwen a few months later. And now he was about to marry her.

She walked over to them. Gwen looked very pretty in a classic blue cocktail dress. She was smiling warmly like the happy future bride she was. It took Romey a bit longer to look at Gray. He wore a suit with no tie, a few of his top shirt buttons open, making him look a little less preppy than usual. He was handsome as always. They looked perfect together.

"Hello, lovebirds," she said as she approached.

"Romey!" Gwen smiled brightly as she reached to hug her. "I'm so glad you made it. You look gorgeous."

"I've got two pairs of shapewear sucking it under here. You should see me without it. I look like a busted tin of biscuits."

Gwen let out an almost startled laugh. "I don't think I've ever heard that saying before. But it's perfect."

"You look very lovely, Gwen," Romey said. "I just wanted to say congratulations before things got too busy. I can't stay that long tonight."

"Why not?" Gray asked.

"Gray," Gwen gently chided. "That's none of our business."

"It's nothing private. I have a really crazy day at work tomorrow."

"Executive pastry chef," Gray said. "The restaurant lured her away from Chicago for this job. I heard from Charlie that

all kinds of politicians come there just to taste your desserts." He was annoyed with her. Most people wouldn't be able to tell. She wasn't even sure Gwen would notice. But she did. His eyes were a little harder; there was the slightest edge to his voice.

"I might not have an important job like you, Gray. But I take my work very seriously."

"I would never say that your job wasn't important. You're amazing at what you do. You've been like a ghost since you've gotten it. I saw more of you when you lived a thousand miles away than I do now."

It was true. And it wasn't because of work. He was serious with Gwen. He and Romey couldn't be friends anymore. Not the way they used to. Not the way they had been for the past twenty years.

"You know how it is. I'm trying make my mark on the world."

"I think that's wonderful," Gwen said. "It must be so nice to have a career you are passionate about."

An older couple came up to them at that moment, and Romey took it as her chance to slip away. It was the last time she would see or speak to Gray for a long time.

* * *

It was one of those days she wished she could stay in bed, Romey thought as she got up the next morning and walked downstairs to put on a pot of coffee for her father. She hadn't slept well last night, which made waking up at four AM even crueler. She had been doing it as long as she could remember. Always at work by five, prepping for the day's menu. It wasn't for everyone, but she enjoyed the silence of the morning, the solitude of being alone with just a pile of flour, the smell of butter, and her thoughts.

Her thoughts had been keeping her awake most nights lately. Sometimes she wished she could turn them off. Have an empty head for once in her life. She wished she could be like a man. Men swore that when they said they weren't thinking about anything, they meant it. She wondered how it could be possible, and if it were, what it would be like to walk around in the world with a head full of nothing.

It must be quiet.

She, on the other hand, thought about the next presidential election, the amount of gas she had in her car, and how much more pizza she could eat before her jeans started to cut off her circulation. Then there was her baby, who was constantly on her mind. And now there was Gray.

He had spent four hours with them last night. Four hours in public where anyone could see them. Yes, they were a little outside of town, but not far enough out that people wouldn't know them. It was odd for her to be in public with him without Charlie or Callahan. He was someone she had seen only at night when they lived close to each other. There was the occasional weekend where they spent the entire day together, but it had always been at his house or hers. Dinners were ordered in. Date nights never consisted of going out. They had been a secret.

One they never discussed. Not even with each other.

Yesterday had been a very odd experience for her. She kept looking around the shopping center to see if anyone had seen them. Gray didn't seem to care if anyone had.

He was oblivious to her feelings. To how anxious she was.

For years they had been so quiet, so careful about everything. Now, to have things in the open just seemed odd.

They'd made a baby together.

Romey had to share Lily with him. And to do that, she had to be around him. He was easy and hard to be with at the same time. There was a part of her that was comfortable around him because they had known each other so long. But there was the part of her that didn't trust him. When he broke up with Gwen and came to her, she was sure that that was it, that they were going to quit dancing around each other, but Charlie died and Gray disappeared, and he'd taken a very important piece of her that she wasn't sure she was going to get back.

Her confidence.

There was a knock at the front door, and Romey jumped as she was pouring coffee grounds into the filter.

"What in the hell?"

The knock came again.

She glanced at the clock. It was just a few minutes after four. Callahan wouldn't have knocked. Gray probably would have come to the back door, just like he did when they were kids.

Romey walked over to the door and saw a tall man in a tan suit standing there.

"Mr. Norton?" She opened the door, her mind trying to catch up with her eyes. "What are you doing here?"

"My grandbaby is here, isn't she? I've come to see her. I've been waiting a long time to become a grandfather. I hope you'll let me see her."

She stepped aside, dumbfounded. "Of course, sir. Please come in."

"I wish you'd stop being so formal with me, Romey. I've told you a million times to call me Carey."

"But I can't," she said, horrified. "You're my elder and the mayor and you used to be my daddy's boss. I can't just go around calling you by your first name. People already think I'm fast. They'll drop dead if they hear me calling you Carey."

He grinned at her. She wanted to say she saw Gray in his smile, but it reminded her of someone else. She just couldn't put her finger on it at the moment.

"Who cares about people? Besides, we're family now. Gray told me you were having a bit of an issue with my grandbaby's childcare. I'm here to help."

"But . . ." She didn't know what to say. "Angela is coming."

"No. She isn't. I'm taking over for the day. Your father and I will be watching Lily. It will give us some time to catch up. Bond over being grandpas."

"I'm having trouble getting my mind to work. Do you know how early it is?"

"Of course I know. You're in the shop by five every morning. But I was so excited about coming here today, I could barely sleep. Go on and get dressed. We'll talk before you leave."

"I was making a pot of coffee for my father." She shook her head. "I feel like my manners have up and vanished. Can I get you anything?"

"Sweet girl." He touched her cheek. "Go get ready. I think I can take over making the coffee."

"I spilled some grounds on the counter." She started the walk toward the kitchen. "Let me clean it up."

He touched her shoulder, stopping her. "I know I have help to clean for me, but it doesn't mean I can't do things for myself. I can manage a few coffee grounds. Now go get dressed. I promise you, everything will be okay."

Romey nodded, still confused, and went back upstairs. Carey Norton was the very last person she'd expected to see this morning. And his presence there was unexpectedly sweet.

* * *

Gray walked up to the back of Romey's house, his shoes slightly wet from the dewy grass, and saw his father sitting at the kitchen table holding a cup of coffee and staring down at his iPad. He lightly tapped on the sliding glass door, alerting his father of his presence. His father smiled at him and stood up to let him in.

"You beat me here."

"I did. Some people believe in being fashionably late. I believe in being the first one on the scene. It's good to know what you're getting yourself into."

"This is your granddaughter's house. Not a crime scene."

"I know that. I was giving you a little life lesson there, son."

Gray took in his father's clothing. "I see you dressed for the occasion."

His father was pristine as usual in his summer suit. Gray didn't know why he was having a hard time understanding how his father had gotten here so early. He should have known better. His father never spent time thinking when he could be acting.

"I know you young people like to dress casually and think it's old and stuffy to be in a suit, but wearing a suit commands a certain amount of respect. But the light color says I'm still friendly and approachable."

Gray laughed. "You've got to start writing this stuff down, Dad."

"I think I should too. I've had a few reporters contact me over the years about a few high-profile cases I worked. But I don't really trust anyone else to get the facts right." He paused and studied Gray for a moment before he took his seat. "Son, I've been trying not to say anything, but I need to know when you plan on dressing like a person who doesn't live under a bridge."

"You don't like my clothes?" He looked down at himself. He wore a black T-shirt and some gray cargo pants.

"Can't say I do. Are you having a problem with your hot water? I've got a guy I can call to fix it. Or if you need a pack of razors, I can run to the store and pick you up some. You just tell your old man what you need, and I'll help you."

Gray scratched his chin. He couldn't remember the last time he'd shaved. His hair was too long. It annoyed him the way it touched the back of his neck, but grooming hadn't crossed his mind.

"There was no need to dress up where I was. I only had a couple of changes of clothes. I had to travel light."

"Well, you aren't traveling anymore, son. You have to have more than a few changes of clothes now. You've got an entire closet full of stuff back at the house."

"I don't think oxford shirts and loafers are my thing anymore."

"No." His father took a sip of his coffee. "You've seen the world now, and not just the fancy parts that your mother liked to send you to, thinking it was cultured. You really saw how some people live."

"I was spoiled."

"Yeah, but a lot of Americans are. That's what makes this country the one people die trying to get to. But I get it. You're a rugged man now. No more pretty-boy doctor with hands that are too soft."

"You taking a shot at me, Dad?"

"Not at all. Merely agreeing with your assessment of your former self." He was thoughtfully quiet for a long moment. "If you want to get Romey back, you've got to start taking care of yourself."

He stared at his father, surprised at his frankness.

"You do want her back, don't you?"

"I think you already know the answer to that."

"She's a gorgeous girl. Looks just like her mother and her aunt."

"Her aunt?"

"Callahan's mother. Celesta. You know they used to be a double act in their family's circus."

"I vaguely remember hearing something about it. Romey and Charlie never talked much about their mother's side. How do you know about it?"

"They used to travel through here with their circus. My friends and I would buy a ticket every single time. The women in this town are just fine, but Luna and Celesta was goddesses. We had never seen women like that before."

"I had no idea."

"You've got to step up your game, son. You want a beautiful woman, you have to put in the work."

Romey walked in before Gray could respond. She wore a denim skirt, a little black T-shirt with skulls on it, and a pair of white Converse on her feet. Her hair was pulled high on the top of her head. It wasn't even five AM, and he found her so damn sexy.

She paused upon seeing him, her eyes going wide. "You're here too?"

"I tried to beat my father here, but clearly no one beats Carey Norton."

"I sure like it when they try," Carey said, grinning. "This is damn good coffee, by the way. Where did you get it from?"

Romey walked over to the cabinet and handed him a package. "I order it from a friend I used to work with. Their shop is based out of Chicago. You can have this one. I have a couple more."

"You are not taking that coffee from her," Gray said to his father.

"But I'm giving it to him." Romey frowned at him.

"He can buy his own damn coffee. In fact, I'm sure he could buy his own coffee-roasting operation and have it run right out of his house."

"Don't be ridiculous, Gray. You know the house isn't zoned for that kind of business."

"You can have the coffee, Mr. Norton. But you do realize, in order to get this coffee, you have to pay for my baby's college."

"Gray is paying for her education. I'm Grandpa. I buy the fun stuff. Like a hot-pink sports car for her birthday. Or a pedigree horse that we'll name something ridiculous like Popcorn Puff."

Romey shook her head. "No sports cars. And nothing new either. I'll be damned if my kid gets a brand-new car before I do."

"I'll buy you a sports car too. Y'all can match each other."

Romey shook her head and smiled. "Give me a sensible SUV that's good in the snow, and I'll consider it." She reached into another cabinet and set out a container of oatmeal and then took out two bowls, one made for a small child and one for an adult.

She then set out a container of brown sugar and some dried fruit and nuts.

Gray knew she wasn't doing this for herself. It was one of the little ways she took care of her father. She turned back to face them.

"I left my father a note on his door so he won't be surprised to find you here. They both get oatmeal in the morning. Daddy loves to eat eggs and bacon every morning, but we are watching his cholesterol. Lily is usually up by six thirty. She eats and then I dress her. I laid her clothes out already. She's a busy body nowadays and tries to head for that back door every chance she gets. She really loves sitting in the grass. If you could take her outside for a little while, it would make her happy. I have sunscreen in the medicine cabinet. For lunch—"

"Romey, there will be three grown men here. We'll be all right," Carey said. "Don't look so worried."

"I can't help it. I've only left her with my family before."

Carey stood up and squeezed her shoulder. "Didn't I tell you we were family now? You're going to be seeing so much of me you're going to get sick of my face. Lily is ours too now. You know we'll take care of her."

Romey nodded but looked unconvinced. "You have my number. Call me if you need me. Or just drop her off at the shop if she gets too much for you. Alice helps me with her after the morning rush."

"We won't be dropping her off, Romey," Gray told her. "I promise, we will be fine."

She nodded once again, the worry not leaving her face, and he hated that ultimately he was the cause of her worry. He hadn't been there with her from the beginning. To her, he was a stranger to their baby.

But she was trusting him with her. He was thankful for that. As mad as she was, as mad as she had every right to be, she wasn't being difficult about his access to their child. He probably didn't deserve the gift she was giving him.

"Let me walk you to your car," he said to her.

She grabbed her bag off the back of one of the chairs and walked ahead of him. He followed her to her car. It had to be ten years old at this point. A perfectly serviceable vehicle, but she should have something newer. Something she wouldn't have to worry about fixing all the time. He could give her that. He could give her so many things, but he knew she would refuse them.

The only woman he had ever wanted to spoil was the only woman who would take nothing from him.

"When did you plan this?" she asked him when they were alone.

"I didn't. I had some legal questions for my father, so I called him last night and mentioned that we were going to start to look at day cares."

"Legal questions? You aren't going to try to sue me for custody, are you?"

He rolled his eyes. "Don't ask me questions you already know the answer to."

"I don't know! That's why I asked."

"Unless I can have a judge order you to move in with me and agree with everything I say, I don't see a point in you and I going to court."

"What legal stuff, then?"

"Life insurance. A college fund. A will. You know, adult shit I have to think about now that I'm a father."

"Oh." She fell quiet. "I guess I can't be mad at you for that."

"Are you looking for reasons to be mad at me?"

"To be honest, yes. Yes, I'm looking for any reason to rip you a new asshole."

He grabbed her by her hips and pulled her close.

"Get off of me," she said as she rested her head on his chest.

"Thank you," he told her. He smoothed his hand down her back, and she shut her eyes. She felt good against him.

Familiar.

Warm.

Right.

"For what?"

"Not punching me in the face for trying to hug you."

She grinned. Her eyes were still closed. Her face relaxed. "No one hugs me. Cally and Daddy aren't the affectionate type. They are sweet to Lily, though, but it's not the same."

He wanted to say something witty or even empathetic, but he just stayed quiet and hugged her a little tighter. It was his fault she had been alone.

A car drove past, and it broke the moment. She pulled away from him, looking up at him with almost sadness in her eyes.

"We'll be okay today," he told her.

She nodded. "If anything happens to her when she's on your watch, I'm going to kill you, cut you up, and feed you to the gators in the lake."

"There are no alligators in the lake."

She shrugged. "I'll find something to feed you to then."

"I'm going to try to avoid that fate. Go to work. We'll see you this afternoon."

She briefly shut her eyes and took in a breath. Her armor came back on then, and he found himself feeling so damn bad that she had to do that to face the world every day.

CHAPTER TEN

A good cook is like a sorceress who dispenses happiness.—Elisa Schiaparelli

Romey's cell phone buzzed in her back pocket. She glanced at Alice to make sure she was okay tending to her customer and then stepped into the back to check the text. She had looked at her phone probably two dozen times today, waiting to see if Gray had called or texted. But he never had.

She didn't know why she was such a ball of anxiety. Gray was a responsible adult. He was a doctor. And he wasn't even alone with Lily. His father had been there as well as hers. Of course three men, three fathers, could take care of one little girl.

It was just so odd for her to see them there. Yes, Gray had been a fixture in their house when they were kids, but that had all ended when he went away to college and Charlie went to the Marines. His father had never spent any time there, only stopping by briefly to pay his respects after Charlie died. The Nortons seemed so out of place in her shabby little house, where the furniture didn't match and the floors were scuffed. They hadn't seemed uncomfortable. But she'd looked at Carey Norton in his suit with his quiet man-in-charge air about him and knew that their worlds didn't line up. That there were experiences her family had had that his would never know.

And now Carey was saying they were part of her and Lily's family.

She looked at the text. It was from a number she didn't recognize.

Hey, baby. It's Mama. I got a new phone number. I've really been missing you. Please send me some pictures of my grandbaby. They were all saved on my old phone and that got destroyed.

Romey just stared at the message before she put her phone away. She didn't feel like dealing with her mother now. Her number changed at least twice a year. So much so that when Charlie died, they hadn't been able to get in contact with her for over a week. It was the day after the funeral when they did.

She had been hurt by Gray, but she had been mad at her mother. Callahan had to call in a few favors with some government agencies to find her. She was in Mexico that time, at some wellness retreat, and when she whisked herself into town after hearing the news, Romey was so mad she could barely look at her. But it wasn't Romey who laid into her. It wasn't even Callahan who was spitting mad that most of their family couldn't pull their shit together enough to be there for them. It was her father who blew up at her.

"You don't want to live in a small town? Fine. You don't want to stay settled and raise our kids? That's fine too. You can go traipsing around the whole goddamn world, for all I care, but you better be reachable when the kids need you.

You better make yourself available when they ask you to come. You better put someone else first for the first time in your entire selfish life."

Her mother just stood there, looking beautifully wounded.

"I'm sorry, Cy."

"I don't want to hear your apologies anymore. Change, Luna."

Ever since then, her mother had always made sure they had a number to reach her at. She had lost a son too, but Romey hurt more for her father than for anyone. He'd had to raise them alone, with no support from the woman he'd married, only fights with her when the disagreements over how they wanted to bring the kids up got too big.

Romey's mother had never agreed with sending her children to school.

The world is your school.

Life is your university.

She'd hated that Charlie decided to go into the Marines. She said he was becoming a hit man for the government. She'd also never understood why Romey went away to college. She told her to move to France if she wanted to learn how to bake. Romey had found the thought intriguing for a while. But in the end, she knew she wasn't like her mother. Starting over in a new country wasn't for her. She liked the idea of roots. Of familiarity. Of having a home.

"Romey," she heard Alice call from the front of the shop. "There's someone here to see you."

She slipped her phone back into her pocket and walked back out to the front of the shop.

The first person she spotted was a tall, handsome man standing on the other side of the counter. He was tanned and clean-shaven. His hair was a little on the longish side but fashionably cut. He was dressed in a fitted black T-shirt and light-wash jeans.

"Mama!"

And he was holding her baby.

"Gray?" She walked out from behind the counter and went up to him. He didn't look like his old self, the man she'd known before he left. But he certainly wasn't the man she'd driven away from this morning either.

"Hi, Mommy. We thought we would come pay you a visit so you could see we were fine," he said to her.

Romey took Lily from him and kissed her chubby warm cheek. "Are you having a good time with your daddy today?"

"Daddy?" she heard Alice gasp from behind her.

"Oh." She turned around and looked at Alice. "I guess I forgot to tell you. Gray is the one who knocked me up."

"Ramona," her father warned. She turned to see him and Carey sitting at a table near the window. She hadn't noticed them when she walked out. Her eyes were on Gray.

"It's true, Daddy. He did get me pregnant. I didn't even know anything about that kind of stuff. He's a bad influence on me."

"You're the worst," Gray said softly as he leaned down and kissed the side of her face. His skin was smooth now, no more bristly facial hair to scratch her face. He smelled heavenly too, like some mixture of soapy shaving cream and spicy aftershave. She would love to wrap herself in him, bury her nose in his neck, and just inhale him. But she couldn't. And she wouldn't. She was always so incredibly attracted to him. It wasn't the way he looked, but whatever body chemistry he was made up of pulled her in and wouldn't let her go.

It was how she'd ended up with a baby in the first place.

Kissing her, even as innocently as he had in front of both their fathers and motormouth Alice, was a statement. And she wondered if he had any idea of how it would change things. Soon everyone would know he was Lily's father.

She walked over to the table that her father and Carey were sitting at. Her father looked a little more like his old self. His eyes still held that heavy sadness, but he looked present. He was wearing one of his button-down shirts, which was neatly tucked today. His hair was shorter too.

"You got a haircut, Daddy. You look so handsome."

He nodded. "I took Gray to my barbershop. Almost didn't recognize him this morning. Thought he was there to rob me. The boy better be glad his father was there. Saved him from getting his behind kicked."

"Pa." Lily reached for her grandfather, who without hesitating took the baby from Romey. It didn't escape Romey that Lily had spent almost her entire first year in the care of her father. She loved him, and not spending the day with him was probably difficult for her too.

"You've probably been playing musical arms all day, haven't you?" she said to her daughter. "Two granddaddies now. How am I ever going to stop them from spoiling you?"

"You can't," Carey said. "It's like trying to stop the sun from shining. Impossible."

"Are you all hungry? I was trying out some new savory pie recipes, and I need tasters."

"I would love to be a taster," Carey answered. "That oatmeal we had this morning is wearing off."

"They wouldn't let me make them bacon and eggs," her father said, looking up at her. "Both said they'd rather eat oatmeal. Now I've heard some pretty big lies in my life, but a man telling me he prefers oatmeal over bacon is by far the biggest."

"I guess there's no accounting for taste, Daddy. I've got to finish up those pies. It will be a few minutes, but you can go help yourselves to something to drink while you wait."

She'd started to head to the back of her shop when she heard Gray say, "I'll help you."

She looked back at him, starting to say that she didn't need help, but she didn't.

She paused once she got in the kitchen and looked up to him expectantly.

His eyes widened. "What?"

"What do you mean, what? Didn't you want to tell me something?"

He shrugged. "I need to know what you think about my haircut."

He caught her off guard with his question. After a moment she shrugged. "It's fine."

"It's fine?"

She put her hand on her hip and shook her head. "It's not like you to fish for compliments. What's going on?"

"I want you to think I'm cute," he said.

She grinned at him and then went to her counter to put the finishing touches on the chicken Florentine pie. "Every girl in our high school thought you were cute. I was included in that every girl. I was so mad at myself when I realized I liked you."

"Why?" He came to stand by her, watching her while she brushed the top layer of phyllo with butter.

"I don't know. You were Charlie's friend. You were the most popular boy in school. Everyone tried to get your attention. I didn't want to be like everyone else." She placed the pie back in the oven to warm it up.

"You didn't have a crush on me from afar. You actually knew me. We were friends. You weren't like everyone else."

"Were we really friends, then? You didn't just think of me as Charlie's sister?"

"I thought of you as Romey. You existed outside of your brother. We also did things together without your brother around. That's what friends do."

"You mean we had sex. Well, we couldn't do that with Charlie in the room, now, could we?"

"I wasn't talking about sex, you pervert. You would go out on the lake with me every summer."

"Charlie hated rowboats. He always thought he was going to fall out."

"We would go to the store on ice cream runs. You would stay up late with me and watch old movies. We were friends."

"Such good friends I let you take my virginity."

He wrapped one arm around her and pulled her into him. "I was so nervous," he told her in a whisper. "I thought I was going to screw it up and you would never want to speak to me again."

She shook her head. It was the second time that day she had found herself in his arms, and just like before, she found herself unable to pull away from his warmth. He made her feel safe when she was with him. It was a stupid, untrustworthy feeling, but it was there and she wanted to settle into it. "You didn't mess it up. You didn't mess it up so much that I slept with you two hundred more times."

"I was too embarrassed afterward to ask you about it."

"You could have asked me anything."

He looked at her for a long moment and then lowered his lips to hers. She allowed him to kiss her, at first just standing still, letting his lips move over hers. She was just trying to experience rather than participate in this kiss, but there was always that little spark, that little something that made her insides go all warm and melty and her body start to hum. She kissed him back but only briefly before she pulled away.

"We can't do this," she said to him, her lips still close to his.

"No. Not right now." He straightened up. "Nobody's lips ever felt as good as yours."

"You saying stuff like that is how we ended up in this mess in the first place." She walked away from him. The smell of the pie she had in the oven was starting to fill the air.

"It's not a mess. And if I recall, you are the one who kissed me first all those years ago."

"I kissed you first? Ha! You were going to kiss me and then you paused. I just closed the space between our mouths. I didn't want you backing out of my first kiss."

"You made me nervous. I think I knew back then if I kissed you that there would be no turning back."

"Yeah," she said, looking up at him. She really did like his haircut. His beautifully formed face. His lips. She had never been so attracted to another man. Not even close. "Look at us now."

"I'm very glad you kissed me first."

"Speaking of firsts. I don't think you ever told me who your first time was with."

A little bit of surprise filled his eyes. "You definitely know who my first was."

"No, I really don't. I thought I heard you and Charlie talking about some girl you met while you went to visit your mother's family. But you stopped talking when you noticed me. You kept that kind of stuff quiet. Who was it?"

He looked at her with disbelief. "Are you serious?" he asked her.

"Why won't you tell me? Are you embarrassed?"

"No." He laughed. "I'm not embarrassed. I just can't believe we are having this conversation."

"Do you think I'm being tacky for asking? I just don't go around asking people these things. We had a baby, Gray. I think you could trust me with this information that doesn't even matter. I don't even care who it is. I was just curious."

"You already know who I lost my virginity to because you were there when it happened."

"What are you talking about?" She shook her head. "I couldn't have been there. I never hung out with you when you were with another girl. You and Charlie never let me go to any of the parties you guys went to."

"Romey, you were there because it was you. You were my first."

She blinked at him, still not sure she was understanding what he was saying. "That can't be." He was the most popular boy in their school. He had had girlfriends before her. He'd been nearly eighteen when they were first together.

He touched her chin. "You're shocked. I can't believe you didn't know!" He laughed again. "You couldn't tell how nervous I was?"

"I . . . I . . ." She didn't know what to say. Too many emotions bubbled in her chest. "What a loser." She walked away from him, needing to have her eyes off him for a moment. She checked on her pie, knowing she shouldn't keep the oven open for so long.

"Loser?"

"Yeah. Big, macho Gray Norton. Girls were throwing their panties at you. I thought you had been with at least half a dozen girls before me. That's why I chose you. I thought you knew what you were doing." She was lying to him. There was no choice when it came to him. He was the only one she had ever wanted to be with.

She took the pie out of the oven, not sure if the insides were fully warmed through again. After placing it on the cooling tray, she glanced at him. He was studying her. His head tilted to the side. His arms folded over her chest.

She walked over to him and impulsively threw her arms around him and kissed his lips. "I like your haircut. Okay? But I still hate you and I think you're dumb."

"You drive me insane," he said to her. "And that's why I can never stay away from you." He pulled away from her. "I'm going to see how the old men are doing. Don't hide too long in here."

CHAPTER ELEVEN

Cooking is like one failure after another, and that's how you finally learn.—Julia Child

Gray pulled up in front of the little white house with black shutters. The house was located on a quiet street not far from his home. He must have walked down this street hundreds of times as a kid. It was the one they'd had to take to get to the center of town. Not much had changed in the past twenty years. People have moved in, others had moved out. The houses had pretty much stayed the same. Neat little houses with small fenced-in backyards, so close to each other that neighbors could probably hear each other's conversations.

It was a real neighborhood. He remembered being kind of fascinated by it all those years ago. He hadn't lived near anyone in his house on the other side of the lake. Sure, he'd had neighbors. Other people who owned lakefront estates. But no one was within walking distance. There were no yard sales or block parties. There were no kids to play with.

He hadn't realized that this was how most people lived until he'd met the Michaelses. And he hadn't realized that some people weren't lucky enough to live in a neighborhood like this.

Charlie had sometimes spoken of how much he missed New Orleans. But Romey never had. She had told him the reason they had ended up moving to Sweetheart Lake. A man had broken into their house one night while their father was at work and their mother was somewhere performing. She had told them they would be fine at home. They were nine and ten years old. The man locked them in a closet while he ransacked the house. Their father found them after he finished his shift as a hospital custodian. Their mother didn't come home until the early hours of the morning. That fight between her parents had cemented their move.

"Daddy was so mad at her," Romey had told him. "She wasn't supposed to leave us. She always leaves us."

It made him think about Luna Michaels. About what his father had told him about her and her sister, Celesta. Callahan's mother. He had seen her only once when she came to visit Callahan at his high school graduation. Life had been rougher on her. She wasn't as beautiful as her younger sister anymore. But he could see the traces of what she had previously been. He could see that she had been gorgeous. Her hair was a faded auburn. Her dark, creamy skin was lined with creases. There was none of the overly carefree spirit that Mrs. Michaels had possessed. She didn't smile once, even though the day had been so big for Callahan. It was as if life had sucked all the joy out of her. He could remember thinking she was dried up, like flowers without their moisture.

Callahan hadn't seen his mother in years. Their relationship was incredibly strained. Callahan never said a bad word about her, but from what Gray could gather, he had been left on his own a lot. He'd fed himself. Fended for himself. Raised himself.

There was a kind of loneliness in Callahan that Gray could identify with. If they were to line up their two childhoods, Callahan had clearly had it worse than Gray. But Gray had been without parents as a kid too. His mother hadn't been a kid person. She didn't play with him. If he got hurt, his first instinct was to go to his nanny for comfort. He couldn't remember hugging his mother as a child. He couldn't recall her smell. Which was odd, because he could remember Luna Michaels's sweet, earthy scent. He could recall her kissing him good-night when she came to kiss her children. His mother had never done that. Callahan's mother hadn't either.

He'd thought a lot about Callahan while he was gone. If anyone asked him who his best friend was, he'd always said Charlie. He had known Charlie longer. Callahan had come into his life later—a quiet, angry teenager who had just been released from juvenile detention when they met. Word had spread quickly through town about where he had been. No one was sure how the word had gotten out. It wasn't the Michaelses who'd told. Probably some bigmouth teacher or counselor at the school.

Everyone had whispered, gossiping as to what he had done to earn almost a year away. Gray had learned the truth only after a year of knowing him. If the rest of the town knew, they wouldn't have been so quick to bestow that bad-boy reputation on him. But Callahan never defended himself. He never explained the reason he had spent so long locked up. His mother's boyfriend had grabbed her by the throat and slammed her into a wall so hard that the plaster crumbled around her. And Callahan, who was just fifteen at the time, had beaten the man unconscious.

I would have killed him if the neighbors didn't stop me.

It seemed vicious. But Gray didn't know many people who would stand by and let their mother be abused. No matter what their relationship was like.

The front door of the little white house opened. Callahan walked out and looked directly at Gray.

"You going to stay in the car all damn day? Or are you coming to speak to me?"

No one could ever accuse Callahan of not being direct.

Gray got out of his car and walked up to Callahan. He had been back in town for days, but he had been thinking about this meeting for long before that. He had been thinking about what it would be like to face his friend the moment he'd gotten on the plane and left the country.

Callahan's brown face was stone. His arms were crossed over his chest. Even in jeans and a T-shirt, he looked every inch the police chief he was. He wasn't giving a single clue as to how he felt, but Gray knew he was angry. Callahan always kept tight control over his anger. Only a few people knew how bad it could be when he let it rage out of control.

"I wasn't sure you would see me," were Gray's first words to him.

Callahan's eyes flicked over him, quickly taking him in, assessing him. "Come inside," he grunted as he turned away from him.

Gray hadn't been here since Callahan first moved in after his divorce. The house had been sparsely decorated then, and not much had changed in the past few years. There was a large flat-screen television mounted on the wall and dark-brown serviceable furniture. No clutter in sight.

"Say what you came here to say."

"I missed you."

Callahan recoiled as if Gray had punched him. "What?"

"Charlie and I were best friends as kids, but Callahan, the truth is that you were my best friend when we grew up."

Callahan shook his head, and for the first time Gray could see emotion slip out of his friend. "You left without a word, without warning."

"It was a spur-of-the-moment decision. I was booked on a flight a half hour after I decided to take the job with Doctors Without Borders."

"I don't give a shit if it was a spur-of-the-moment decision. A quick call. A text. Anything. We thought you were dead."

Those words made his stomach roll. He'd never thought about how his decision would affect everyone else. But he'd only been thinking about himself then. His self-loathing over the things he'd said to his friend right before he died had ended up driving him away from the people who were most important to him. "I was in the wrong."

"Is that all you have to say? You were gone almost two years!"

"Do you want an explanation? An apology? Saying sorry feels like an insult. It's not enough. I know I was wrong. You tell me what you want from me."

"I don't know what I want." Callahan paced away from him. "Actually, I do know what I want. I want to knock you on your damn ass. Not even for Charlie. For Romey. For Lily. You're supposed to be better than that."

"I'm not better than anybody! That's part of the reason I left. I was engaged to the perfect woman, but I couldn't love her. I had the perfect cushy job, but I hated it. Everyone kept expecting me to be a certain way, and I just couldn't do it anymore."

"If you had feelings for Romey, you shouldn't have proposed to Gwen."

"I didn't realize how deep my feelings were for Romey until I proposed to Gwen and Romey removed herself from my life." He sat down heavily on the couch. "She stopped talking to me, Callahan. Even when we lived hundreds of miles apart, we talked all the time. And then suddenly she was gone. It started me spinning."

"I guess I kind of knew you had a thing for Romey, but I had no idea how . . . involved you two were."

"No one knew. Charlie never wanted me with Romey. He said I was wrong for her. He made me promise to stay away from her."

"He never told me that," he said quietly.

"Charlie started to hate me. You had to have noticed that. After he was discharged, he could barely hide how much he hated everything about me."

"He resented the hell out of you, Gray. You don't know how hard it was for him to watch you go off to college while he got sent to war."

"I do know how hard it was for him. I wasn't stupid. My parents had money. I had tutors and connections and the right background. I had everything. You think I'm an idiot? You think I don't know that most poor eighteen-year-olds don't sign up for the military because they want to die for their country? They do it because they lack choices. I made the mistake of telling him that we could use my trust fund to pay for his college. He shoved me against the wall and told me he didn't need my charity."

Callahan was quiet for a moment. "Where was that offer when I decided to go to college? I worked like a dog to send myself to college and still paid back loans for years."

"How would you have reacted if I offered to pay for your school?"

"I would like to think I wouldn't have been angry about it."

"He stayed angry at me. And then he came back home addicted to oxycodone. I didn't recognize him after that anymore."

"I did the research. There's more people in rehab for pills than alcohol. It's not like cocaine or meth. We can't go arresting doctors for writing prescriptions."

"I won't give anyone a prescription for it. I never have. It doesn't matter who they are to me."

Callahan looked startled. "Charlie asked you to write him a prescription?"

"I thought you knew. Romey seemed to know already."

He grimaced. "I guess it makes sense. This must have been around the time he started asking for money."

"That he never asked me for. We . . ." He trailed off. The next words were hard for him to say. "I pulled away from Charlie as he got deeper and deeper into his addiction. I was relieved when he didn't show up at my engagement party. I was angry when he refused my offer to get him treatment, but I wanted him to know how I felt about Romey. I thought I owed it to him. He punched me when I told him I was going to be with her. It got ugly."

"He was in rough shape after that. I saw his face. You got him good."

"And then he spiraled out of control and started drinking. That combined with the oxycodone caused respiratory distress and led to his death. I was the one who made them rush the toxicology reports. They never put the cause of death as a drug overdose, but that's what it was. I had a hand in that death."

"You think you loving his sister contributed to his death?" Callahan asked. "You're more self-absorbed than I thought."

Gray was genuinely surprised. "You don't blame me at all?"

"What exactly did you do? Shove pills and alcohol down his throat? It also wasn't your fault that you were born with privilege, but the fact that you recognize that you have it means a little more. Charlie was on a path to self-destruction. We all thought if we had done something differently, maybe we could have saved him. But addiction is a nasty, unpredictable bitch, and the only way for a person to beat it is if *they* want to. His death had nothing to do with you and everything to do with himself."

Gray hadn't been expecting that from Callahan. He'd been expecting his anger. He'd been expecting him to accuse him of disloyalty, but there was none of that.

"How do you feel about me and Romey?"

"Romey is a smart woman and tough as hell. If she wants to be with you, it's her decision."

"Do you think I'm wrong for her? The thing that bothered me the most was that Charlie thought I would just throw her away when I was tired of her. He never thought I would be able to treat her well. What was it about me that made him think that way?"

"You're asking the wrong person. If she was happy, I would have been happy. But she hasn't been happy. She's been putting on a good show. It was hard for her to go through her pregnancy alone. It was hard for her to give birth alone, to raise her baby alone. She's got us, her family, to back her up, but she needed you there. It might have been different if you were some random guy she got pregnant for. But it was you. You were the last person who was supposed to hurt her."

Gray set his face in his hands. "I only planned to be gone for six months. I missed my baby being born. I'll never stop feeling guilty."

"Romey says you took the news well."

"I love that baby, Callahan. One smile and I was done for. Romey was worried that I wouldn't believe her."

"I had the same concerns as Romey. If you had rejected Lily, if you would have hurt Romey again, you and I were going to have major problems."

Gray looked at Callahan for a long moment. There wasn't even a little hint of humor in his words.

"In all those years, Romey and I never talked about us. After I broke up with Gwen, I still wanted to keep things quiet for a while. It would seem like a slap in the face to go public with Romey so soon after I had broken my engagement with her."

"That's understandable."

"And then Charlie died."

"And then you started to blame yourself."

"I needed to go figure out who I was and what I wanted."

"And did you?" he asked.

"I did. Now the only thing left to do is figure out how to get what I want."

"You're on your own there." Callahan started to walk toward his kitchen. "Turn the TV on. I was watching a game before you pulled up in front of my house and sat there like you were casing the place."

"You want me to leave?"

"Not unless you plan on talking through the game. I'm going to get us some beer."

* * *

A well-dressed man walked into the Crusty Petal. He wasn't a local. Romey didn't know everyone in Sweetheart Lake, although it seemed like it, but she knew this man didn't come from her town. He wore cornflower-blue trousers and a button-down shirt with little blue checks that matched the color of his pants. If she had to guess, she would say he was from DC, maybe on a day visit. Carey Norton had done a lot to draw people to Sweetheart Lake. It seemed to be working.

The man walked up to the counter, taking in the selection. They had been fairly busy today. Usually only a few customers came in after the morning breakfast rush, but they'd had a steady stream today. She had customers at nearly every table. Sipping coffee, chatting. There was no rush for anyone to go anywhere. She loved that she had made the kind of place that customers wanted to sit and relax in.

"Hello." She smiled at the man.

He looked up at her, seemingly startled by her greeting. "Oh, hello," he said. "You have quite an impressive display."

"Thank you. What are you thinking about getting? Maybe I can help with your choice."

He seemed a little distressed. "I really don't know. Sometimes when I'm presented with too many choices, I can't decide."

"Well, we have fruit pies, cream pies, nut pies, and savory pies. Today I've got three different kinds of apple, because everyone loves apple pie. Traditional, crumb, and caramel apple if you want a little bit of a kick. Cherries and strawberries are in season, so I have great cherry pies and a really good strawberry-rhubarb, if you like rhubarb. I also have a strawberry cream pie that folks go wild for. I usually only sell those on Tuesdays, but I can make an exception for a man who knows how to dress as well as you do."

The man smiled softly at her. "You aren't making my decision easier. Please tell me more."

"I've got pecan pie, peanut butter pie, and if you're feeling naughty, chocolate bourbon pie. If you're looking for a cream pie, I've got chocolate cream, which is one of my best sellers. I've got coconut cream and my limeade pie. It's new. I'm experimenting. No one has bought it yet today. And then I have my savory pies. All the breakfast ones sold out this morning, but I have my chicken Florentine pie, which my daddy loves. I use a crap ton of butter, so I know why. I also have my super supreme pie, which is filled with meatballs freshly made from Carter's Butcher Shop, a layer of mozzarella cheese, onions, red and yellow peppers, all covered in a garlic-butter-infused crust."

"That sounds incredible. I wasn't planning on savory pies."

"The super supreme pie is new. How about I give you a little piece of it on the house and you give me your honest feedback? I asked my cousin to taste it, and all he said was that it was good."

"I would gladly pay for it, ma'am."

"Don't call me ma'am!" She grinned. "I'm barely out of my teenage years, and if you call me a liar, I'll kick you out of my shop."

"I would never," he said, grinning back. "I'll accept your offer, and I've decided I would like to try a small piece of your traditional apple pie, your chocolate bourbon pie, and your limeade pie. I would be happy to be the first person to buy a piece. You're the one who makes the pies?"

"I do. I just have the supreme pie coming out of the oven. Would you like your apple pie warmed up?"

"No, thank you."

"You can pay the pretty lady at the counter, and I'll start dishing up. Have a seat anywhere you want."

He thanked her, and she plated his sweet pies in to-go boxes. Even the hungriest of people couldn't eat all that pie in one sitting.

She served him the steaming super supreme pie and watched him as he dug his fork in and pulled up his first cheesy bite. Upon putting it in his mouth, he shut his eyes and moaned. "High-quality mozzarella. The vegetables are fresh and perfectly seasoned. The meatballs tender and just the right size. And this crust . . ." He opened his eyes and looked at her. "What did you put in this crust?"

"If I told you that, you might try to make it, and I can't have people going around trying to make their own pies now. I've got a business to run." She touched his shoulder. "You enjoy your food. Let me know if you need anything else."

She had started to walk back to her side of the counter when she heard the bell over her door tinkle. She looked back to see Gray striding toward her with their baby.

Of course, her stupid heart started to act up when she saw them. Lily was with her father. Lily liked being with her father. Gray loved her. As hard as Romey looked for signs to see if Gray was putting on a show, she found none.

He wanted to be involved.

He had been back two full weeks. Every morning he would show up at her house just as she was leaving for work. She'd told him a dozen times that he didn't have to, but he came every day to watch Lily and ultimately her father as well. He was getting him out of the house. Most days they went over to Gray's house. Her father had taken over the painting, apparently unhappy with the way Gray was doing it.

He was still quiet, still so inside himself, but he seemed to have more of a purpose. The other day he'd mentioned being excited to tackle the ugly floral wallpaper that covered one of the bedrooms.

"Hey. What are y'all doing here?"

Gray looked upset. His eyes were full of worry. "I didn't mean for it to happen. I wasn't quick enough."

Immediately Romey's heart started to pound. "You didn't mean for what to happen? Is my father okay?"

"He's fine. He said I was being ridiculous. I was sitting outside with Lily, and she saw a bumblebee in the grass and grabbed it. It stung her before I could stop her." He kissed her forehead. "She cried a lot, and it almost killed me. But she's okay. No allergies. I checked her thoroughly."

"My poor baby!" Romey said, feeling relieved.

"Show Mama your hand," Gray prompted.

Lily extended her hand to Romey. "Ow," she said.

She had a small red spot in the center of her palm. Romey took it and kissed it three times. "Mama's kisses make things better. Good thing Daddy is a doctor, or we would be going to the emergency room right now," she joked.

"You're not mad at me?"

"Why would I be mad at you, dummy? She's always touching everything. It's what babies do. She's perfectly fine."

Gray exhaled, but he still looked distressed. "I didn't like seeing her in pain. I almost cried. Your father was making fun of me."

She found Gray to be absolutely adorable in that moment. "You're a doctor. I'm sure you have seen people in more pain than this."

"Those people weren't my baby. You're letting me take care of her. I didn't want to mess this up."

She impulsively kissed his cheek. "You are doing a good job, Daddy."

He wasn't content to let her get away, and he wrapped his arm around her waist and pulled her into him. "I got a very big grocery delivery today," he said into her ear. "I wonder who ordered it?"

She had used the card he'd given her and sent the delivery to his house. She had held on to the debit card for days, not wanting to use it, but she did have the right to. He was Lily's father. He should be buying her diapers too. When she'd checked the balance, she'd almost had a heart attack. He had told her that it should cover any expenses she'd had during the past year. She had expected a few thousand at the most. What she'd gotten was more than a year's salary at her highest-paying job.

She knew there was no use arguing with Gray. So she'd sent him groceries. She would keep sending him groceries.

"I've never had so much food in my house my entire adult life."

"Daddy said your new refrigerator came the other day. I figured you hadn't filled it yet. Also, if you are keeping my baby and my father at your house all day, I want to make sure they have enough food."

She also wanted to make sure he had enough food. He had put on a little weight since he'd been back. She was relieved, but she still worried about him. He still looked exhausted. And there was just . . . something was different about him. But she couldn't name it.

He set a quick kiss on her lips. "We have to go."

"You do?" she said, feeling out of sorts.

"Meeting with the tile guy."

"Which ones are you going to choose?" Every night he asked for her opinion on something different. Tiles, appliances, carpets.

"The ones you liked," he said, as if it were obvious.

"But it doesn't matter what I like. It's your house."

He looked at her as if she'd said something stupid. "Text me what you want for dinner. I'll see you tonight. Say bye to Mama, Lily."

"Bye-bye." And then they were gone, and Romey felt as if a storm had just blown through the room.

CHAPTER TWELVE

Cooking is like making love, you do it well or you don't do it at all.—Harriet Van Horne

The smell of sweat and body odor stung Gray's nose. He looked down and his hands were now a grayish color from the dirt, and he realized that the smell could only be him. He couldn't remember the last time he had bathed. They had been holding him and his colleagues for months. He didn't know who "they" were, or which side they were on or what they were fighting for. But there weren't just Syrians at the camp. There were a few British people here too. Expats who had abandoned their country and their old way of life to be here. Others fought alongside the terror group. He would never understand why they had given up their lives of relative comfort, but it was clear to see that they thought they were doing what was right. They didn't seem to think that keeping a group of doctors and humanitarian workers, people who were just trying to help, as captives was wrong.

As prisoners, he and his colleagues had been treated better than the others. They were doctors; therefore, they were useful to their captors. They weren't tortured for information. They were allowed to leave their cells when someone needed treatment. Some days it was just minor stuff around the camp that needed tending to. Other days it was major medical events that required many of them to treat the wounded. None of them wanted to help; they felt compelled to. There were children at the camp as well. Innocents who had nothing to do with the fighting. They also served their captors to protect Rachel. She was the most at risk.

If any of them refused, they would take it out on her. They had witnessed it firsthand. The poor girl had had a black-and-blue face for weeks at a time.

Gray wondered what the purpose of keeping them there was. What did they want? No one was paying a ransom. There would be no trade for them. They were all from different countries with different governments. They weren't important enough to be saved.

They would die here.

He heard a commotion. Standing up, he went to the bars of his makeshift cell and looked out. He could see two guards, heavily armed, dragging a weeping woman across the ground. She was covered from head to toe, but her identity was clear. Her words were in English. Her accent U.S. American.

"No. No. Please," she begged.

"Where are you taking her?" he screamed from his cell. "Leave her alone!"

* * *

Gray jolted awake. He glanced at his cell phone, which was lying on the coffee table. It wasn't even ten yet. He had fallen asleep on the couch, tired from his day. Cyrus Michaels had taken over the renovations from Gray. Apparently Gray wasn't handy enough to be trusted with his own house. It was fine with him. Cyrus seemed to like having something to do. And Gray got to spend his days with his daughter.

He missed her when she wasn't there. It felt wrong to be here in this big house alone while Lily and Romey were just a yard away. He got up from the couch and went over to the window. He could smell rain in the air. It had been humid all day. The house felt stuffy, and even though the living room was large and open, he felt like he was trapped in the room. He shoved his feet into his shoes and stepped outside, hoping the slightly cooler air would settle him. It didn't. The air was still too thick.

His body needed to move, and so he started to walk, his mind not knowing where he was going until well after his feet decided on the path. He had made this walk before. At night. In the dark with not even a flashlight to guide him. He hadn't wanted to be seen then. Getting caught would have meant enormous trouble for him.

He saw the old tree in the same spot it had been for hundreds of years. The one that had been perfect for climbing when he was a teenager. He hopped to grab a branch and then swung his legs up. It had been much easier when he was a kid. But still he climbed until he reached the window. A flickering light could be seen. A television. She was still awake.

He tapped on her window. He heard a small, startled yelp, and then there she was. She opened the window wide and poked her head out.

"You scared the crap out of me!"

"I didn't mean to."

Romey's lips curled at the corners. She was gorgeous in the moonlight. Her hair was loose, falling over her shoulders. Her body was clad only in a little nightie. He could stare at her for hours.

"Well, what do you want?"

"I don't know. I guess I wanted to see if I could still climb this tree."

"Come inside, dummy. I refuse to watch you fall and break your neck."

He climbed in her window, grunting as he landed on the floor. "This used to be easier when I was a kid."

"Yeah. Getting old sucks, doesn't it?"

"It's not all bad." He got up off her floor. "We can buy liquor and rent cars and we don't have a curfew."

"I wouldn't mind a curfew. All I wanted to do when I was young was stay up late and experience the world. Now all I want to do is be in my pajamas by eight thirty and experience my bed."

"It's after ten. Shouldn't you be in bed now? You get up so early."

"I couldn't sleep. I'm watching one of those investigation channels where they have all the murder shows. I don't know why that would put me to sleep. And then here you come, knocking on my window. Scared me half to death. Now I'll probably never get back to sleep."

"I should have warned you that I was coming over. Like old times."

"I used to sit by that window, waiting for you to appear. Praying to god that my father or brother wouldn't catch us."

"We were so quiet. Why aren't we being quiet now? I don't want your father to hear us."

"He's not even here. He's staying with Angela tonight. And even if he was here, he wouldn't hear us. His bedroom is downstairs, and he doesn't hear as well as he used to."

"Well, that kind of takes the fun out of it. I could have walked in the damn door."

"I'm glad you didn't. I got a kick out of seeing you struggle to climb through my window."

"I didn't struggle! It's just smaller than I remember." They smiled at each other for a long moment before their smiles faded and awkwardness settled between them.

Why was he here? He didn't know. He just didn't want to be alone. "Can I see Lily?" he asked. "I promise I won't wake her. I got the urge to check on her."

"Sure. I used to check on her eight hundred times a night when she was first born. I was terrified that she was going to stop breathing." She led him down the hall to the room that used to be Charlie's. When he'd first gone in there last week, he'd been nearly overwhelmed by painfully conflicting emotions. He had spent so much time here growing up. He'd never thought things would end up the way they had.

The room looked much different now. Romey had painted it a soft yellow, with accents of cream and light gray. On the wall above the crib was a hand-drawn picture of a baby elephant sleeping on a cloud. The room was sweet, not the messy boys' paradise it had been years ago.

They walked over together and looked down at their daughter. Her little fist was curled under her cheek. "She looks so peaceful, doesn't she?" Romey whispered.

"I wish I could sleep like that."

She turned around to look at him, studying his face in the moonlit room. "You don't sleep well, do you?"

He was hesitant to answer. The truth was, he couldn't remember the last time he'd slept more than three hours in a row. "That's a funny question coming from someone who should have been asleep an hour ago."

He had been diagnosed with PTSD. It was another reason he had been gone longer than he'd planned. They'd been in rough shape after being rescued. If Romey thought he looked bad now, she should have seen him in the months right after he left Syria. Unrecognizable to himself.

"I was talking about you."

"Let's go. I don't want to wake Lily."

They walked back to Romey's room without exchanging a word. He could feel her questions hanging in the air between them, and when he entered her room again, he expected them to pour out of her, but they didn't. She sat on her bed.

Thunder rolled in the background.

"It's been humid all day," she said, more to herself than to him. "I was wondering when it was going to start."

And just like that, he heard the rain start to fall. "I should go. I just wanted to see her."

"You going to climb out the window? It would give me a good laugh to see your old ass shimmy down that tree."

"Old? You're only a year younger than me."

Her eyes widened. "A year is a lot."

Sometimes she was adorable. He had missed her. Not just these past twenty or so months, but longer than that. He hadn't seen her when he was with Gwen. He hadn't talked to her. There was a huge empty space in his life, and it had been her.

He bent down and kissed her cheek. "Good night, Romey. I'll see you in the morning." He didn't want to go. Every time he left her, every time she walked away, it was like watching a piece of himself go.

She grabbed his hand. "Keep me company for a little while."

* * *

She didn't know what had possessed her to say those words. She hadn't meant to say them. And judging by the expression on Gray's face, he sure as hell hadn't expected to hear them.

She didn't want to be alone right now.

"It's raining," she said softly. "Stay until it stops."

He sat on the bed beside her. "Want to play cards? I bet I can still kick your ass in rummy."

"I think you cheat."

"Me? I never cheated in my life! You were just a sore loser."

"Take your shoes off," she ordered softly. She climbed beneath the blankets, silently inviting him to join her. He looked so unsure, as if maybe she was trying to trick him. She wasn't. She didn't know what she was doing either.

There was still a mixture of hurt and sadness that filled her when she was around him, but overall, she just wanted to be near him. She had purposely stayed away when he started getting serious with Gwen, when their daily text exchanges ended. They had no longer spoken on the phone. She'd treated him like she would have treated any of Charlie's and Callahan's friends.

And it had hurt her.

She should have known then that her feelings ran so much deeper than she wanted to admit. There was no one else in the world she had to force herself to stay away from.

He tentatively climbed in bed beside her, as if she might change her mind any moment. She wouldn't. It had been lonely this past year. Yes, she had her father, Angela, and Callahan to help her with Lily, but their support didn't ease the bone-aching loneliness that filled her.

She had felt rejected when he left without a word. Unlovable for a long time.

She reached for him, inviting him to hold her. She felt safe in his arms. She shut her eyes and let the sound of the steady rain soothe her. She hadn't been able to sleep lately, her mind unwilling to shut off.

It was odd that the person causing her uncomfortable swirling thoughts was also the one who could calm her.

They had been each other's first. It had been hard for her to believe when he first told her. She had thought about that night so many times. He had been nervous. But she'd thought it was because they had broken into the green house and lied to everyone about where they would be. She'd also known that he had always felt uneasy about being with her due to Charlie. She certainly hadn't wanted her older brother to know she was infatuated with his best friend.

He had been so gentle with her. He just kissed her for a while. Softly. No tongues down throats. No aggressive pawing, like other boys had tried. He touched her, his hand moving in slow strokes all over her body. She thought he was a practiced lover. She thought he knew how to touch her because he had touched other girls.

She had been wrong.

Gray pulled his mouth away from hers, and it was then that she realized she was kissing him. "I didn't come here for this," he said to her, his voice low, his tone husky.

"I know," she said, her lips pressing themselves against his. "I like how you kiss me."

He continued to kiss her. Gently, as if it were her first time all over again. He was keeping tight control over himself. She could feel him holding back. She deepened the kiss, touching her tongue to his, pressing her breasts against his chest. She started to feel hot beneath her clothes, her nipples hating the feel of fabric against them, needing to feel skin.

She pulled her lips away from his. "Undress me."

He looked at her for a brief moment and pulled her nightie off over her head. Her body had changed after Lily. Her breasts were bigger. Her hips fuller. Her belly rounder. His eyes drank in her body.

She hated herself for thinking of Gwen in that moment. They were polar opposites. Romey had thought that Gwen's trim, fit figure was what he preferred, but his eyes told her that she had been wrong to judge her own body so harshly. His rough hand stroked up her thigh to her hip and then to her breast. He cupped it in his hand, felt the weight of it, gently squeezed it. His thumb came up to stroke her nipple.

She moaned, feeling sad for how much she had missed his touch. She kissed him again as she reached for his hand and placed it between her legs. He knew what she needed and began to slowly stroke her. But it had been too long, and his touch was too precise. She fell apart almost immediately, crying out into his mouth as the waves rolled over her. He held her for a while after her breathing returned to normal.

She felt his hard length pressed into her thigh and waited for him to climb on top of her, but he never did. He just kissed her forehead and continued to hold her.

"You don't want me, Gray?" she asked him.

He looked stricken. "Don't ask stupid questions, Romey."

"I'm serious. Why won't you be with me?"

"Because I don't want you thinking I came here for this."

"I don't. I asked you to stay."

"It's been a long time for me. I haven't been with anyone since you. I'm afraid I might lose control."

"Lose control, Gray. Sometimes doing the exact thing you want when you want it makes you happy."

He looked so tempted. So torn. She couldn't allow him to battle with his decision any longer. She slipped her hand into his sweatpants as she straddled his body and slowly pushed her way onto him. She moaned as he filled her up. She rose and slid down on him again, her eyes locked on his.

His control snapped then. He rolled her onto her back and gave her what she had been seeking—hard, raw, emotional, pounding sex.

It didn't last long, but it didn't need to. She came again, her nails digging into his back. He collapsed on top of her. It was only then that she could sleep.

He stayed the entire night. It crossed her mind to tell him to go home when she woke up in the middle of the night, but it seemed unfair. Not just to him but to her, because his hard, heavy body felt good nestled against hers.

He slept deeply, so much so that when her alarm went off at four, he didn't stir. She went about her normal routine, never disturbing him. When it was time for her to leave, she decided she would wake him. Sitting on the edge of the bed, she looked down at him for a long moment. As much as Lily looked like her, there were definitely parts of Gray there too. They looked very much alike when they were asleep. Peaceful.

She ran her fingers through his hair. She liked it longer. He somehow was more handsome than he had been before. He was slowly putting on weight. She shouldn't be worried about him, but she was. She wanted to rage at him for coming in and out of her life, but she couldn't find the will.

He opened his eyes and looked at her.

"Hey," he said.

"I'm going to work. I sent a text to my father and told him to meet you at your house. You can stay here and sleep as long as you want, just don't let my father catch you in my bed if he decides to come home before he heads to your house."

He nodded and took her hand in both of his, stroking her fingers. "You want to talk about last night?"

"No." The word caught in her throat.

"Do you regret it?"

"I said I don't want to talk about it."

"We don't ever talk about us. Not once in twenty years have we had a conversation about us. I think we could have saved each other some grief if we did."

"What do you want me to say about last night? That I haven't had sex with anyone since you left? That I needed it? That I needed to be with you? I don't regret it. But this doesn't change anything. I'm still so damn mad at you."

To her horror, tears spilled out of her eyes and ran down her cheeks, so hot they burned her skin. She tried to get up and walk away, but he grabbed her hand and pulled her into his arms. She cried even harder then.

"I missed you, Gray. I'm so mad that I missed you."

He didn't say anything, just held her while she sobbed.

Somehow not saying anything was exactly what she needed from him in that moment.

She wasn't sure how long she cried. It seemed like hours, but it couldn't have been more than five minutes or so. And when she was finished, he gently kissed her lips and told her he would see her later. She went off to work that morning feeling exhausted but somehow lighter than she had felt in months.

* * *

"Alice," Romey said as she sat down at one of the empty tables. "I want you to cash your paycheck this week."

"You know I won't." Alice eased into the chair across from her.

The Crusty Petal had been busy that morning, so much so that she and Alice had barely had time to catch their breath. She had sold out of her pie of the day before ten o'clock. There was only one apple crumble left. The coffee was completely gone. The customers had even drunk all the decaf. After the regular morning rush, there had been a steady flow of customers, many of them staying to enjoy their food but many of them taking whole pies to go. It was the time of the year when school was ending. Picnics, graduation parties, and luncheons were being held all over town. If things kept up like this, she was going to have to take on more help.

She had already inquired at the high school's culinary program, hoping to take on a future baker to work with her this summer. She was going to have to start making more pies to keep up with the demand.

The bell over the door sounded, and Romey and Alice started to get to their feet.

"Sit, Alice. I'll take care of this customer."

Alice didn't argue and slumped back into her chair with a sigh.

"Hello, sweetheart!" It was Carey Norton.

Romey smiled, happy to see him. "I missed you this morning. I tried to save you a piece of home-fry pie, but I sold out very quickly this morning."

"Don't you worry about. I had oatmeal this morning. I stopped by Gray's house and ate with your father. Gray made us all eat oatmeal and fruit." He shook his head. "Gave us turkey bacon. Tried to fool us, can you believe that? Like I wouldn't know the difference."

"I'm glad you're spending time with Daddy. He's enjoying working on Gray's place. He looks forward to getting out of the house."

"Your father is a man who needs to keep busy. He reminds me much of myself. It's probably why we get along. Just because you get past a certain age doesn't mean you need to stop working. Us older folks have a lot to offer the world."

She believed him. She couldn't imagine Carey sitting down and letting the world move on without him. "Did you want a little something to take back to the office? I don't think you've tried my new salted caramel pie. I know you like the fruit pies better, but I think you'll like this one too." She turned away to go fetch him a piece.

He grabbed her arm. "I didn't come here for pie." He paused. "Of course I'll take a piece to go, but I came to talk to you about my grandbaby."

She hadn't been expecting that. "Do you want to see her more? You can come by anytime. You know that."

"I know. Her first birthday is coming up, and I would like to have the party at my house."

"At your house?"

"Yes. I want to throw her a party—with your permission, of course. The house sits empty, and it shouldn't. There's some people at city hall who have babies around Lily's age. I thought it would be nice to invite them and their families. Nothing big. I figured we could grill us some hamburgers and hot dogs. Let the kids splash in the lake. Take out the boat."

She didn't know what to say. Well, actually she wanted to refuse, but her mouth wasn't letting her. Many grandparents threw parties for their grandchildren. There wasn't a logical reason she could think of not to let Carey throw the party. Except that he was rich, and his home was an estate.

"If I say yes, you have to promise you won't go overboard. You won't hire a giraffe or bring in some stupid fancy food that I can't pronounce."

"I'm not my late wife. I'll even let you plan the menu."

"I get to make the cake."

"Of course." He nodded.

"And no expensive presents."

"Hey, now. That's my only grandbaby."

"Carey . . ."

"Okay!" He put up his hands. "That look you just gave me could curdle milk. I'll buy her a reasonably priced present." He leaned down and kissed her cheek. "I'll be in touch with you later this week about some details. Can I have my pie now?"

She shook her head and grinned at him. A few minutes later he was gone.

"You know," Alice drawled, "I would happily forgo a paycheck for the rest of my life if you tell me the story of how you ended up snagging Gray Norton."

"They are your paychecks. You earned them. Cash them." She sat back down across from Alice. "I didn't snag Gray. We aren't a couple."

"That boy can't keep his hands or his eyes off you. I don't believe you're not a couple. You had his baby! Do you know how many women in this town would love to be the mother of his child? Gwen must want to scratch your eyes out."

"You think?" Romey asked, feeling guilty. She had tried not to think about Gwen. It had always been hard to run into her in town after Gray left. "Gray is not a cheater. He had broken up with Gwen when we started up again."

"Again?"

"Yeah. You ever hear of the term friends with benefits?"

"I may be over fifty, but it doesn't mean I don't know things. Of course I know what that means."

"Well, me and Gray had that kind of relationship for the past fifteen years."

"Fifteen years! That's longer than my first marriage lasted."

Romey wasn't one to talk about her private life. She kept everything to herself. She didn't know why she was being so open with Alice now, except that Alice was her friend and it felt good to confide in someone. "Gray is so damn cute. I can't seem to help myself when he's around. I'm very mad at him for disappearing for almost two years and leaving me to raise my baby alone, but I also find him very sexy and ended up sleeping with him when I told myself I wasn't going to."

"You'd be a fool not to sleep with him. I bet he's good in bed."

"Fifteen years, Alice. Fifteen years."

Alice giggled. "I don't know, Romey. Good sex isn't everything. There has to be more between you if you keep going back to each other."

"There's a baby now. I don't think I'll ever be rid of him."

"Why should you be rid of him? You need to throw caution to wind. Be a little reckless. Get rid of the thing between you two that has stopped you from making a go of it all these years." Alice got up and squeezed Romey's shoulder. "I'm going to fix my face. I probably look a fright."

Romey watched Alice walk away, thinking about what she had said.

Would she ever be able to completely trust Gray? She wanted to, but she refused to be blindsided by a man again.

CHAPTER THIRTEEN

Cooking is one of the greatest gifts you can give those you love.—Ina Garten

Gray was just closing the oven door when he heard his doorbell ring. He was trying his hand at cooking. Tonight, he was making honey garlic chicken. Last night he had made salmon. It was a little dry, but overall, the meal was decent for someone who could barely boil water a few years ago.

Being with Lily and Cyrus every day was good for Gray. When he was captured, he hadn't eaten regularly. Maybe it was once a day. It was never at a regular time. It was always just enough to keep them from being malnourished. His body had been knocked off track for so long that he'd continued not to eat regularly long after food was readily available, but now that he had Lily and her grandfather with him for most of the day, he had to make sure they were fed, and when they ate, he did as well.

He was starting to feel better. His mind was more alert. His body no longer felt as if he were dragging it through mud.

He walked over to his front door and opened it, expecting to see Romey's father or even his. No one else came by the house unless it was a delivery person or a contractor, and it was too late in the evening for that.

"Gwen." He froze for a moment, shocked to see her there. "Would you like to come in?"

"No." Her face didn't hold the pleasant neutral expression it had the last time he had seen her. He didn't recall ever seeing her angry in the little over a year they had been together. They had never had one fight, not even a small disagreement. He'd thought she would be the perfect woman to marry because of that, before he realized that perfection didn't exist in anyone and that he didn't know her at all. "I heard you were the father of Romey Michaels' daughter."

"Yes." He nodded. "Lily is mine."

"Did you cheat on me, Gray?"

He shook his head, not sure he was hearing her correctly. "I never cheated on you."

"I did the math, Gray. She had to have been conceived very close to the time you broke our engagement. Is that why you did it? You felt guilty about sleeping with Romey?"

"I never slept with Romey when I was with you," he said firmly. "I do not cheat. There is no reason for me to lie."

"But you left me for her, didn't you?"

He opened his mouth to speak, but he couldn't find the right words to say. He was going to sound like an asshole either way. He refused to lie to her. "It wasn't fair of me to marry you when I wasn't sure. I didn't have some grand plan to leave you for her. I didn't even know how she felt. We were barely speaking at that time."

"You two had a thing before we got together, didn't you? It makes perfect sense now. Things were awkward between you two. She could barely be around you for more than five minutes without making an excuse to scamper away. I thought I was out of my mind at our engagement party. You got so quiet after she left early. I knew I had to be wrong. I knew you couldn't have been pining over another woman when it was supposed to be our night."

"I'm sorry, Gwen. It was unfair of me to put you through that. I have so much history with Romey. I've known her since I was ten."

"And you've been in love with her the entire time, haven't you?"

He nodded. "I thought we could just be friends. I tried to be her friend. I couldn't."

She stared at him for a long, hard moment, as if she had come to a realization. "You and I were never even friends, were we?"

"Think about our relationship. You can't honestly say you were in love with me. We were polite to each other. We looked good together. Our mothers thought we would be the perfect couple, but never for one moment did I ever think you loved me. Hell, I can't even say that I know you. You never let me see the real you. You only let me see the perfect you that the rest of the world sees."

"What does 'in love' mean anyway?" She threw up her arms in a burst of emotion he hadn't expected. "It's a bullshit excuse people use to let their emotions run away with them. We got along. I would have been a good wife for you. I would have made a comfortable home for you. What else do you need?"

"What about what you need? You should want someone to love you. You should want to be in love with the man you're going to marry. Don't you think you deserve that?"

She flinched at his words, and then he saw her shake herself, pulling herself back together into the composed woman he had known all along. "Congratulations on being a father, Gray. I'm sorry to disturb your night."

She turned and walked away. He closed the door and returned to the kitchen to find Romey standing by the counter, her eyes wide. She had been giving Lily a bath while he started to cook.

"How much of that did you hear?"

"Gray, are you in love with me?"

"Goddamn it, Romey. Of course! Of course I'm in love you. My whole damn life."

"Holy shit, Gray." She turned away from him and went to go sit in a chair. "Holy shit. You should have said no."

"You want me to lie to you?"

"Yes. No." She shook her head. "When the hell did you figure it out?"

"I don't know. I guess I always knew." He sat down across from her. "I denied it for a while. For years. But then you stopped talking to me."

"I didn't, though!"

"We used to talk every day. You used to text me funny pictures and tell me about your day. We used to talk on the phone and watch TV together. And then you stopped. And then there was this hole in my life."

"I didn't know that it mattered so much to you. I thought you could do those things with Gwen."

"Could I? Could you do those things with anyone else?"

"Yeah." She shrugged. "I do those things with everyone."

"Liar."

"I was trying to be respectful. I wouldn't like it if my man was talking to some other chick. It wouldn't matter how long they had been friends."

"Because we were such good friends, Gwen asked me to ask you to consider making our wedding cake."

"She did?" She wrapped her arms around herself. "Ugh. I'm so glad you didn't ask me. I don't know what I would have said."

"I couldn't bring myself to ask you. That's when I knew for sure. I showed up at your door a couple days later."

"You really think you're in love with me, huh?"

"Not *think*. I know. This is not one-sided. We are in love with each other."

"I never said I was in love with you." She stood up. "I think the chicken is burning. I'm starving too." She went over to the oven and pulled it out of the now-smoking pan. "Damn it. We're going to have to get Chinese food."

Somehow, he knew it wouldn't be that easy with Romey. She wasn't sure of him, and after everything he had done to her, she had every right to feel that way. The only thing he could do was convince her that they needed to be together.

* * *

"I want you to do everything she says, you hear?" Callahan said to the teenage boy he had brought by Romey's shop this morning. "This is my cousin. She's more like my sister, and if you piss her off . . ." He paused. "She'll destroy you because she's feisty as hell and doesn't take any shit from anyone, but if she tells me about it, then I'm going to come after you too."

"Cally, you're going to scare the boy," Romey interjected.

"That's the point, Ramona," he said, glancing at her and then back at the boy—whose name, she learned, was Abel. "Let me hear you say you understand."

"I understand, chief." Abel nodded. "Thank you, ma'am, for letting me work here. I promise I won't cause any trouble."

"I know you won't. Callahan wouldn't bring me someone I would have to worry about. You do look sleepy, though. You want me to make you some coffee before you get started?"

"He doesn't need coffee. He'll get used to getting up early."

"It's no trouble. I was going to make you some coffee too."

"Okay. I'll take some." He looked back to Abel. "Bosses don't make their employees coffee before they start work. Don't expect it. Don't get used to it."

"Would you stop barking at the child? It's his first day."

"It's okay, ma'am. It doesn't bother me. If he was nice, I would think something was wrong." He grinned at her. He was a large boy, right on the verge of manhood, but there was a babyish quality to his face that gave him a bit of sweetness. He was well over six feet tall and could probably run through any man that stood in front of him, but she could sense a gentleness in him.

She smiled back. "Can you start peeling those apples for me while I make the coffee? When you're done, I'll show you how we prep the breakfast pies."

"Yes, ma'am." He immediately went to work.

Romey left the kitchen with Callahan and returned to the front of the shop, where her coffeemaker was. "I think I should invest in one of those fancy coffee machines. A lot more people are starting to dine in. I could offer them some more options that cost a little more. But then again, Alice can just barely handle making coffee. I don't know how she would respond to making a latte."

"You aren't going to ask me why I asked you to take Abel on."

"Nope." She turned away from him and started the coffeepot.

"I brought you a kid the size of a linebacker that most people cross the street to avoid and you don't think twice about."

"Most people are stupid. I think he's sweet looking. He got dimples."

"He's been in trouble, Romey."

She shrugged, having already figured that out. "I know you wouldn't bring me a thief, so I don't really care what he did. You were in trouble when you were a kid, and look at you now. Putting the fear of God in all the citizens of the land."

"You don't care at all? What if I told you they found seventeen people buried in his basement?"

She glanced back at him. "I would say he had a really good defense attorney. I always wonder how killers manage to lure people into their homes. You know how some people say to come from a place of yes? Well, I come from a place of no. No, I'm not helping you move your furniture. No, I won't help you look for your lost cat. You'd have to pick me up in order to kidnap me, and my heavy ass is going to make sure you get a workout in trying to get me."

He frowned at her. "Sometimes I really think you are out of your goddamn mind. You're the person who hired a kid off the street without asking him a single question."

"Cally, you aren't like my brother. You are my brother. You are also the chief of police. If I can't trust you, then I'm shit out of luck, aren't I? But if you're so hell-bent on telling me what this kid's deal is, then tell me."

"He's got some anger issues. I don't blame him, though. He has been put in the position where he had to be the adult in the house when he should have been a kid. He was taken in by an aunt when his birth mother placed him in foster care. That aunt is married to a woman, and when anyone says anything about them, Abel is ready to smash some heads. They came from a very small town with backwards-ass people before they moved here. He broke a man's arm. Overheard him say something like his aunt hadn't experienced a real man yet."

"I would have broken his arm too, Cally. I hate men like that. They're the ones that will harass you when you're walking down the street and then call you a bitch for not wanting to talk to them."

"I got involved with him when I saw him lift a kid into the air. I was sure he would have flung him halfway across the parking lot if I hadn't stopped him. Some of the kids call him slow. He's quiet. He might not have as many experiences or the opportunities as some of the kids in this town do, but the boy isn't stupid."

"Do you think it's gotten any better here in the last twenty years? There was a noticeably clear divide between the people with money in this town and the people without. It seems to have gotten better," she asked.

"It has gotten better. I think Gray had a hand in it. He broke the unwritten social rules by being friends with us."

"He brought Charlie into the popular crowd. Sometimes I wonder if that ended up doing more harm than good. When Charlie was around those other kids, he saw them getting new cars for their sixteenth birthdays. He heard about their fancy summer vacations and then their college acceptances to schools their parents could pay for. He was surrounded by their privilege, and there were times he started to believe that he could have what they had."

"I remember him having the conversation with Uncle Cy about him going away to college. He had his heart set on that private school in California. He genuinely seemed surprised when he found out there was no money for him to go."

"Daddy had to save for months just so he could pay for half of Charlie's car. I don't know how he could have thought there was money to send him to a forty-grand-a-year university. He was raising three kids and paying a mortgage on the house with no help from my mother," Romey reminded him.

"I think he just got wrapped up in the crowd. You and I didn't. Charlie resented the hell out of Gray for it."

"I know. It's like Charlie's dreams dying somehow became Gray's doing. It wasn't fair to him."

"Charlie could have gone to college if he wanted. He could have gone to a state school like I did. He could have lived at home. He could have worked his way through."

"It wasn't about the education for Charlie. He never liked school. He wanted the experience. Like your friend who is peeling apples in the back of my shop, he was lacking the opportunities and the experiences that some of the other kids in this town had."

"You ever feel resentful that we never got to go on vacations as kids?"

"No. Damn, I'm a full grown-up and haven't been on more than a weekend trip. I really would love to go to

Disney World one day. I would wear the hell out of some mouse ears."

"You should go. Money isn't an issue anymore."

"What do you mean, money isn't an issue anymore? My shop is doing pretty well, but I don't have the kind of money to drop on a trip like that."

"You do. Gray set up that bank account for you."

"That money is to buy stuff for Lily. I can't use Gray's money to go on vacation."

"The vacation would be for Lily. Listen, you know I'm not one to ever take anything from anyone, but you are going to have to let Gray do something for you."

"He is doing something for me. He's watching Lily."

"You mean he is taking care of his daughter. He is supposed to do that. He gets no pats on the back for that, especially since he wasn't there for your entire pregnancy or most of the first year of her life. He should have been the one buying the crib and car seat. He should have been the one covering the part of the hospital bill that wasn't covered by your shitty insurance. He should have been buying diapers and formula and wipes every week. He should have just been there."

"Money doesn't make up for that."

"Of course it doesn't. But you're not taking anything from Gray that he's not fully willing and able to give you."

"I don't want people thinking I got pregnant to trap him. My kid is no paycheck."

"Who gives a shit what people think? Gray wants to be with you. He's not hiding it."

"He says he's in love with me," she admitted. She had played those words over and over in her head since she'd heard them.

Of course. Of course I'm in love with you.

She had wanted to hear them for so long, but now that she had, she felt kind of empty.

"Why do you say it like you don't believe him?"

"How do you walk away from someone you're in love with? I always wondered if I was just someone he passed the time with." She shook her head. "I don't want to talk about him anymore. I get sick of having my thoughts consumed by some man. Tell me more about the boy."

"He's going to graduate soon. Next week. He's eighteen and directionless. I'm hoping that he can gain some job experience from you. College isn't in the cards for him right now, but I'm looking into some job training programs. Or if he really likes working with you, I'll see about getting him into the local culinary school."

"Cally, you're really going out of your way for this kid."

"Uncle Cy went out of his way for me. Hell, I can't imagine where I'd be without him."

"Go see him. He's at Gray's house. He's always at Gray's house. He's taken over the renovation. What he managed to get done in two weeks, Gray wouldn't have managed to get done in six weeks. It has been really good for him."

"I'm glad."

The door from the kitchen swung open, and Abel walked out with a bowlful of perfectly peeled apples. "Ma'am, I finished these. What can I do for you now?"

"Be still my heart!" She clutched her chest. "Those are the most beautiful words a man can say. I think you are going to be a perfect assistant."

* * *

"You two think you'll be okay here by yourself for a couple of hours?" Romey asked her two employees a few days later. It was odd to her that she had more than one now. She hadn't been sure how Alice was going to respond to Abel, but she liked him and got a kick out of watching him lift heavy things.

"Yes, ma'am." Abel nodded.

"How many times do I have to tell you to stop calling me ma'am? I'm young, damn it."

"Sorry, Miss Romey. We'll be good."

"Abel is going to show me how to get on that Tock Tick that all the kids have been talking about," Alice said, lifting her phone.

"Only when there are no customers," Abel said quickly. "But I won't do it at all if you don't want me to."

"It's okay." Romey smiled at him. "It's the slow time of day, and Alice will bug you to death if you don't. Y'all call me if you need me."

"We won't." Alice shooed her away. "Go do what you have to do."

She left her shop and walked the few blocks to city hall. Abel had been working out great so far. He showed up for work early nearly every morning. She'd found him waiting outside her door today. She would love to have a son as sweet as him.

It struck her then that she might actually want a son. She had been pretty much team no kids all through her twenties, but now . . . She had a baby who was soon to be a year old. What would it be like to have two babies to love? She shook off the thought. Now was not the right time to get a case of baby fever.

City hall was quiet, and when she walked up to Carey's office, she was sent in right away to find Carey sitting behind his desk with Lily on his lap.

"Mama!" Lily clapped her hands and grinned at her.

"There's my baby!" She noticed Gray as she walked around Carey's desk to pick up Lily. "How's my sugar? Is your granddaddy spoiling the mess out of you today?" She held Lily close to her and gave her a little squeeze.

"Well, give her back," Carey demanded. "She just got here. I haven't even started spoiling her yet."

"Fine." She handed Lily back and gave Carey a kiss on the cheek. When they were kids, he'd seemed like a mythical being to her. He was the famous lawyer her daddy worked for. He had been on television and everything. Mr. Norton had seemed larger than life to her, but this past year she had seen him as a man—a bold man, but still a man who at his core cared deeply for others.

"Do I get a kiss?" Gray asked.

"You've got cooties." She sat down in the chair beside him. "I didn't know you were going to be here."

"He's the daddy," Carey said. "I figured he should be here to hear all the decisions you are going to make."

Gray lifted a brow as he addressed his father. "Are you implying that I won't be making any decisions today?"

"I'm not implying, son. Romey will get her way. Now let's talk about the menu. I was figuring we could have a menu just for the kids. I can order chicken fingers, fries, them little pizza things that D'Amato's makes. We can also do chicken quesadillas and tacos."

"You don't have to order all that. I can cook all those things."

"You will cook nothing," he said firmly. "We agreed that you would make the cake and make the cake only. You, young lady, are going to wear something pretty, put a smile on your face, and be the hostess of the party. I will not have you running back and forth to the kitchen all day. You will not be serving anyone else. You are the mother. You will enjoy your daughter's party."

She looked at Gray. "He's getting firm with me."

"He is. You going to take that from him?"

"I feel like he might sue me if I don't agree. Joke's on him, though. I'm broke."

Gray grinned at her, and she was once again reminded of how freaking hot he was.

"Your mama is funny," Carey said, looking down at Lily. "I see why your daddy loves her. Two smart behinds."

"Okay. I won't cook, but pizza and chicken fingers should be enough. I thought you said we were going to grill hamburgers and hot dogs."

"There will be some of that there as well. I'm going to order some special burgers for the adults. I need the contact information for the guy you get your beef from."

"You don't just get it from the supermarket?" Gray asked.

"To feed the family, yes. When I'm charging for it, I get it from a local farmer." She looked back to Carey. "How many people are coming? You said just a few people from here and their kids."

"This is not going to be like one of Mom's parties, Dad," Gray said. "This is my kid's first party. It's not going to be an event."

"I am inviting the people from city hall. I'm sure you and Romey have some people you want to invite too. Only people who live in town are coming. I want to show off my grandbaby. In fact, I told everyone she was coming in today, and they all want to see her. Can you two go somewhere for an hour?"

"You set up this meeting," Romey said. "Now you're kicking us out?"

"I can't have a meeting with my grandchild here. I need to be paying attention to her. We can talk later." He stood up and pulled some cash out of his pocket and handed it to Romey. "Go feed my boy. Get him some ice cream or something. He's still a little too skinny."

"I have money, Dad."

"Go with Romey, son. She's going to buy you a treat."

"You said the same thing to me when I was six."

He shrugged. "Some things never change, and if I recall, you never turned down a treat."

They left the office just as one of the town clerks walked in to see Lily. "I can't believe he kicked us out of his office," Gray said. "And we listened."

"He has a way about him, doesn't he?" She looked down at the cash in her hand. "He gave me fifty dollars. That's one hell of a treat."

"Let's go to the general store," he said, once they got outside. "We can get a bunch of stuff."

They used to go there a lot as kids, stopping there before they went to the town beach to load up on snacks. She remembered the last time they'd all gone together. She had just turned twenty-one. Charlie had been on leave. Gray was on a semester break from medical school. Callahan had been off that day.

A small wave of sadness washed over her as they walked up to the entrance. She had been here a hundred times since then, most of the time thinking nothing of it. But walking in here with Gray today was bringing up memories.

It was an old-fashioned-looking place, with penny candies lined up around the wooden counter. There was a little deli in the back, a cooler full of drinks, and a special counter to buy coffee and pastries. There was also a weird mishmash of gifts you could buy. Candles, handmade jewelry, a talking fish. Every time she shopped here, she saw something new.

"I'm going to get a sandwich. You want one?"

"I'm going to eat half of whatever you get."

"Of course." He shook his head and smiled at her. "Can you grab the snacks and drinks while I order?"

"Is there anything special that you want?"

"You know what I like. Surprise me." He walked away from her, trusting her to get him the right thing.

She did know what he liked. Kettle-cooked chips, sweetened iced tea with lemon, any candy bars with peanuts and chocolate in them.

She was studying a row of chips, trying to determine which flavors she should get, when she heard footsteps behind her. She glanced behind her to see Pastor Collins from the Baptist church approaching. His wife regularly came to her pie shop.

"Hello, Pastor."

"Hello, Romey. It's good to see you. My wife can't go a week without one of your pies. If she doesn't bring one to the church on Sunday, there's a small revolt."

"I'm happy to see her every time she comes in," Romey said, turning back to study the chips.

"You should come to our services. We would love to see you there."

"I might," she said in a noncommittal way. She had heard the invitation from his wife many times. She wasn't very religious, and her father's family was Catholic. The few times she had been to church, she had gone to a traditional mass.

"We also have a woman's group that you might be interested in."

"That's nice," she said, hoping he would go away. The people of this town had been trying to get the Michaels family into church since they had arrived. Her mother had been wildly against it.

We're circus folks, not cannibals, she used to complain when they were kids and she had another run-in with a well-intentioned but overstepping member of the community.

"I know being a single mother can be difficult. Our group can show you the teachings of our Lord and Savior so you can learn from your mistakes."

"What mistakes?" She had heard Gray walk up on the other side of her. His body was stiff, and his eyes held a sort of deadly glare that she had never seen in them.

"Gray." The pastor laughed uneasily. "How are you? It's so good to have you back in town."

"What mistakes did Romey make?"

"Maybe *mistake* isn't the correct word. We know it's difficult for unwed mothers out there, and with our teachings, we can show women the right way of going about things."

"I'm sure you know that I'm the father of her baby. Why didn't you come to talk to me about my 'mistakes'? I'm the one who got her pregnant. No one comes to me and tries to tell me the right way of doing things."

"Well, Gray," the pastor started nervously, "you're a very educated man. A doctor. We know your position in the community and how women can sometimes get men in these difficult situations."

"Romey's educated. She went to the best culinary school in the country. Not only does she have a degree in pastry arts, she has one in food business management. She runs her own business. She's no wayward sixteen-year-old. We're both over thirty. She didn't get me into a difficult situation. She didn't trick me or trap me. And if you ever imply my daughter is a mistake again, I will knock you on your self-righteous sexist ass."

"I . . . I meant no disrespect."

Gray gave him a look so hard, Romey nearly shook. "Come on, baby. Let's pay and get out of here," he told her.

"I still didn't get the chips," she said softly.

He yanked two bags off the shelf and led her to the front of the store. He didn't even give her the chance the use the money his father had given her. He slapped his own cash on the counter as soon as the food was bagged, took her hand, and left the store. She followed him silently, barely able to keep up as he took long, angry strides. She had never seen him so upset.

They ended up in the park that overlooked the lake. He finally led them to a bench in a nearly deserted area and sat down.

"I can't believe that asshole. Who the hell does he think is he, talking to you like that? He's the worst kind of religious hypocrite. I've seen men of God in poor countries feeding the hungry, living in hovels, offering comfort. That fucking guy lives in a huge house, drives a damn Bentley, and would sooner cut off his foot then spend the day with truly needy people, and yet he can sit here and judge you. Judge us! For what? Having a baby. Fuck him."

Romey didn't know what to say, so she slipped her arms around Gray and kissed him. He was surprised at first, but soon she felt him relax. He took over the kiss, deepening it, flipping that little switch inside her that made her want more of him. She slowly pulled away. They were in public, in daylight, and it was clear that some people in this town already thought she was a temptress.

"I thought I had cooties," he said, his eyes still half closed.

"You do. I got my cootie shot though. So it's all good. I figured I had better kiss you before you gave yourself a heart attack."

"I could have smashed that guy's face in. If he ever speaks to you like that again, I will. You better let me know if he does. Has it been this way the entire time I was gone?"

"Most people aren't bold enough to say anything. There's a few, though. I think it was killing them not to know who Lily's father was."

"They can come to me if they have any questions."

"I'm finding this pissed-off version of you very sexy." She found him being protective of her very sexy. She rested her head on his shoulder.

"Stay over tonight. The whole night. I miss you when you leave. The house feels so empty."

It was hard for her to walk away too. They had dinner every night together, though it wasn't necessary. Gray was spending the entire day with Lily. Romey could pick her up as soon as she finished with work and spend time with her at her father's house. But she never left. She spent the entire evening with him. Two nights ago, she'd allowed Lily to stay with Gray, in her new bedroom that he and her father had so painstakingly renovated. She had fallen asleep, and Romey hadn't had the heart to move her. She also felt bad making Gray leave his bed so early in the morning. He didn't have to; Lily was always sound asleep when he came, and her father was in the house. Gray could come closer to her waking up time, but he was always there, a little before five in the morning, to see her off to work.

It was nice to be alone with him for those few minutes every day.

"Say something," he urged.

"You're my favorite person to have sex with," she said. She couldn't think of an excuse not to stay over, but she just wasn't ready yet. If she started staying, things would change again. They were already changing faster than she had anticipated.

"I knew I shouldn't have had sex with you again," he said. "I always felt like you were using me for my body."

* * *

"I was. I'm going to keep using you for your body," she said. "We should eat. Your father told us an hour."

"You know he doesn't mean an hour. We could stay away for three and he wouldn't notice. He loves showing Lily off." He opened up the bag, unwrapped a thick sandwich on a hard roll, and gave her half.

He was glad that his father had sent them off. He was crazy about his daughter, but he loved his quiet moments alone with Romey. He had never been able to spend this much time with her. Before, the most time he'd gotten to spend with her was a week. It had felt like stolen time, him quietly sneaking off to wherever she was. Lying to people about where he was going. Lying to himself about them being just friends.

His father was hoping to push them closer together. He suspected that was why he'd invited him to the meeting without telling her.

"Why didn't you tell me you were coming to the meeting when we FaceTimed this morning?" she asked him before biting into her sandwich.

"You didn't want me there?"

"You have every right to be there. I just wasn't expecting to see you."

"I thought you might like to see Lily. I know it's hard for you not being there when she wakes up in the morning."

"Thank you for calling me every morning. I like seeing her when she wakes up. My father doesn't know how to FaceTime. I would call every day, but it's so much better for me to see her."

"Don't thank me. I'm doing it for selfish reasons. I want to look at you every chance I get."

She leaned against him. "Don't flirt with me, Gray."

"Don't tell me what to do."

They both ate their sandwiches in silence for a few minutes. He could be quiet with her. There was no awkwardness. He could just be with her.

She reached into the paper bag and pulled out the two bags of chips. "Sweet onion and white cheddar horseradish. Interesting."

"I was so mad, I didn't even look at the flavors."

"That's okay. We can try new things. This will be the exciting part of my day." She opened the white cheddar horseradish bag first, offering him a chip before she tried one herself. He watched her put the chip in her mouth, then saw her eyes go wide and her shoulders do a little shimmy. It made him laugh out loud.

"You like it?"

"It's got a kick to it."

He found her to be ridiculously attractive. She wore a simple T-shirt dress today and her little white sneakers. Most people would have simply found her cute, but he found everything she did to be sexy, from the way she held her head to the way her lips moved when they formed words.

He watched her take a long sip of the lemonade she had bought before he took her chin between his fingers and kissed her. He had to touch her every time he saw her. That had been the hardest thing for him when he was gone. He'd missed having contact with her body, just feeling her warm softness pressed against him.

They hadn't had sex again since the night he'd come through her window. Every sleepless night he lay in his bed, forcing himself not to go back to her room. He didn't want her to think any of this was about sex. He just wanted to be near her.

"I want you so bad," he said as he lifted his lips from hers. "Every part of me. Every day."

"People think I'm a seductress that led you down the wrong path, but here you are trying to talk me out of my panties right here in this park."

"Stay over tonight. I know the bedroom still looks rough, but it's the next room we're going to tackle."

"It's not about the bedroom. Tonight is family dinner night. I want you to come this time."

"You sure? I don't want to intrude."

"I got you, a very educated man, a doctor, into this 'difficult situation.' The least I can do is invite you to family dinner. I enticed you into fathering my child. You're family now."

He knew she was joking, but he also knew there was hurt there. This was his fault. He had left, and she'd had to face all the judgment alone. He had wanted to escape the pressure of being the perfect son. He'd never thought about what she had faced. He wasn't sure he would ever be able to forgive himself.

"If you married me, it would stop all of that. No one would ever say another word to you. But then again, I would find a perverse satisfaction in throwing it in their faces. We could live in sin and just keep having babies. We could give the rest of our kids funky names like Rainbow and Jet. You could be like your mother was and homeschool for a while."

"You want another child?" she asked seriously.

"With you? Absolutely. A son would be nice, but I would be fine with another girl."

She was quiet for a moment. "I was planning to go hunting for the second richest son in this town and have him get me pregnant. If I have another baby with you, it will ruin my street cred as a seductress."

He was going to say some smartass remark in response, but he didn't have the heart for it. "I came back home for you, Romey. There was no other reason. I'm here to be with you."

He had gotten her. She had no quips. No slick comments. So she just rested her head on his shoulder and reached for the chips.

He took it as a victory in this long battle they had been fighting.

CHAPTER FOURTEEN

After a good dinner one can forgive anybody, even one's relations.—Oscar Wilde

"So Gray is here," Angela said to Romey as she checked on the white lasagna she had made for dinner.

Romey paused and looked at Angela. She hadn't said much about Gray since he returned. "He is. Do you mind?"

"Of course not. I saw him grab you and pull you in for a kiss when he thought no one was looking. I had to stick my head in the freezer to cool off. Your father never kisses me like that. Maybe I could have Gray give him a few tips?"

Romey grinned. "Now you know how I ended up pregnant."

"I'm really annoyed that I had no clue about you two! You both used to bicker all the time. Now it seems obvious. I feel like a fool."

"Why? It was a secret. Nobody knew. That was the point."

"I don't know, Ramona," she sighed. "I've been in your life for over fifteen years. You're like a daughter to me. I wish you could have talked to me about this. It must have been incredibly hard for you to keep everything to yourself."

"I always wondered why you never asked me about Lily's father. I was fully expecting to be questioned when I told you all I was pregnant."

"It's not like you were a kid. Sometimes a woman just wants a child and she finds a way to get herself one. I figured you wanted a baby and it was none of our business how you got pregnant. Plus, I didn't want to embarrass you. We've all had our flings that we'd rather forget."

"I'm grateful that you respected my decisions enough not to ask me, but I probably would have told you. Next time I get pregnant, feel free to ask me who the father is."

"By the looks of that kiss, I don't think there will be any question of who got who pregnant."

Gray had told her he wanted to have more children with her. He wanted a son. He wanted marriage and to be a family. But . . . "It's complicated. I'm not planning on having another baby anytime soon. I'm just getting used to the idea of not parenting alone."

"I understand. You can't go away for two years and then expect everything to be all right in a few weeks."

Gray walked into the kitchen from the backyard. They both went quiet and stared at him. He paused. "Were you talking about me?" he asked.

"Yup. Angela caught you kissing me. You aren't sneaky enough."

He shrugged. "No regrets. You need help with anything?"

"I do. Can you grab some wineglasses and the bottle chilling in the fridge? We are going to be fancy tonight."

"You bought wine?" Angela asked.

"Good wine too," Gray said, taking the bottle out of the refrigerator and studying it.

"I didn't buy it. Someone sent it to the shop yesterday. It was from a customer. The note said, 'Thanks for taking the time to talk to me about your pie. Be prepared for big things.' "

"Do you remember the guy?" Gray asked. "He's probably trying to hit on you."

"If he is," Angela said, "he's very good at it."

"I'll talk to anyone who'll listen about pies. Poor Abel. Not only does he have to listen to me ramble on about baking all day, I've been making him taste every crazy concoction I think up. Alice wouldn't do it. She doesn't want to gain weight."

"Poor Abel?" Gray shook his head in disbelief. "The boy scored a dream job at eighteen. He's got a sexy boss who feeds him all day. Callahan told me you treat him like a king."

"I do not. Callahan thinks it's not hard work unless you have to suffer a little. It's why I wanted to open my own place. Some executive chefs can be such pompous assholes. Screaming at folks. Slamming pots and pans. I can't put up with that shit."

"Yeah, didn't you get fired for pointing a knife at your boss?" Angela asked.

"Yes. He said maybe I should consider being a stripper because I had more tits than cooking skills."

"And if I recall correctly, the rest of the staff threatened to walk out if he didn't get you back," Gray added.

"Everyone wanted to pull a knife on him. I mean, how stupid do you have to be to yell that at someone who is chopping a block of chocolate with a very sharp knife? I could have sliced his face off if I wanted to."

"That's my girl," Angela said. "Don't take shit from anyone."

Gray nodded. "I wish you would have laid into that pastor today. He deserved it."

"You came to my rescue before I got the chance."

"I love you. I don't want him treating you like you some stranger who trapped me."

"He shouldn't be treating anyone like that. There are a ton of unmarried mothers. There's nothing wrong with it. Or having sex."

"You're right." He kissed her cheek and then turned to get the glasses.

A few moments later he was back outside and out of earshot.

"He loves you?" Angela said.

"Yeah." She didn't know what else to say. It felt good to hear, and yet it still hurt at the same time.

"Complicated or not, I believe we'll be welcoming another grandchild in the not-too-distance future."

* * *

It had been many years since Gray had been to dinner at the Michaelses' house. Things had changed. The house had been updated a bit. They were all older. There were some new members of the family and some members that were gone. But the feeling he'd had as a kid was very much the same. He was with a group of people who loved each other. It was the opposite of how he'd grown up. His father was always working. His mother was just somewhere else. He was fed dinner made by someone who was paid to care for him. On the rare occasion his parents were home, there was no warm chatter. His parents were almost businesslike.

His father had said he and his mother were friends, and maybe they were at one point, but it became very clear to Gray from an early age that their marriage was just for convenience. It was the kind of marriage he would have had with Gwen. He eventually would have made excuses to work longer hours. She would have been preoccupied with whatever she wanted to do. They probably would have had one child because that's what was required of them by their world.

He didn't want the kind of life his parents had. He didn't want to be the kind of father his was. He wanted to be with Lily for dinner every night.

He looked over at her in her high chair. She was chewing on a piece of bread, looking as content as could be. She must have noticed his eyes on her. She looked up at him and smiled. Her smiles never failed to catch him right in the heart. How many of them had he missed?

"Do you want more, Gray?" he heard Romey ask him.

"It depends on what you're offering."

The rest of the family weren't wine drinkers, so it was just him and her sharing the bottle. She always got a little giggly when she had wine, more relaxed. It was nice to see her this way. It could have been because she was around her family. He and Romey ate together every night but there was always that thing there between them. How he had hurt her standing in the way of her ever being truly relaxed.

"Lasagna. Garlic bread. Wine? Anything?"

"Is there dessert?"

"I've got brownies." She started to stand, but he caught her hand and wouldn't let her.

"Relax. After me and Callahan clean up, we'll bring out the brownies."

"Callahan?" Callahan said. "How did you get to volunteer my services?"

"Angela and Romey have been working all day serving people. We can do the dishes."

"I've been working all day serving the community," he said in protest, but he got up anyway and took his uncle's empty plate as well as his own.

"Thank you, boys," Angela told them.

A few minutes later the plates were cleared, the dishes were in the dishwasher, and they were all back on the patio enjoying the breezy evening with the pan of brownies Romey had made.

"We have to start talking about what you're going to do with your patio and deck area. It's a mess," Cyrus said to Gray. "You'll want to enjoy the summer out there, so it probably should be next on the list of things to tackle."

"The deck needs to be completely rebuilt," Gray was starting to say when he noticed a woman opening the sliding door that led out to the patio. Callahan noticed the direction of his eyes, and they both stood up at the same moment. Callahan moving toward the intruder first, but suddenly he paused.

Romey gasped.

Cyrus cursed.

It took Gray a moment to recognize who was walking through the door.

"Mom?" Romey stood up. "What are you doing here?"

* * *

Romey almost couldn't believe what she was seeing. Her mother was walking toward her with a huge smile on her face and arms stretched wide. She looked gorgeous. Her long curly hair was loose around her shoulders. The silver-gray strands that had started to form glittered in the sunlight. Her body was fit and trim, and on it she wore her signature maxi skirt along with a white button-down that was knotted at the waist.

Romey couldn't return her smile or muster up any joy at seeing her. Gray hadn't been the only one missing at Lily's birth. Her mother hadn't been there either. Romey had asked her to come—if not for the birth, for the first few days after.

She had been somewhere. Romey couldn't remember where. It didn't matter. She had tried to make up for her physical absence by video calling in. But it wasn't what Romey needed or wanted.

Instinctively, Romey reached for Angela's hand, who took it and squeezed back.

"What are you doing here?" she managed to ask again.

"You told me you were having a birthday party for my only grandbaby, and I wanted to be here." Her smile never dropped. "Don't just sit there. Give your mama a hug."

Romey stood and allowed her mother to wrap her arms around her. It was a tight squeeze. All Romey could manage to do was loosely return the hug.

Luna let her go and stood back to study her. "You look like a lush goddess. Our family blood is strong in you." She turned to Callahan, whose face had turned to stone. Romey didn't know what was going through his head, but she couldn't imagine it was happy thoughts.

"Callahan! Look how handsome you are. Come give your favorite aunt a hug."

"You should have given us a warning, Luna," Cyrus spoke. "You can't just pop up here whenever you want." His face looked as stony as Callahan's.

"It's a surprise, Cy. Relax."

"Every time you decide to surprise someone, all hell breaks loose."

"You're being dramatic."

"And you're only thinking about your feelings like you always do."

Callahan moved out of Luna's path and stood next to Cyrus. Romey knew Callahan didn't have it in him to pretend. He wasn't thrilled to see her. This wasn't some grand family reunion. Did she expect them to be happy?

"Well, I'm here to see my grandchild."

"You mean meet her?" Cyrus said. "You made a big promise about being there for the kids after Charlie died, but of course it was just as empty as the others. You couldn't tear yourself away from your bullshit to be there for your only living child."

"Cy." Angela rubbed his back. "Calm down. You're getting yourself all worked up."

"It's okay, Daddy," Romey said quietly. "I had who I needed there."

Angela had stayed with her through her entire labor. Callahan and her father had been in an out of the room for brief moments. But Angela held her hand. Angela walked her up and down the hallway of the hospital. Angela fed her ice chips and wiped the sweat from her brow. Angela was the first person to see Lily.

She couldn't repay her for that.

Gray had taken Lily from her highchair and walked her slightly away from the table. He was speaking softly to her, probably trying to distract her from the tense energy that flowed through them all.

Romey walked over to them, feeling very out of sorts. She had told herself that she was no longer mad at her mother. That she had accepted her for who she was, and yet . . . seeing her in person now dredged up every forgotten, tamped-down feeling she had pushed away. Her insides felt like they were churning.

"Is that my Lily?" her mother cooed as she came over. "Hello, my gorgeous girl. I'm your Nana."

"Angela is her Nana," Romey said quickly, and to her own ears she sounded petulant. "I mean, Lily calls Angela that name. You'll have to pick something else for her to call you."

"What does she call her other grandmother?"

"Nothing," Gray responded. "My mother passed before she was born."

"Gray Norton, is that you?" Luna's eyes went wide. "I haven't seen you since you were a kid."

"It was Romey's college graduation, but yes, it has been a very long time."

"You said your mother?" She thought for a moment. "You're telling me that you are the father of my grandchild?"

"Yes. Lily is our daughter."

"I'm shocked." She turned away. "Absolutely shocked."

"Why?" Gray's eyes narrowed, and he started to get that dangerous look that he'd had earlier in the day with the pastor.

It occurred to Romey that speaking his mind, letting his actual feelings show, was new for him. He had always been the peacemaker in public. The one who was always polite and never ruffled anyone's feathers. He wasn't that man today.

"I'm not surprised that you would want to sleep with my daughter. Men of your kind always lust after women like her. I never thought she would let her head be turned by some old-money, spoiled trust fund baby. You'll probably be gone before her second birthday. It happens to all of my sisters. I never thought it would happen to my daughter."

"Excuse me? The woman who walked out on her kids multiple times shouldn't be accusing me of anything."

"Gray," Romey warned. "Not in front of Lily."

Her mother had always been anti-Norton. She'd hated that her husband had to work for the richest family in town. She'd hated their generational wealth. She'd hated his mother, who very clearly thought the Michaelses were beneath them. It made sense that she would be displeased with Gray as Lily's father.

It was probably why Romey had avoided telling her.

"Mama, I think it's best that we go to neutral ground."

"This is my house too. I picked it out. Why should I have to go?"

"This *was* your house," Cyrus retorted. "It stopped being your house when you walked out of it and left your kids."

"Okay, we're going!" Romey took Lily from Gray. Things had never been this bad when her mother came to visit, but her mother hadn't been back since Charlie died. Their world was completely different without him in it. "Mama, we need to leave here. Where are you staying? Lily and I can visit with you there for a while."

"Well. . . . I haven't exactly figured that out yet. I just felt the urge to come see my baby, so I jumped on the first flight."

Of course she hadn't figured it out. Of course she was the same impulsive person she had always been. Leaving the logistics to someone else and only running by emotion.

"Take her to the Sweetheart Lake Inn," Gray said. "Ask for Mona when you get there. Tell them I sent you. She's the manager on duty. She'll take care of everything."

Romey looked up at Gray, puzzled by his orders, but she nodded and for once did what he asked without question. He'd taken the awkwardness out of the situation. Her mother couldn't be near the family. It was best that everyone separate and cool down.

* * *

Romey looked out the window of her mother's room to see the gorgeous purple-and-orange sunset and clear, glistening water. When they'd pulled up to the inn a few hours ago, she'd been thinking there was no way her mother would be able to afford a stay here. But she should have realized that Gray had taken care of everything by the time she pulled out of the driveway. When they arrived, a woman had met them at the entrance. She had been expecting them and told them that all Romey's mother's needs, from food to entertainment, would be taken care of.

It was odd for Romey to be there. It was one of those places in town that people from her side of the lake didn't frequent. It was the only hotel in town with a lake view. There was a little five-star restaurant attached to it where people in town went to have their special-occasion dinners.

When they were kids, it had been run by an elderly couple, but when they passed away it closed. Someone else had purchased it about ten years ago, renovating it and updating and in the process attracting more people from out of town to come stay.

"Mama, I think we need to be going." She turned around to see Lily sitting quietly in her mother's lap. Her hair had gone silver in some places, but her mother hadn't aged much. Her skin was smooth and clear. She looked natural holding a baby in her arms. "It's past Lily's bedtime."

"I guess your father rubbed off on you. Bedtimes and schedules. You're not going to let a child just be."

"Routines are good for kids." She crossed the room and took Lily from her arms. "I'm not making that up. It's a fact." It had been a difficult couple of hours for Romey. Her mother hadn't seemed to notice. She spent the majority of the time chattering away about her travels, about the man she was seeing, about her performing for crowds.

She had preferred it when her mother talked about herself. It kept Romey from having to talk to her.

"It's a fact that we live in the most repressed country in the world. The schools are like prisons. People are robbed of creativity and free thought."

Romey didn't want to have this discussion with her mother. She had heard it a hundred times. She had the aching need to be out of there. "I'll be at my shop starting at five. You can stop by during the day. I would love for you to see it."

"But what about my grandbaby? I came here to see her. I was hoping I could babysit for you tomorrow."

The idea of her mother spending the entire day with Lily unmonitored shook Romey. She and Charlie had survived their early childhood but only because their father's will kept Luna from going too far off the deep end. A lot of her memories from their time in Louisiana had faded. Their father had worked multiple jobs and was never home. Luna left them to fend for themselves. They were free-range children before that was even a thing.

"Lily stays with Gray, Mama. If you want to see her tomorrow, you'll have to check with him."

"I have to check with him? You're my daughter."

"And she's his daughter. I don't think he'll let you take her, but I'm sure he'll let you visit." It was incredibly nice for Romey to have Gray as a scapegoat in this situation. She wouldn't allow herself to feel guilty. Every word she said was true. Gray had every right to make the decision.

"I'm surprised he's actually spending time with her. The Nortons are notorious for pawning off their kids on other people."

"Gray's not like his parents. He's not working right now, so he can spend time with Lily."

"Why didn't you tell me he was the father? You told me it was a fling."

"It was a fling. Or at least it started out as one fifteen years ago. Listen, Mama, you text me tomorrow morning and let me know what your plans are. I'm sure you're tired after traveling all day. Make sure you sleep in a bit tomorrow."

She escaped the room before her mother could say anything else. She returned home fifteen minutes later. Callahan was gone, but Angela's car was still in the driveway. Romey was sure she was there trying to soothe her father.

She walked in the house with Lily asleep on her shoulder to see Angela walking toward her father's bedroom with a mug of tea in her hands. "You okay, kid?" she asked. "You look like you've been put through the ringer."

"I'm just tired."

She heard heavy footsteps on the stairs and looked up to see Gray coming toward her. "He wanted to say good-night to Lily," Angela explained.

Romey was surprised at the way her heart lifted when she saw him. He took sleeping Lily from her arms and kissed her cheek. "I'll go get her ready for bed. You relax for a moment."

He disappeared back upstairs. "I wanted not to like him for your sake," Angela said. "But I do."

"Now you know how I feel. It's exhausting to have all these feelings." She shuddered. "I much prefer being numb."

"You only go numb when you're in survival mode. You don't have to be there anymore. That's a good thing."

"If you say so." Romey impulsive reached over and gave Angela a tight squeeze. "I love you."

"I love you too."

Romey went upstairs to find that Gray was changing Lily's diaper. She didn't say anything, just sat in the rocking chair and watched him work. It was hard to believe that a month ago he'd had no idea that he was a father. He looked like he had been doing this for years.

When he finished, he brought Lily over to her to say good-night, and then he put her to bed. She took his hand and led him to her bedroom, shutting the door behind them.

"How was your visit?"

"I don't know." She shook her head. "My mother . . ." She didn't have the words to explain. "Can you stay tonight?"

He nodded and sat on the edge of her bed to remove his shoes.

"I . . . I don't want to have sex tonight," she blurted out.

He paused for a moment, a small frown crossing his face. "Shut up, Romey," he said softly. "Go get ready for bed."

She left the room to brush her teeth and wash her face. When she returned, he was in her bed beneath the covers. His shirt and jeans were gone, neatly folded on top of her dresser.

She stripped off her clothes, very aware that he was watching her. She had put on weight in the time he was gone. Her hips had grown wider and rounder. Her stomach had the little pouch from having a baby. Her breasts were larger and lower than before.

She glanced over to him. He was looking at her, not with heavy arousal but with interest. She knew he liked her body. She could tell by the way he touched her. "You're okay with not having sex tonight?" she asked him as she slipped her nightgown over her head.

"I'm trying hard not to be insulted here, but you're bugging the hell out of me."

"Why?" she asked seriously.

"A few reasons. Sex is not the only thing on my mind. I understand that you have had a rough day, and I have the ability just to be here without expecting an orgasm. Plus, your father and Angela are downstairs."

"My father and Angela have been downstairs before when we've done it." She climbed into bed beside him. "That never stopped us before."

"I was eighteen then. Now I have no desire to sneak around to be with you. And have you considered that maybe I don't want to have sex tonight either?"

She slid her hand under the blanket and cupped the bulge in his boxers. "Liar."

"Hey!" He pushed her hand away. "That doesn't mean anything. You took off your clothes in front of me. I'm not dead."

She laughed and moved her body closer to his so she could rest her head on his chest. "Is it weird for you to have everyone know about us?"

"No. I like that everything is in the open. We were lying before."

"In a way. I guess a lie of omission is still a lie. My mother wasn't happy that I never told her that you were Lily's father."

"I don't think it was the fact that you never told her. I think it was that you had the nerve to have a baby with me. A Norton. All mothers like me. I guess I finally found the one that doesn't."

"Don't take it personally. My mother is not a normal mother."

"Why didn't you tell her?"

"I didn't tell anyone, remember? I thought you should be the first to know."

"I meant after you told me. Why didn't you tell her?"

"Our relationship has kind of deteriorated in the last two years. Not that I think she's noticed."

"I heard your father say she wasn't there for you."

"I asked her to come down to be with me when I had Lily. She couldn't make it." She shook her head, trying to ignore the dull throb of pain that surfaced whenever she thought of that time. "Angela was there. It was fine. I needed someone who was calm. My mother always makes me feel chaotic."

He kissed her forehead. "I'm sorry."

She wasn't sure what he was apologizing for. For her mother not being there? Or for him not being there? She wasn't sure whose absence stung more.

"I know you're from a fancy family, but the manager of the inn almost broke her neck to accommodate my mother. You must be paying a fortune for my mother's stay."

"I'm not paying anything for it."

"Gray . . ." She sat up. "You know my mother can't afford to stay in a place like that. I could have taken her to a cheap hotel."

"Relax." He pulled her back down. "I own the inn."

"You what?" Just when she'd thought he could no longer shock her, he somehow managed to.

"I didn't want to touch my trust fund. I lived in my parents' guest house and saved my paychecks. I started buying small investment properties. I bought the inn just before it went to auction. I was going to sell it, but there were some foreign investors looking to buy it and I couldn't let it go. I wanted to keep the ownership in the community."

All that wealth. It almost annoyed her that he had been gifted with so much that he could afford to turn it down. "So what you're telling me is that you're double rich?"

"No. I'm not rich. I only use the money I've earned. The money comes from my mother's family. My father hasn't ever used it either, only the money he earned as an attorney. My father worked countless hours to grow his practice. I resent him, but at the same time I understand him. He had to prove himself."

"What are you proving yourself for? No one would blame you for using the money your family gave you. No one knows you're not using it now."

"I had to prove things to myself," he said. "I'm sick of talking about me. Let's talk about something else."

"Like what?"

"I don't know. Baseball?"

She shook her head. "Boring."

"What about television?"

"I love murder shows. You know that."

"I do. You like the ones where the women kill their husbands. I'm kind of afraid you're plotting to kill me."

"Not until I'm sure I'm the beneficiary of your life insurance policy."

"Remind me to put a clause in there that if you murder me, you don't get anything."

"Did you really make me the beneficiary of your insurance policy?"

"You know I did. As soon as I found out about Lily, I had it all changed."

It was hard for her to come to terms with how serious Gray seemed about everything when it came to her and Lily. She was afraid to let herself fully trust him. She wouldn't allow herself to be hurt again. But everything he was doing was slowly luring her into feeling secure again. She couldn't let it happen. She always had to stay on her toes. "I'm really going to have to start thinking about how to kill you. You're a doctor; how do you feel about a slow but gentle poisoning?"

"You are insane." He kissed her lips and then reached behind him to shut off the lights. "I couldn't fall in love with the nice woman who always agreed with me. I'm stuck on the feisty one who jokes about killing me slowly."

"Who said I was joking? I'm seriously considering it."

She could see his grin in the moonlight streaming in from her window. He never failed to be gorgeous to her. "Go to sleep, Ramona."

She sighed, and a few minutes later she had drifted off. That was another annoying thing about him. She always slept the best when he was sleeping beside her.

CHAPTER FIFTEEN

Never eat more than you can lift.—Miss Piggy

Gray woke up the next morning when Romey got out of bed. It was four AM, the ungodly hour she got up for work. It was now when he got up too. He made it a point to see her off every morning before she went to work. He wanted to be the first one his daughter saw when she woke up in the morning. He was going to have to decide what he was going to do about going back to work eventually. But not now. It was foolish to think he could make up for lost time, but now that he was here, he couldn't hand his daughter off to someone else to care for her.

"Go back to sleep," Romey said softly. She was looking at him through her vanity mirror as she beat her curls into submission and styled them into a bun. "You don't have to be up just because I am. Lord knows I would love to sleep in. Sometimes I dream about sleeping in."

"When are you going to have a day off?" he asked her seriously. Her shop was open seven days a week.

"I'm off Sundays and I close early on Saturdays."

"You are not off on Sundays." She opened her shop only for people who wanted to pick up specially ordered pies on Sundays. "You're still working for four hours. You come home exhausted."

"I love my job."

"You're working too hard."

"I'm growing a business. I can't afford to close the shop for an entire day."

"What about for Lily's birthday? You going to work that morning too?"

She paused and looked at him. "It's only for a few hours."

"It's her first birthday."

"Do you know how many pies I sell on Sundays?"

"Have them order on Saturday. Or don't have them order at all. You can afford to close one full day."

"You don't know that!"

"I do know that. You don't have to worry about money anymore. I'm here now, and even if I disappear, there's enough money in the account to last you a lifetime because you won't spend it."

"I'm spending it," she said weakly.

"On groceries for a house you don't even live in! I'm not trying to act like some white knight that is trying to swoop in and save you. You're doing fine. You would have been fine if I had died in Syria and never came back. I didn't die there. I came home, and I want you to lean on me a little."

Her eyes narrowed. "Why did you say you could have died there? What happened?"

"Clearly I didn't die." He had almost said too much. He needed to be careful. "Don't change the damn subject. You can be mad at me forever for leaving. I can understand that. I get that you don't want the world to see you as some gold digger who trapped me, but who gives a shit what the world thinks? Let me do something for you. Not for Lily. For you, even if it's taking away the burden of worrying about everything alone."

"I don't want to argue with you, Gray."

"You're not. But how long are you going to work seven days a week? How successful does your business have to be before you give yourself twenty-four hours? How long is Lily going to have to wake up every single day to a face that's not yours?"

"Guilting me is a really shitty thing to do." She got up and left the room. He had touched a nerve, but he had no intention of running after her and trying to fix it. If they were ever going to have a chance, she was going to have to give a little.

* * *

"Miss Romey?"

She looked up from her bookkeeping software to see Abel standing there.

"Yes, sir?" She hoped she didn't sound like a miserable bitch. She *was* a miserable bitch today, but she sure as hell didn't want to sound like one. Her mood had been sour when she left for work this morning. And it had only gotten worse as the day went on.

"Will you try my pie? I've been practicing."

"Of course I'll try your pie." She got up from her chair and walked into the kitchen. She was sick of looking at her books. They had just put her in a fouler mood. Gray was right. She could afford to close her shop for a day. With Abel's help in the kitchen, she was making and selling more pies each day. He had also convinced her to buy the fancy coffee machine, which meant she was making a higher profit on the drinks she was selling. He'd installed it and spent an hour teaching Alice how to work it. He was worth more than the ten bucks an hour she was paying him.

"It's a five-berry pie. I think it tastes better warm." He cut her a slice. "Maybe with a little ice cream it would be good?"

She looked at the pie. Overall, it would make any home baker proud. Appearance wise, it needed a little finessing, but that was something he would learn with time. She took a bite.

"Please be honest with me, miss. I want to get better."

"I think it tastes good. It's a little soupy, though. That just means the water in the fruit makes it a little too juicy. There's a few ways to fix that."

"I don't think I let it bake long enough."

"Maybe, or you could use a little bit of cornstarch to thicken it. You can also put your fruit in sugar for a half hour and let the juices drain out before you make your pie."

"Hold on. I got to make notes." He retrieved a little notebook. "Can you tell me again?"

She did as he asked, watching him write notes in his barely legible handwriting. It was very adorable.

"Keep practicing. I'm still thinking about those cinnamon-sugar pie crust cookies you made from the scraps the other day. We could sell those."

His eyes went wide. "You think so?"

"Yes. We can sell them with our coffee as a special."

"Thank you for teaching me."

"You're welcome." She squeezed his arm and walked away to the front of the store to check on Alice.

"We're almost out of everything," Alice told her. "A man came in here and bought every whole pie we had left."

"Really? Was he from town?"

"Didn't recognize him. Said his friend told him about the place."

"That's good. Word of mouth is always a good thing."

The door opened, and a very familiar face walked through it. Her mother. Her stomach was annoyingly flat for someone in her late fifties. All those yoga retreats must have done her some good. She wore a blousy white crop top with intricate long floral sleeves and another long skirt, this one in a soft pink color. Her silver-streaked curls were perfect ringlets all over her head.

"Hi, Mama. I'm so glad you decided to visit my shop."

"This is your mama?" Alice said. "She's stunning."

"Thank you." Luna smiled widely, which made her even more lovely. Romey was used to this reaction to her mother. Her beauty always drew people to her. It was part of what made her such a captivating performer. "I'm Luna Michaels." She walked over to shake Alice's hand.

"I'm Alice. It's nice to meet you."

Gray walked in at that moment, holding Lily in his arms. She certainly wasn't expecting to see him there. He was pissed at her. He'd FaceTimed at his normal time with Lily this morning. But the call had been shorter than usual. He'd done it so Lily could see her. There was no lingering. No chatting. He'd hung up after a brisk good-bye.

She didn't like that he was mad at her.

"Mama!" Lily reached her arms out to Romey.

"Hi, baby girl!" She left the counter and took Lily from Gray. Lily rested her head on her shoulder and sighed sleepily.

"She was asking about you, and your mother wanted to spend some time with both of you, so I figured I would kill two birds with one stone."

"You brought my mother here?"

"I did."

"Thank you. You didn't have to do that."

"I'm pretty sure he's trying to impress me," Luna said. "The inn just might do it. I got to take a class with a yoga master this morning, and then I was treated to a massage."

"That's nice, Mama. I'm glad you enjoyed yourself this morning."

Lily shut her eyes. Romey kissed her cheek, which felt slightly warm to her.

"She's teething," Gray said, reading her mind.

"Isn't it a little late for that?" Luna asked. "Romey and Charlie already had their front teeth by now."

"No. She's actually within the normal range. Her incisors are coming in."

"Well, excuse me," Luna said. "Looks like we have a smarty-pants here."

"He's a doctor, Mama," Romey said, not missing the bite in her mother's words. "Board certified in family medicine. He knows what he's talking about."

"A doctor, huh? Big-pharma-pushing, drug-dealing doctor."

"Mama." Romey started feeling annoyed. "Quit it. Gray was overseas doing humanitarian work for the past two years. You can relax with your demonization of him." Gray was a big boy, he could take a little ribbing from her mother, and yet Romey still felt the need to defend him. She was the only one allowed to talk shit about him.

"I don't prescribe those kinds of drugs. It's why I prefer working with children. They don't even bother to ask for it."

"Okay." She threw her hands up. "I guess I'm done picking on you for the day." She spun around in a slow, dramatic circle, taking in the shop. "This place is absolutely charming."

"Thank you. Can I get you something? Coffee? Pie? Juice? We don't have much of a selection left, but please let me know what you want."

"I would love a matcha latte."

"A what now?" Romey asked.

"Matcha. Come on, Romey. You went to a ridiculously overpriced school and you don't know what matcha is?"

"It's the green stuff," Gray offered. "I think it's made from ground tea leaves."

"Dr. Smarty Pants is correct again."

"No, Mama. I don't have matcha. I have regular tea."

"Do you have oat milk?"

"No, ma'am."

"Soy?"

"I think I have almond milk, but frankly, people here aren't asking for many nondairy alternatives, so we don't keep it in stock."

"I don't consume dairy products. The dairy industry is truly awful."

"That may be. But I can't live without butter, so me and the dairy industry are going to have to stay on good terms."

"I'll take a regular latte and some raw sugar if you have it."

"Okay, Mama." She didn't have raw sugar, but she wasn't about to get into that discussion. "You want try some of my pies?"

"I'll take care of your mama, Romey," Alice volunteered. "It looks like your baby has no plans of letting you go."

She looked down at Lily, whose head was planted firmly on her shoulder. "Do your teeth hurt, sugar?" She kissed her too-warm cheeks again. "Maybe a frozen strawberry will help. I've got some in the back."

She left the front of the shop to head into her kitchen area. Gray was right behind her. She didn't have to look to know he was there. She felt his presence.

Going right to the freezer, she pulled out a large frozen berry for Lily. Abel was there washing dishes.

"Abel, stop washing those dishes for a moment and come say hi to my baby."

He turned around and smiled. "I've met her before, Miss Romey. Chief had him with her one day when I went to see him at work. Hello, Miss Lily. It's nice to see you again." His large hand gently touched her arm.

"She isn't feeling too good. Her teeth are bothering her."

"Mouth pain is a special kind of pain," he said to her softly. "I feel for you."

"The man over there is Lily's father. Dr. Norton. He's who I talk to every morning."

"It's nice to meet you, Dr. Norton."

"My name is Gray," he said, shaking Abel's hand. "No Mr. Gray. Or Dr. Gray either. You call me by my first name only."

"Yes, sir."

"Abel is unfailingly polite," Romey explained. She looked back over to him. "Can you go to the store for me?"

"Yes, ma'am. What do you need?"

"I need for you to stop calling me ma'am."

"You're too young to be called ma'am." He grinned at her.

"That's right. I want you to go to the supermarket and buy oat milk and soy milk. I'm pretty sure they keep it with the other milks." She slipped her hand into her back pocket and pulled out a twenty. "See if you can find matcha. It might be with the tea stuff. It also might not be in the supermarket at all. So don't worry if you can't find it."

"It might be at the little health food store at the end of the plaza." Gray pulled more money out of his pocket and handed it to Abel. "It's not cheap. It doesn't come in tea bags either. It's a powder. But don't worry if you can't find it, and only go to the health food store if you want to."

"Is it for you, sir?"

Gray pulled a face and shook his head. "I personally think it looks like baby vomit. But some people love it."

"It's for my mama," Romey explained. "She's not a regular mom. She's a cool mom."

Abel grinned again. "I'll bring you back everything, Miss Romey. The receipts too."

"You can keep the change, Abel," she told him. "We're sending you on a little bit of a trek."

His eyes widened. "No, ma'am! You're paying me over minimum wage. This is part of my job. I need to do what you tell me. Chief would kill me."

"Chief won't know. Now go on, Abel. I don't want to hear another word about it."

He nodded his head and walked out the back door, looking a little bewildered.

"He's a nice kid," Gray said.

"Forget about having another baby. I want him as a son."

"He's a full-grown man, Romey."

"He's eighteen. There's an innocence about him that I find very refreshing."

Lily seemed to have given up on the strawberry and was quietly resting her head on Romey's shoulder. Gray gently extracted it from her hand and tossed it in the garbage.

"Daddy wasn't cutting it today, huh? Sometimes we just need our mamas, don't we?" she told their daughter.

The irony of her words wasn't lost on Romey. She had been back here in the kitchen far longer than she needed to be, avoiding her mama.

"You're softer than I am. I'd rather lay on you too."

"You still mad at me?" she asked him.

"Yup."

"Good. I don't care." She glanced at him and then looked away. "Stupid face."

"I'm a stupid face? Well, you have a big butt."

"That's not an insult, stupid face. I like having a big butt."

"I like you having it too. I just couldn't think of a comeback for stupid face."

She turned away from him and smiled for a moment. "I'm closing the shop the day of her birthday."

"It's not about just her birthday, you know."

"I know."

"You're eventually going to need to take one full day off every week. I don't know if that means hiring more staff that can work for you or just closing the shop for an entire day. But working seven days a week isn't good for anyone."

"Some people don't have the privilege of taking days off."

"You do, damn it."

"Okay." She relented. She knew he was right. "Eventually, I will."

He walked over and placed a soft kiss on her lips. "Don't you ever storm out the door first thing in the morning. It messed up my whole damn day."

"You shouldn't pick fights with me before five AM."

"We should probably go out there and save Alice from your mother."

"You're right." She steeled herself. "Let's go."

CHAPTER SIXTEEN

There are only three things women need in life: food, water, and compliments.—Chris Rock

"Thanks for coming with me," Gray said to Callahan as they drove to the inn.

"Don't thank me. I have been avoiding my aunt all week. The least I could do is take a ride with you to get her."

"I don't remember her being so intense when we were kids."

"I actually don't know what she was like when we were kids. She was long gone by the time Uncle Cy took me in."

"How did he come to take you in? I never knew the story behind it."

"My time at the juvenile detention center was up, and my mother was nowhere to be found. I called the only family member I knew was in the same place. I didn't know that Aunt Luna was gone. I was hoping she knew where my mother was. I was told by my social worker that if my mother didn't come get me, I was going to become a ward of the state and they would place me in a group home for troubled boys. I figured that's where I was going. I told Uncle Cy to let Luna know the next time he got in contact with her. The next morning, he was there. He became my legal guardian that day."

"Do you know where your mother is now?"

"Don't know and don't care," Callahan said in a way that let Gray know the conversation was over.

"How long do you think Luna will stay?"

"Hard to tell. She goes through these weird spurts of missing her kids. It's funny that she wants to be a grandmother now. She couldn't sashay her ass down here to meet her only grandchild before now."

"She makes Romey tense. It's like she's bracing herself the entire time she's with her. I keep waiting for her to tell her to cut the shit, but Romey just acts like nothing is bothering her."

"Their relationship is complicated."

"Clearly. I just don't remember it being so strained."

"She wasn't at Charlie's funeral either."

"What?" Gray took his eyes off the road for a moment and looked at Callahan. "Romey never told me that."

"I'm not surprised. We couldn't get in contact with Luna until the day after. She was in a jungle or a desert somewhere doing some stupid shit. I don't remember the excuse, but it wasn't a good one."

Gray had been a friend who wasn't there, and he knew that had felt like a betrayal, but not having your mother there . . . He could only imagine the hurt.

"Romey never told me that," he repeated.

"She's been through a lot. She never complains. She just takes everything in stride. Sometimes I worry she's going to pop under all that pressure."

"I'm trying to prevent that. We had a big argument this week because I wanted her to take today off."

"You won the battle. She closed the shop. She's one stubborn-ass woman. Congratulations."

He shook his head. It didn't feel like a victory. "I never meant to be gone so long."

They were quiet for a long moment. "I was reading an article about a bunch of doctors that were held captive in Syria for nine months. They were taken with an American humanitarian worker. The terrorists held her for ransom and made the doctors treat their people in the camp."

Gray kept his eyes on the road. "I heard about it too. It was a terrible situation. I feel bad for the girl's family."

"There was a picture with the article. It was showing the French doctor being reunited with his family at the organization's headquarters. Names weren't mentioned, but . . . I don't know. One of them looked kind of familiar."

Gray swore. It was no use lying. He had been caught. "What do you want me to say?"

"I don't want you to say anything."

"How did you find out?"

"You told me. You said you were in Syria when you weren't supposed to be there and had trouble getting out. I remembered the story about the American woman that was killed and did a little digging. The timeline works out."

"Stop being a cop all the time. It's annoying."

"I got curious. I looked."

"Don't tell Romey."

"I won't." He nodded. "But you will."

"I'm not going to tell her."

"Why the hell not? She needs to know why you weren't there for so long. Being a prisoner during a civil war is a hell of a good excuse if I've ever heard one."

"It doesn't change the fact that I left in the first place. I don't want her to forgive me because she feels sorry for me. I want her to see that she can trust me again."

"You're wrong about that. If you keep this away from her, you'll never be in the right place with her. You can't start a new life together by keeping the old one a secret."

Gray fell silent as they pulled up to the inn. He didn't want to talk about it anymore. He was trying to forget that part of his life. Telling Romey about it would only make him relive it.

"Why didn't you tell Romey I owned the inn?"

"Why would I tell her things that aren't my business?"

"Technically, it is your business, because you're part owner."

"I gave you some of my savings a few years ago. It doesn't make me an owner. I'm a silent partner. Very silent."

Callahan was more involved than he would ever let on to anyone. Gray had made sure to hire the best hotel manager he could find, luring one away from a resort in Nantucket. He'd given her the freedom to execute her vision. Gray just wanted to be kept informed and approved the expenses. Callahan was the one who had taken over approving the expenses when Gray left, but he'd turned the responsibility back over to Gray as soon as he landed.

Gray didn't see Luna waiting in the front. He had asked her to be waiting for him so they could go right to his father's house. He didn't know why he had expected her to do as he asked.

"We're probably going to have to go in and get her," Callahan said, reading his mind.

"Can anything ever be easy with a Michaels woman?"

Callahan laughed. "You should have met my grand-mama. She was a bareback horse rider. Still rode well into her seventies after suffering a heart attack. Stubborn isn't enough to encompass a Michaels woman."

"Romey and Charlie never talked about their family's circus background. I would love to hear it one day."

"They were embarrassed about it. Our family used to perform here every summer. People remembered Luna when she decided to move her family here. We've all heard the term *circus freak* more than once."

"Your family history is much better than mine. My mother's side of the family were members of the original Jamestown settlement. They act like it something special, ignoring the fact that they probably were cannibals and slaughtered a group of indigenous people that tried to teach their dumb assess how to farm."

Callahan chuckled. "You're sounding woke in your old age."

"Don't say that. I hate that word. I'm probably ass back-wards about a lot of things, but I can absolutely recognize the shitty stuff my mother's family did to get the kind of wealth they have."

"What about your father's side of the family?"

"They were immigrants from Ireland. Horse people. Bred thoroughbred racehorses for a few generations. My grandfather was a dentist. His brother was a state senator. As far as I can tell, they were a well-respected family in town."

"It's important to know your history. Even if it's bad. It helps you learn who you are."

"You don't know who you are?" Gray asked him. "You seem to have figured it out long before any of the rest of us did."

"It doesn't matter how sure of himself a man seems, I don't think any of us a hundred percent know who we are."

They parked the car and walked through the front door of the inn. The employee at the front desk smiled warmly and greeted them.

"We're looking for Luna Michaels. Could you call her room and see if she's there?" Gray asked.

"No need. She's at the restaurant. Sitting at the bar."

Callahan and Gray exchanged looks before they both went off in the direction of the restaurant.

She was easy to spot. Earthy and gorgeous. Still maintaining the sex appeal she'd had in her thirties.

"Do yoga with me tomorrow," she purred at the older gentleman sitting at the bar.

"I couldn't." He laughed away the suggestion.

"Are you leaving tomorrow? I was hoping to see more of you before we both had to go."

"I'm here for another couple of days. I would love to spend some more time with you, but honey, yoga isn't going to happen."

"Why not?"

"I'm far too old to be bending and posing. My body doesn't work that way, and I would look like an old fool."

"Old? You aren't too old!" She hopped off her barstool, stretched her arms, and then proceeded to bend her leg behind her head. "We're the same age, and I can do it."

"Well, I'll be damned," the man said. "I haven't seen anything like that in person. Only on television."

"I used to be an acrobat in my youth. I don't spend too much time on trapezes anymore, but some skills you never lose."

"I've had about enough of this shit," Callahan grumbled. "Luna," he barked with the authority only a man in charge possessed. "Birthday party. Grandchild. Let's go."

Everyone, including the bartender, jumped. "Good grief, Callahan. If my hair wasn't already gray, you would have turned it."

"Car. Now."

"I'm coming. Let me say good-bye to my friend." She turned back to the man and gave him her most dazzling smile. "I have to go to a family party. Hopefully I will see you again." She extended her hand, which the man brought to his lips and kissed.

"You can count on it."

Callahan fixed them both with a look that could have burned through the wall, and Luna finally walked toward them.

"You were supposed to be waiting for us outside," Callahan said.

"Oh, relax. It's a one-year-old's party, not a state dinner."

"It's not just any one-year-old's party," Gray said. "It's your only grandchild's birthday party, and we wanted to be there to greet the guests."

"Don't you get huffy with me, Dr. Know-It-All." She walked slightly ahead of them. "My beautiful daughter could have been with an artist or a musician, someone with beauty in his soul, but she had to procreate with the most establishment guy."

"I'm a doctor. Callahan is the head of the police force and works for the local government. Your son was a Marine. And I'm the establishment one?"

She dramatically threw up her hands in disgust. "I can't even talk about that. I cried for weeks when I saw them in their uniforms. I blame Cyrus. He brainwashed them into thinking they needed to conform. They sold their artistic souls for the promise of a pension and health benefits. If they just gave health care to everyone, they wouldn't have needed to resort to such things."

"That's one thing we agree on. Everyone should have equal access to health care. You shouldn't have to sign up to risk your life in order to earn it."

"Don't try to get on my good side by agreeing with me." Luna looked back at Gray as they exited the inn. "You're still from that family."

"I didn't become a police officer for the health care," Callahan said through clenched teeth. "Instead of blaming Cy for brainwashing us, you should consider that maybe after spending our childhoods with mothers who flitted off in whatever direction the wind blew, we craved some structure, security, and order. No kid should have to move ten times in one school year."

"We grew up in the circus. We never stayed in the same place for more than two weeks for ten months of the year. You all have hundreds of years of performance in your blood. I don't know how all that creativity got stamped out of your souls."

"Creativity doesn't pay the bills," Callahan said.

They approached the car. Luna slid into the passenger seat and shut the door. Callahan growled but didn't say anything and climbed into the back seat. Gray looked back at him when he got into the car, silently apologizing for asking him to tag along.

"Creativity absolutely can pay the bills. If it didn't, there would be no famous actors or musicians."

"There are more starving artists than there are famous actors and singers."

"I wish you never stopped singing. You had such a beautiful voice."

Gray looked back at Callahan again, floored by what he'd just heard. "You can sing?"

"Shut up, Gray."

"He's got a beautiful voice. My Charlie could dance. He had such beautiful movement in his body. If my family were still touring, he would have been an acrobat for sure."

Gray started the car and pulled off. "Why did your family's circus stop touring? Your kids never want to talk about it. I'm curious. From what my father tells me, you were very good."

"My brother fell off a high wire and broke his neck and died during a performance. It made the news. People started looking into us. Digging up information on some of our troops' pasts. People who leave their families to join a traveling circus don't often have the most spotless pasts, but we never judged. We took in all kinds. But the scrutiny was too much. There was infighting, and frankly, no one wanted to do the wire act anymore after they saw my brother die in front of their faces."

Callahan swore under his breath. "We're going to a baby's birthday party, for fuck's sake. You think we can keep things a little lighter?"

"Sorry for asking," Gray said. But he wasn't. He was glad he'd been able to get a little more insight into the family that half of his daughter's genes came from.

* * *

They pulled up at Gray's childhood home, and he let out a string of silent curses. They had talked to his father about his plans for the party. They'd wanted to keep it simple. Carey had promised them he would keep it simple.

He walked into a jungle-theme setting with life-sized cutouts of wild animals. He spotted a lion, tiger, and orangutan as he walked beneath a huge balloon arch. There was a photographer there, a team setting up the catering, and in the middle of it all was his father, who was in a full khaki costume as if he were about to depart on a safari.

"Dad, you promised to keep things simple."

"I did!" He sounded offended. "Everything is local. I didn't fly anyone in. I didn't get a tiger. I do have a guy who is coming with a couple of ponies and another guy who is bringing some reptiles, but that's it."

"Dad . . ."

"It's my only grandbaby's birthday. What did you expect?"

"Are you going to do this for every grandchild?"

His eyes widened and he grinned. "Are you going to have more children? Does Romey want one?"

"Let's not get ahead of ourselves. Where is she anyway? Is she mad?"

"Didn't seem like it to me. She's in the kitchen putting the finishing touches on the cake. It's gorgeous. I made the photographer take about fifty pictures of her with the cake when she got here."

"I'm going to go see how she's doing. Where's Lily?"

"Cy and Angela have her. They're taking a walk around the backside of the house. Angela's never been here before. Seems to like the place. I'm going to have them over again. They're good folks. We can become better friends."

"My husband was here every day," Luna said, making her presence known to Carey. "You think he wants to come back here and socialize with the man who signed his checks?"

"Well, hello, Luna. Still gorgeous as ever. I haven't signed your husbands checks since the kids graduated from high school. We share a grandbaby. I don't see him as an employee. I see him as a man who shaped my son's life when I was working all those years. I see him as a friend."

"Always a charmer. It won't work on me like it did my sister."

To his father's credit, he didn't lose his cool. "I admire your fire, Luna. I always have." He looked at Callahan and gave him a genuine smile. "There's the best chief of police in the whole damn country. I heard you turned down an interview with Richmond."

"I have no wish to move to Richmond, sir."

"Good!" He clapped him on the back. "I can't be losing my best people."

Luna make a funny little noise, which Gray chose to ignore. He walked away in search of Romey. He needed a break from Luna.

She was in the kitchen at the island, placing tiny animals around the perimeter of the three-tiered cake. She might not have made pies that morning, but she still had escaped to her shop incredibly early to work on the cake. His father's housekeeper, Anna, was standing on the other side of the island looking at her work with amazement.

"Oh, Miss. It's like watching a live version of that British baking show. You sure those little animals are edible?"

"Yes. They're made from sugar paste. The young man who works for me helped me make them. He's quite good at it. He made this elephant this morning." She gently lifted it to get a closer look. "See how intricately he did the trunk and tusks? I was so proud of him."

"Abel was at the shop this morning?" Gray interrupted. She hadn't noticed he was there and looked at him for the first time.

"He surprised me. I invited him to the party. I think he feels like he would be intruding. I'm going to ask Cally to go get him."

He quickly greeted Anna, who excused herself and left them alone. "I can go get him."

"You sure?"

"You have to find someone else to take your mother back to the inn later. I'm sorry, Romey, but I won't survive another car ride with her today."

She nodded and sighed, seeming defeated. "Thank you for helping me with her. I appreciate it. I owe you."

"You don't owe me anything. I'm supposed to be doing this kind of stuff for you."

"No, I really owe you. I know putting up with her can be a lot."

"If you owe me, then I already know what I want in return."

"What's that?"

"I want us back together. Or just together officially for the first time. We never spelled things out before I left. But I want us to now. I don't want there to be any doubt."

"Gray . . ." She looked heartbroken for a moment. "Please, don't do this to me right now."

"It's doesn't have to be complicated. You need to decide if you want to be with me."

She removed her hair from the clip that was containing it. She had done something different to it. Instead of the normally wild mass of ringlets, she had large soft curls. Her apron was the next to come off. Underneath it was a white sundress with a cornflower-blue floral pattern. She looked distinctively southern. She was the most beautiful thing he had ever seen.

She walked over to him and leaned against him. "Your father rented two of the biggest bounce houses I have ever seen. There's a cotton candy and popcorn machine. A man is coming with ponies! I want to be very mad at him. But I can't because he is so happy to be doing this. My mother is here for this. Can we get through this day and not focus on us? I think about us so much it makes my head hurt. I don't want to think about anything but my baby and enjoying her day."

"Okay." He relented. "Let's get through this day."

CHAPTER SEVENTEEN

Let's face it, a nice creamy chocolate cake does a lot for a lot of people; it does for me.—Audrey Hepburn

Romey had been very anxious the entire morning. It was just a party, she kept telling herself. One that Carey Norton was throwing for her daughter at his lakefront mansion. Lily was a Norton. He wanted everyone to know. It was a very public acceptance of Lily. It was the best she could hope for.

Now that the party was in full swing, she could relax a little. There were no elite guests. No other politicians. No millionaires. It was just people from Sweetheart Lake. The ones who worked for the town and their families. The ones who lived on her side of the lake. As they entered the party, she had seen awe of their faces. It wasn't every day they encountered this kind of wealth. Carey had opened his home to them.

The kids were having a blast. Some were splashing in the lake under the careful watch of a hired lifeguard. Others were in the bounce houses. There were children lined up at the cotton candy machine and eating freshly popped popcorn. They all had big smiles on their faces. Carey had done all this with little help from her. She felt a little bad that she hadn't had more involvement in planning her daughter's first birthday, but Lily was all smiles too.

"Alice and Abel are actually friends," Gray said, walking up to her. "They've been laughing and talking the entire time he's been here."

"I know. Half the time I find them with their heads together in a corner, staring at her phone. If I didn't know how old Alice was, I would think she was a teenager."

"She said she would drop him home tonight. Anna said she would drop your mother off. She lives not far from the inn."

"That's nice of them. Remind me to send Anna a pie. She's sweet."

Gray touched her chin. "How are you feeling? You want me to get you something? I don't think I've seen you eat anything all day."

"I was supposed to be doing that now. Callahan took Lily from me and ordered me to sit down for an hour. There was a woman with him. I'm pretty sure I've seen her around town, but he shooed me away before I could ask her name. I wonder if he's interested in her."

"Stop thinking about Callahan. He sent you away to take care of yourself. I'm going to make sure you do so. You're going to sit someplace quiet and eat. You're not allowed to worry about anyone for that time."

She stepped closer to him, wrapped her arms around his neck, and kissed him. He was doing a damn good job making her feel like she wasn't in this alone. It was almost overwhelming.

"What was that for?" he asked her.

"I don't know. You're very sexy when you try to order me around."

He grinned at her and led her toward the food stations set up on the patio. As soon as Gray stepped up, a woman appeared with a foil-covered tray.

"Mr. Norton, your father had me make this for you and your wife. It's all still hot. We just finished plating."

Gray didn't flinch at the word *wife*, and he definitely didn't try to correct the server's mistake. He just smiled and thanked the woman as he took the tray from her hands.

Callahan walked down the steps toward them. He had changed into his bathing suit and so had Lily.

"Are you sure you are okay with her, Cally?" Romey asked him, even though Lily was perfectly content with her uncle. "Gray and I can take her with us while we eat."

Callahan frowned at her and looked at Lily. "I'm not even going to answer your mama. She's ridiculous sometimes. We're going to go swimming, and then both the grandpas are going to take us and some of the kids out in the boat. After that we're going to watch the man with the lizard do his little show. We don't need Mama, right, Lily? She's been trying to hog you all day."

"Ignore her, Callahan," Gray said. "I'm making her sit down right now."

"Good. She was in the shop working on that cake this morning. I just spotted it when I walked through the kitchen. It's incredible, but I can see in her face that she's exhausted."

"Can you not talk about me like I'm not standing right here?"

Callahan shrugged and looked back at Gray. "She could use a drink. There's some adult jungle punch the bartender is serving. Make sure she has one of those." He walked away toward the lake, where Carey and her father were already standing.

"Ass," she said, feeling a little annoyed.

"Come on, Mama." Gray laughed. "Let's go get some drinks and eat."

She was expecting to sit at one of the many tables that Carey had set up outside. But Gray, seeming to know that she was overwhelmed, took her a little farther onto the property. The guest house where he had lived before he went away was still there, looking even more pristine than ever.

"My father should have changed the code to the door after I left," he said as he let them in. "Anna told me they clean in here once a week."

It was the same as he had left it. His degrees were framed on the wall. Various pictures were still around. She spotted one: the four of them. It was a candid shot. Charlie had a big goofy grin on his face. Callahan had his arm slung across his and Gray's shoulders. He was smiling too, as big a smile as she had ever seen on Callahan. And then there was her and Gray. She was on the end, looking at the camera. Her arm wrapped around his waist. But Gray was looking at her. She put down the drinks she was holding and picked up the framed photo. It was one of the rare times they had all been home. Christmastime, judging by the Santa hat Charlie wore on his closely shaved head.

"You haven't seen that picture before?" he asked, walking up behind her.

"No." She had been to his house before, but never when they were sleeping together. He always had come to her, away from anyone's eyes on his parents' property. "The way you're looking at me . . ."

"You had just moved to Chicago. I had missed you so much that year, I thought I was going to die. I was very much in denial about being in love with you. I told my girlfriend at the time that she was being crazy. It's turns out I was the crazy one."

"I feel dumb now."

He took the picture from her hand and set it back on the end table before grabbing her by the waist. "Why should you feel dumb? It wasn't the right time for us. I was an overworked, stressed-out resident. You were just starting your career. We weren't ready then."

"My career was very important to me. It's still very important to me."

"It's your passion. You had to make your mark on the world. I never wanted to be in the way of that. I had started to think about a future without you in it, and then you threw me for a loop when you decided to move back home. I was so mad at you. You knocked my plans off track."

"I didn't mean to. I stayed away as much as possible as soon as I realized that you were serious with someone else."

"And that's the part that kills me. Having you so close and not being able to see you drove me off the deep end. I was never so confused in my life."

He was right. There had always been confusion with them. Things had never been clear. They'd never told each other how they felt or what they wanted. They hadn't been a couple right after his engagement ended. He'd just shown up at her door with a black eye, telling her he had broken off his engagement, and he'd kissed her. She had been too afraid to bring it up, to ask him what that meant for them. She didn't want to be seen as the other woman. She didn't want to go public with him so soon after his breakup with the woman the world thought was perfect for him. So yes, she did have the right to be mad at him for leaving, but she also had been so damn mad at herself.

"You're not confused now, right?"

"You're my family," he said in response. She kissed him and started to undo the navy-blue stripped button-down he wore.

He briefly broke their kiss and looked at her, checking to see if she was sure. She wanted him all the time. Every night she left him to sleep in her bed alone, and it was becoming more and more difficult to leave him. It had started to feel wrong.

He unzipped her sundress, tossing it aside before unhooking her bra. She knew there was no turning back now. The look in his eyes . . . he wanted her. He had always wanted her. She unbuttoned and unzipped his shorts as he was walking her backward toward his old bedroom door. She slid her hand down his hardness, and he swore. Stopped walking and picked her up, carrying her to the bed. They weren't even fully undressed. He tugged at her underwear so hard they ripped, but she didn't care. She was ready for him, wrapped her thighs around his hips, pulling him to her. He complied, giving her what she wanted, entering her in one swift hard motion. Sex between them was so often like this. Pent-up frustration from being denied each other that spilled over into this. It was always deep and satisfying and sexy.

But it didn't have to be like this anymore. Sometimes she so desperately missed the summer he had first made love to her. The summer she had fallen in love with him. It wasn't a hurried explosion. Life had been so much simpler then.

It could be that way now, if she allowed it.

"Look at me," he whispered when her eyes drifted shut. He knew exactly how to love her. She just wanted the sensation of him being inside her body to take over. But she did look at him, into his eyes. "I love you," he said.

The words came so easy for him. Why couldn't it be as easy for her? A moan escaped her lips. His slowed his pace but plunged into her deeper, slower. It somehow managed to turn her on more and drove her right over the edge. Her climax came then, and he kissed her through it, still moving deeply inside her until his own came. He collapsed, burying his face in her neck for a few moments.

"Are we bad parents?" she asked him. "Sneaking away to have sex during our child's first birthday party seems wrong."

"We were ordered to go relax for an hour." He rolled on his side and pulled her into his arms. "We didn't sneak off. And nobody said how we had to spend the hour."

She sat up. "We need to start doing that more often. You think the food is still warm?"

"I'll go get it. You stay here."

"We can eat at the table."

"No. I really would like to see you eating barbecue naked in bed. It's one of my fantasies. Indulge me. You said you owe me a favor, remember?"

She smiled and lay back in bed as he got up. Life could be fun with him. She wanted her life to be fun with him.

CHAPTER EIGHTEEN

Part of the secret of a success in life is to eat what you like and let the food fight it out inside.—Mark Twain

Gray looked over at Romey later that evening. Lily was sleeping peacefully on her chest, her little lips slightly parted. She was exhausted from the day's events. They all were. The party had ended a little over an hour ago. The guests had all gone; just family remained behind. They all sat around a large table on the back deck that overlooked the lake.

His father had brought out wine that his mother had probably spent a fortune on and poured each of them a glass.

"Special wine for a special occasion," he said as he popped the corks.

It had been a good day. One of his best memories at this house. He had hated the parties his mother threw here. Everyone dressed in gown and tuxedoes, pretending to be important, thinking they were better than the poor unfortunate souls gathered there to help. His mother threw events where people came to see and be seen. His father had thrown a party for people who worked to keep the town going. There was a vastly different feeling in the air.

"We are never going to get these presents home," Romey said to him. "We should have told people to donate to the food pantry instead. What kid needs all this stuff?"

"People like to buy presents for children," Carey said. "I went into the toy store the other day and had to stop myself from buying out half of it."

"Carey, you must have spent a fortune on this party. You better not have bought her anything else," Romey warned.

"Oh, hush. You don't get to tell me how to spend my money. Everyone had a great time."

"We did, Carey," Angela said. "I took so many pictures today, I filled up all the storage space on my phone."

"You and Cyrus have to come back and have dinner soon. Hell, y'all can stay the night if you want. This is a house that is meant to have people in it. We need to start getting together more. Now that Lily is here and Gray is home, we need to start making some traditions."

"I would like that," Cyrus said. "Family is important. The best times of my life were when I had all my kids with me."

"Sometimes I wish I had more kids." Carey sighed. "But then I would have had more than one resent me for working all the time. So I guess it's good I just had the one, right, Gray?" he said, winking.

"I don't resent you," he said honestly. "At least I don't anymore. You're good to Lily. That's all I need."

Luna made a little annoyed noise. Gray had spent most of the day avoiding her. She'd seemed to be keeping herself enough occupied during the party that she wasn't bothering anyone else. But now it looked like she needed some attention. Gray didn't want to give it to her.

"I would like some more grandchildren. Since you're the only kid I've got, I'm counting on you to give them to me," Carey said.

Gray looked over at Romey. "What do you say? I think we should try to make my father happy. What about you, Cyrus?" he asked Romey's father. "You want more grandchildren?"

"Of course. A grandson, perhaps. But another granddaughter would be nice."

"I would love to have another baby," Romey said. "Which one of you men is going to carry it for me? I only think it's fair for someone else to go through pregnancy this time. I'm still having flashbacks to when the doctor was stitching me back up after this one."

Gray shuddered. He'd had to perform that procedure a few times while he was overseas. He had always felt sorry for the mother.

"Stitches, huh?" Carey said with a shake of his head. "How about a surrogate, then? We can pay a girl to take the pain for you."

"Talk to me in a year," Romey said, kissing Lily's sleeping face.

"That's fair. You didn't ask for my two cents, but I'm going to give it to you anyway. I don't think Lily should be an only child. I always felt bad for Gray."

Luna made another noise. This one was more like a strangled laugh. Carey looked over to her. His attorney face was on, the one he used when he cross-examined witnesses. "Do you have something to say, Luna? You've been making little noises and comments under your breath all night. If you have something to say, then say it."

"I just find it incredibly funny that you are sitting here talking about your son being an only child, when that's clearly not true."

"What the hell are you talking about? Gray *is* my only child."

"You still won't acknowledge him? Even though he's sitting right at this table across from you?"

"What are you talking about?" he asked, bewildered.

"Callahan. Why won't you acknowledge your older son?"

Gray couldn't believe what he was hearing. The table seemed to explode all around them with voices and shock and statements of disbelief. But Callahan's voice rang out the clearest. "What the hell are you talking about, Luna? Carey Norton is not my father."

"She never told you?" It was Luna's turn to be shocked. "She said she told you."

"No, she never told me who my father was. But it's impossible for Carey to be my father."

"It's not impossible, is it, Carey?" She looked at him.

He looked at her, not one to ever back down. "Impossible? No." He turned to look directly at Callahan. "Your mother and I were involved off and on over the years. The last time was the year before I got married, which could very well line up with the timing of your birth, but I assure you, Celesta never told me that I was your father. The last time I saw or spoke to her was about thirty-six years ago. I didn't know you existed until Cyrus brought you to Sweetheart Lake."

Callahan was quiet for a long time. It was probably moments, but it felt like an eternity. Gray looked around the table at Cyrus and Angela, who were stunned. And then at Romey, who didn't have much of an expression on her face. Her eyes were glued to Callahan. Gray was too absorbed in how everyone else was reacting to think about what this meant for him. But if this was true . . . it meant that he had a brother.

"When did my mother tell you this?" Callahan asked Luna.

"I don't know. I think it was when you graduated from high school. She said she told you."

"She's a liar. She's always been a fucking liar." He got up. Clearly angry. "Where is she, Luna?"

"I . . . I don't know. I haven't heard from her in a while."

"How do I get in contact with her?"

"You know it's not that easy. Your mother lets herself be found only when she wants to be."

"We don't need her," Carey said. "We'll take a test. They sell them at drugstores now. We can get the results in two days."

Callahan looked at Gray. "Is that true? Would it be quicker to do it at the hospital?"

"Yes, they sell them in stores. No, I don't think it's quicker to go to the hospital."

"Callahan," Carey said. "I give you my word that I never knew about you. I wouldn't have denied you. In fact . . ." He stopped himself from talking.

"What? What were you going to say?" Callahan demanded.

"I wouldn't have allowed her to raise you," he said quietly. "Let's leave it at that."

"Why? It's not a secret. My mother couldn't take care of a houseplant, much less a child. Always needed a man, too crazy to keep one."

"Callahan," Luna said firmly. "Do not speak of your mother that way."

"Who the hell are you to tell me not to talk about my mother? Where the hell were you? You think you're better than her? You just managed to marry someone sane. You walked out on your kids too. You weren't there for your son's funeral or your granddaughter's birth. You didn't come to see me when I graduated from the police academy. Even he was there for that." He pointed to Carey. "He didn't even know about me, and he was there for that!"

"You believe me?" Carey asked. "I don't know why, but it's important that you do."

"Yeah." He shook his head and rubbed his hand over his face. "I guess I do. I need to get the hell out of here."

"Gray." Romey stood up. "Take the baby. I don't want him to be alone."

"No." Cyrus stood up. "I think I should be the one who speaks to him."

* * *

Romey was the one who ended up taking her mother back to the inn that evening. She didn't say a word to her. Didn't ask her a question. She barely even looked at her as she got out of the car and went inside. She had shut off her feelings, numbing herself. It had been such a good day, nearly a perfect day. She had felt truly happy during most of it. She couldn't remember the last time when she had felt that way.

She had told Gray to take Lily home. She'd never specified which home, though. Right now Lily had two. She spent much more time at Gray's house. Her house really wasn't hers at all. It belonged to her father. He had been kind enough to let her move back during the last months of her pregnancy. He'd told her she could stay as long as she wanted. Forever, even. She'd known she wouldn't. She'd figured she and Lily would get their own place as soon as her pie shop became profitable.

When she made those plans, she hadn't counted on Gray coming back into her life. She'd been fully prepared to do this all without him. Somewhere in the back of her mind, she still felt that way.

He wouldn't leave Lily. Not willingly. She knew that. She had never seen him love anyone the way he loved their daughter.

She returned to her father's home. Her father's and Angela's cars were both there. She walked inside to find them in the living room. She looked at her father expectantly. He'd been the last one to talk to Callahan. She had made herself go numb, but the worry for Callahan had penetrated that. Callahan hid his feelings so well, but tonight, he was hurt. He was wildly angry. His identity had been shaken.

"He's all right. Callahan would never put his hands on a woman, but I think he would like to strangle your mother. His too."

"Was she always like this?" Romey asked her father. "I remember her being flighty and fun and not taking anything seriously, ever. But now . . . there's a bitterness to her."

"It's my fault. The second time she left, she tried to take you and Charlie with her. She wanted to pull you out of school to live on some commune. I went to Carey Norton for help. He was and still is a powerful man. A judge granted me sole custody. Luna has hated him ever since."

Romey had known some of that story. Her mother had told her that she wanted to take them away, but Romey hadn't wanted to go. She had friends here. She went to school regularly. She liked her town. Her mother wanted to pull them away from all of that. For what? Romey had been relieved when her father told her the judge had granted him custody. "I didn't know Mr. Norton had been involved."

"Maybe I didn't play fair, but I couldn't let you two go with her. Lord knows what Callahan's been through. I couldn't risk Luna doing that to you."

"Did you know that Celesta and Carey had a past?"

He shook his head. "I didn't. I just knew that the sisters had been to this town before and they both liked it. Carey very well could be Callahan's father. But Celesta isn't known for telling the truth."

Romey nodded, understanding who her aunt was. "Gray didn't bring Lily here, did he?"

"No. He looked shell-shocked when I last saw him. I think you should go be with him."

"I will, Daddy." She kissed his cheek and then went to her room to pack an overnight bag.

When she entered Gray's house, the faint smell of paint greeted her. He had had construction crews here every day the past few weeks. The inside of the house was transforming. Even the outside showed improvements. There was a brand-new deck, and the balcony off the master had been replaced. The front porch had been repainted, but the house remained the same old ugly green color.

"Gray?" she called out to him. It was a moment before he responded. But she saw him pop his head out of Lily's bedroom.

"She just fell back asleep. I don't want to wake her."

Romey peeked in at her daughter, who was peacefully sleeping in her crib. Gray and her father had done a beautiful job decorating the room. It was similar to the one she had at her father's house, but there were little touches that Gray had added. The rocking chair in the corner. Lily's name spelled out in large wooden letters on the far wall. The state-of-the-art baby monitor system with camera that was set up overlooking the crib, that Romey would never in a million years have thought to buy.

"Thank you for getting her ready for bed," she said to him as they were leaving her room.

"You need to stop thanking me." There was an undeniable edge to his voice. "I didn't do you a favor. It's what I'm supposed to do for my child."

She didn't say anything to that. He took her overnight bag from her and brought it to his bedroom. The master bedroom had been transformed. The walls were now a soft cream color. The furniture had been replaced with the pieces she had told him she liked when he asked for her opinion. But the biggest change had come with the bathroom. There hadn't been one there before. Where there had been a closet, there was now a door.

"Go take a look. They have been working double time to make sure this was done."

She walked inside to see a dream bathroom. There was a huge tub, big enough for two people, and on the other side was an enormous waterfall shower complete with a panel of buttons she had no idea how to work. Further down was a walk-in closet that was a clothes lover's fantasy.

She looked back at him.

"I figured a bigger bathroom was a better use than a small office."

"It's beautiful, Gray."

"I'm glad you like it." He went into the bedroom and sat on the side of the bed, taking off his shoes.

She leaned against the wall, watching him for a moment. "How are you feeling?"

The revelation tonight would change his life too, if it were true. "I don't know. Better than Callahan, I guess. I always knew who my father was."

"Do you think it's true?"

"He looks like him, Romey. More than I do. I never noticed it before because I wasn't looking for it, but now it's slapping me in the face. Callahan looks like my father did when he was a young lawyer."

"But how do you feel about it?"

"How am I supposed to feel about it? This isn't some stranger. This is Callahan we're talking about. I have known him half my life. He was closer to me than Charlie these last fifteen years. I already love him like a brother."

"So you're happy?"

"No. I'm mad I didn't know. I'm mad that your mother had to reveal it there like that. It was Lily's birthday party. She couldn't just act like a regular grandmother. She has to drop bombs everywhere she goes, causing explosions in everyone's lives. She said she's known about this since Callahan was eighteen. That's eighteen years she had the chance to say something. She hasn't said a goddamn thing. She hates it that now our families are even more intertwined than before. She hated seeing us happy and all together tonight."

"Do you really think she did it because she doesn't want to see us happy? How could she accomplish that?"

"Why don't you ever put any blame on her?"

She looked at him for a long moment, not sure how to respond to his question. "She shouldn't have done that. Especially today. I'm not making excuses for her. But she has no power in whether we are happy or not."

"But she could contribute to your happiness or she can take away from it. Your mother has never been a neutral party in your life. I see how tense you've become around her. You don't speak your mind. You cater to every stupid bullshit thing she wants."

"She's my mother! Don't act like you didn't do that for yours. You almost married another woman to please her. Sending Abel out for matcha was no big deal."

"Don't compare your mother with mine. She may not have been the greatest nurturer, but she never took off and left me for years."

"That's a low blow, Gray. Especially coming from you. You left me too. When I was grieving and pregnant."

"You know I didn't know you were pregnant," he said, his eyes flashing with anger. "I never would have left if I had known. Hell, I never would have left if I knew what you wanted. You still can't make up your mind." He shook his head. "You have every right to be mad at me. But why aren't you mad at her? Why is it okay for you to be mad at me and not at her?"

"Because you were the one who wasn't supposed to leave me!" she yelled at him, and to her horror, her eyes filled with tears. "I trusted you. I let myself feel around you. I don't expect anything from her."

He crossed the room and pulled her into his arms.

"You're allowed to be mad at her. To hold her accountable. To tell her how you feel. I was there each time she took off when we were kids. I saw how hurt you were even though you didn't want to admit it."

"It was better with Daddy. He was stable. She was chaotic."

"She isn't allowed to be chaotic around my child. I won't stand for it. Hell, I won't stand for her being chaotic around you. I don't care if she is your mother. You're not happy when she's around."

"I'm fine."

"You can tell that lie to yourself, but you can't tell it to me. I'm going to talk to her tomorrow and send her back to wherever she came from. I'm not sure my relationship with Callahan will ever be the same after this."

She shook her head. "I'll talk to her, Gray. It will just get ugly if you try to."

His nostrils flared a bit and he looked as if he would argue, but he didn't.

"And for the record, I've always wanted to be with you," Romey continued. "But things have never been simple between us, and they aren't simple now. I got used to idea of doing this alone when you were gone. I had to plan for my life as if you were never coming back. You were gone for two years. You can't expect everything to magically be the way you want right away."

"I know. You want to take things slow with us."

She nodded. She wanted to stay away, but it was too damn hard. "I'll start staying over sometimes."

"I can live with that."

"You're going to have to."

He gave her a tired smile. "Let's go to bed. It's been one hell of a day."

It had been. It would probably be that way tomorrow when she spoke to her mother.

CHAPTER NINETEEN

Life is too short for self-hatred and celery sticks.
—Marilyn Wann

The next morning Romey arrived at her shop a little earlier than usual. She hadn't had to go through her normal morning routine of getting everything ready for her father and daughter before she left for work. Gray had bought a programmed coffeemaker and had it set up to have her coffee ready for her when she woke up. There had been no need to lay out Lily's clothes. Gray was perfectly capable of picking out an outfit. She didn't have to do all the things she had been used to doing when she was alone.

It was weird for her to be able to get up and go. But it was also nice to have someone else to take the little things off her plate. She walked in through the back door and right into her office. She flicked on the lights and immediately screamed. There was a large man sleeping on the love seat she kept in there.

The man jumped up. "Miss Romey!" Abel looked horrified. "I didn't mean to scare you."

Romey backed up into the wall, her hand over her racing heart. She shut her eyes for a moment to compose herself. "I nearly wet myself."

"I'm sorry, Miss. I meant to be up before you came in."

"It's okay, Abel." She opened her eyes and looked up at him. Alice had dropped him at home last evening after the party. "Did you sleep here the entire night?"

"Yes, ma'am. It won't happen again, I promise."

"I don't mind that you slept here. I want to know why you slept here."

"I got put out."

"You got put out of your house? Why? When?"

"My Aunt Nina broke up with her wife and went to Florida. She thought that Aunt Kendra would let me stay there, but she's really mad at Aunt Nina and told me that I had to give her my entire paycheck or I couldn't live there anymore. I'm saving up to buy a car. I can't give her my whole paycheck. I guess I'm going to have to, though. I'll try to get a second job. Maybe you could talk to Mr. Norton for me. He's got a big house. Maybe I could do something for him there."

Romey's heart broke for Abel. People kept leaving him. Throwing him away like he was disposable. He was eighteen years old. He should be hanging out with his friends the summer after graduation. He shouldn't be worried about having to work two jobs.

"How about I try to talk to your aunt first? Maybe she's just upset. I can't believe she would kick you out of the house when you're doing so well. I'm sure she's probably feeling a little guilty by now. You'll be back in your bed in no time."

They were busy that day. So many people who had been at the party came into the shop. They thanked her for inviting them. She could take no credit for that. It was all Carey.

He had surprised them by having the photographer email them the pictures of their families that were taken when they all entered the party. The poor photographer must have been up all night, but knowing Carey the way she did, the man had been more than fairly compensated.

Carey came in a little late that morning after the breakfast rush had died down. He wasn't his normally cheerful self.

As soon as she saw him, she left her place from behind the counter and hugged him.

"How are you?" she asked him.

"Didn't sleep a wink last night. I keep thinking about Callahan. Is he okay?"

"I haven't spoken to him. He texted me this morning telling me he was fine. But I don't think Callahan would ever admit to not being fine."

"Do you think he hates me?"

"I really can't say. But from the way you're sounding, you seem to have no doubt that my mother was telling the truth."

"It never occurred to me," Carey said thoughtfully. "I thought he was from your father's side of the family for the longest time. I never thought Cyrus would adopt his ex-wife's sister's child. But of course he would. It was Callahan himself who told me he was Celesta's son. It still didn't dawn on me. I thought he was the same age as Charlie and Gray. I didn't realize he was two years older than them. You'd think I would have put it together when we made him police chief and I learned how old he was. But I never thought about it. I consider myself a smart man, but I really can be very stupid."

"You didn't take the test yet. It might not be true."

He pulled a picture out of his pocket and showed it to Romey. "That's me in front of my first firm. Our coloring isn't the same, but you can't tell me that he isn't mine."

Romey looked at the picture for a long time. Same tall wide build. Same nose. Same strong chin. Even the same forehead. "Gray said this last night. I didn't know what to think until right now."

"What do you think? It's all incredibly convoluted and a little bit scandalous."

It was so odd to her that he would care about her opinion. But it touched her that he did. "Well, I love you, Carey, but who gives a damn what I think? I'm one of the least important people in this issue."

"How is Gray? I'm planning on stopping by the house after I leave here."

"He's very mad at my mother. I think he's ready to send her to Antarctica."

Carey frowned deeply. "Frankly, I'm not too thrilled with your mama either. Antarctica seems like a great idea right now. But she did finally tell the truth."

"I'm going to talk to her. She has this way of enraging people whenever she's around."

"But not you, huh?"

"Oh no, she does. I just hide it well. And take it out on Gray. But in my defense, he's had a pretty good life; he could use a little hell."

"You know I want him to marry you, right? I haven't said anything to him. His mother really did a number on him with Gwen, but if you want me to start dropping hints, I will. We can have you a big old ring in a few weeks."

She grinned at Carey. "He's dropped a few hints of his own. It's me that's the holdup."

"Make him suffer, baby doll." Carey grinned back at her. "You're good for him. You kept him from getting uppity like his mother's side of the family."

"You're not worried about me?" she asked honestly. "You've dealt with the women in my family firsthand. The insanity is strong with us. None of us have a good track record when it comes to being wives and mothers."

"That's not true. Your grandparents stayed married until they died. And maybe if your mother and your aunt had met and married performers like themselves, it would have been a different story. It's hard to take women who grew up that way and turn them into typical folks. It's not genetic. You take care of everyone who comes into your orbit, Romey. Even me. You never have given me a reason to have a second thought about you."

She sent Carey away a few minutes later with an entire home-fry pie that had just come out of the oven. She had Abel make more of the savory pies when they sold out within the first hour that morning.

He had been noticeably quiet the entire day. Apologetic. There were a few times she thought he was on the verge of tears. It made her feel like hell. Apologizing for being homeless so soon after his high school graduation—it made no sense to her.

She drove him to his jilted aunt's home. It was on the outskirts of town. She'd never realized how far out it was, miles away from her shop. Abel had walked to work every morning. No buses ran at this time. It must have been pitch-black out. Of course he was saving up for a car. It was hard to get around town unless you lived right in the center of it.

"You don't have to talk to her, Miss Romey. I'll get another job so I can pay her. Now that you've hired me, it should be easier."

"I'm talking to her." She got out of the car and followed Abel inside. She found his Aunt Kendra sitting on the couch. She was in a bathrobe and house slippers. There was a carton of ice cream in her lap and a trashy talk show on the television. She looked like a woman who had been broken up with.

"What the hell are you doing here?" she asked Abel. There was no hiding the anger in her voice.

"Um . . ." He hesitated. "My boss wanted to talk to you."

"Why? It's no use. You think I want to be reminded of any part of your lying, faithless aunt? The only way I can stomach looking at you is if you pay me, and I don't even know if your little ass paycheck is enough."

"Hold up," Romey said, feeling the rage build up inside her and not caring to tamp it down. "I don't care if you got broken up with. If your attitude was anything like it is with your wife, I would definitely say you had it coming."

"Excuse me!" The woman stood up. "Who the hell do you think you are?"

"I'm his boss. He already told you that, or are you hard of hearing?" She looked at Abel. "Go get your stuff. All of it. You aren't coming back here."

"Ma'am?"

"Go do what I said, Abel."

"Okay." He looked too scared to disobey.

"You're a garbage person," she said as she turned back to Kendra. "He's eighteen years old. He's a kid. He's innocent in all of this, and he trusted you to be there for him. You just threw him away. You didn't know where he was or what could have happened to him. I will not allow it, and I'm here to let you know that you deserve to be a lonely miserable bitch for treating that boy the way you did. He's got a good heart, and he's going to be something someday. It won't be because of you. It will be in spite of you."

She went to sit in her car. Her anger was fuming off her in hot waves. Able came out with a large black trash bag filled to the brim. He didn't have a suitcase. Callahan had told her how many times he'd had to move before. His mother, then foster care. His aunts were the most stable people in his life, and that had only been for the past five years.

It made Romey even angrier. She took him to her father's house. He was home, and so was Angela. They were sitting in the kitchen with mugs of tea in their hands.

He stood up when he saw her. "Are you okay, Romey?"

"She's very mad, sir," Abel answered for her. "It's my fault."

"It is not your fault!" Romey yelled. "You are not a piece of trash that is to be thrown away. Your aunt better be glad I'm somebody's mother, because I might have knocked her right on her ass."

"What happened?" Angela asked. The horrified expression on her face made Romey realized how fired up she was.

"I need Abel to stay here for a while. Is that okay?"

"Of course," her father said without hesitation. "If it will keep you out of jail."

"Cyrus!" Angela scolded.

"It was a joke. Of course he can stay here. We can clear out Callahan's old room."

"I can pay rent, sir," Abel said quickly. "I'll be real quiet, and I promise I won't eat none of your food or bother you."

"I won't be taking your money." Cyrus waved his hand in dismissal. "You eat whatever you want to. I might give you some chores to do, though."

"Yes, sir." He nodded. "Whatever you need. You can make me a list."

"Go on upstairs and get settled, honey," Angela told him. "I'm going to start dinner. You can tell us more about yourself later."

Romey took Abel upstairs to where Callahan's old room was. It had originally been meant to be an office space. They had rarely gone in there since Callahan moved out. It had mostly been used for storage. Before they moved to Sweetheart Lake, they had never had their own rooms. They had lived in a one-bedroom apartment in New Orleans. Their parents had the bedroom; Charlie and Romey slept in the living room. It had been so wonderful to have her own space. Her own bed. She and Charlie had shared a pullout couch for years, until Romey decided she would rather sleep on the love seat than next to her brother.

Even having an assigned seat at school was something special to her. Her desk with her name on it. Her mother hated the idea so much. She used to complain to their father about them sitting all day, about them having to be quiet and be fed information instead of being able to explore the world.

But Romey had loved going to school. She had loved having a bedtime and a place she could be alone with her thoughts. If her father hadn't fought so hard, she would have none of this. She wouldn't be in the position to help someone else.

"I forgot how tiny this room was," she said as she opened the door. It was a little musty in there after being closed up for months. The Christmas decorations were still there. Romey had sworn to herself she was going to put them in the attic, but she never had. "Callahan probably barely fit in here."

"It's fine for me." Abel walked inside. He was even larger than Callahan had been when he was his age. If he stretched out his arms, he could touch both walls. "I really appreciate you doing this for me, Miss Romey. I don't know what I can do for you, but if you ever need anything from me, I'll do it."

"Just help my father with the housework. Mow the lawn. Take out the garbage."

She glanced at the single bed that had been in there for over eighteen years. Callahan had moved out right after he finished college. No one had slept there for years. She slipped past Abel and put her hand on it to touch it. She could feel the springs poking out. She couldn't let him sleep on this.

"Abel, I want you to go down the hall to the linen closet. There's a clear bag with clean bedding in it. I want you to bring it to me."

"Yes, ma'am."

She left the tiny room, closing the door behind her, and walked into her bedroom. She stripped the sheets and pillowcases off her queen-sized bed.

"Miss Romey?" she heard Abel call.

"In here."

He stopped in front of her bedroom door with the bag in his hands. "Is this what you wanted?"

"Yes. Go on and make up the bed. You'll be sleeping in here."

"But this is your room!" he protested. "I can't sleep here."

"You can and you will." She walked over to the window and pointed toward the ugly green house. "You see that house over there? There's a man who says he's in love with me who lives there. I'm going to stay with him."

"Dr. Norton lives there." Abel looked relieved. "I thought he lived at the mansion with his father. The house is so big, half the town could live there."

"That's where Gray grew up. But he spent most of his time here. He was my brother's best friend when they were kids. I think he brought the house because he had good memories of being here."

The best times in her life had been here. She couldn't see herself being anyplace else.

* * *

Romey pulled into Gray's driveway two hours later than she normally did. He had resisted the urge to call and check on her at least half a dozen times. She had planned to talk to her mother today. He didn't want to bother her, but as it got later and later, he had started to worry, and Lily had begun to ask for Romey every few minutes.

He lifted her out of her high chair when he heard Romey's car cut off. "Mama?" Lily asked.

"I think she's home now." He went to the front door, opening it as she approached. She was rolling a large suitcase behind her.

"Please tell me your mother's body isn't in there."

She grinned at him. "She's flexible, but I don't think I could bend her enough to fit in here. Hi, Lily. Mama missed you today."

"Take her," he said, handing her to her mother. "She's sick of me." He picked up her suitcase as she went back to the car to retrieve a smaller bag.

"My beauty supplies," she said, when he looked at her curiously. "Let's take this stuff to the bedroom. I have some things to fill you in on."

They went upstairs to the master bedroom. Romey set her bag down, kicked off her shoes, and climbed into bed, snuggling with Lily. She looked exhausted. He would love for her to be able to sleep in once in a while. To not have to take care of anyone or anything else. To just relax. But she wasn't wired that way.

He climbed into bed next to his little family and looked down at Romey, waiting for her to speak.

"Did your father come by today?" she finally said.

"Yes. He stayed for a little over an hour."

"He's worried about you. How you're feeling about everything . . ."

"The worst thing that could happen is that one of my best friends is my brother. I'm good with that."

"You aren't afraid you'll have to share your father's attention?"

"I've seen my father more in the last two months than I saw him in the first thirty years of my life." He laughed. "I think I'll be fine. Now stop asking about me and tell me what happened today with your mother."

"Nothing happened. I didn't talk to her. I didn't have time." She opened her eyes and looked up at him. "I'm moving in here. I hope you're cool with that."

He blinked at her. Part of him didn't believe what she was saying.

"I'm not. You said you wanted to take things slow. You can't live here," he said, not meaning it. He couldn't let her know how much this news affected him. He was tired of being without her. He had waited half his life to be with her, only for her to keep him at arm's length when all the obstacles were finally out of their way.

"Too bad. I'm not going anywhere. I don't have anywhere else to go."

"What happened to your father's house?"

"Abel is living there."

"Abel? How did that happen?"

"I found him asleep in my office this morning. His aunt kicked him out a week ago when his other aunt left her. She told him that he either had to give her his entire paycheck or he had to go. Abel left."

"That poor kid." Gray shook his head. "I picked him up on the side of the road yesterday. He told me that his house was hard to find and it would be easier to meet me there."

"He's been wandering around town after work every day or hanging out at his friend's house until he thought it was safe enough to sneak into the shop for the night. I went to his aunt's house, thinking I could talk to her, but that was dumb on my part. Anyone who could treat a kid like that is an asshole. I got so mad, Gray. I really could have hurt her."

"Luckily for us, you didn't. I'm not sure how Callahan would react if you showed up at the station in handcuffs."

"I didn't want to be away from my baby overnight, so I decided against hitting her. She just didn't care where he was for an entire week. He's lived with her for five years, and she just put him out."

"What about the other aunt? She's no better."

"Maybe not. She told him he could come down to Florida and live with her as soon as she got settled in an apartment. She's sleeping on a friend's couch for now and doesn't have a place for him. Abel didn't want to go to Florida. He didn't want to give up his job here."

"Your father was okay with you bringing him there?"

She nodded. "Daddy helps people. I think that's why he originally fell for my mother. He probably thought he could help her."

"If your father ever does have an issue with it, Abel can stay here. The work hasn't started on the basement yet, but there's already a bathroom and a kitchenette there. He would have his own private entrance."

Her eyes widened. "You would do that?"

"As long as you promised not to move back to your father's house when your room becomes free again."

"The bathroom was a game changer for me. I might stay just for that."

"I could also talk to my father. He lives alone in that big house and has a staff of bored people looking for someone to take care of. Abel would have run of the house."

"Is your old car still at your father's house?"

He nodded. "Still parked in the garage. Why?"

"Would you consider giving it to Abel? He's saving up for a car. If one is just sitting there, it might as well be used."

"I don't mind, but it's a little sports car. I'm not sure Abel would be comfortable in it."

"Oh, well, maybe I could drive it and give him my car."

"It's not good in the snow and it's not good for transporting Lily. You could get a new car."

"I can't—"

"No more *I. We.* We can afford a new car for you. An SUV. With four-wheel drive and all the boring safety features that neither of us cared about until we became parents."

She looked as if she was going to argue. But she just nodded. "I would like that."

"Okay. We'll start looking tomorrow." This was a huge step for her. Letting him do something for her. Letting him take care of her. They were finally heading in the right direction. He wanted to marry her. He wondered how long it would take before they got there.

CHAPTER TWENTY

Stressed is desserts spelled backwards.—Unknown

The shop was finally quiet. It was about an hour before closing. There was nothing left to sell but coffee and juice. Romey had sent Alice home early. Abel was in the back, prepping for tomorrow. He'd told her that her father had asked him to meet him at the hardware store after work. There was some kind of project he wanted to do in the garage that he needed help with. Her father was putting him to work already.

It was what he had done with young men. When Callahan came to live with them, Daddy had made sure he had something to do. They had built a shed that summer. Even Gray hadn't escaped the same fate. If he was at their house when there was work to be done, he had to participate. The shelves that were in what was now Lily's bedroom at her father's house had been built by Charlie and Gray.

It was no wonder she hadn't been able to get him off her mind all these years. Even when he wasn't with her, while she was at home, there were little reminders of him everywhere. He had been such an ingrained part of her life for more than half of it. She couldn't be rid of him if she wanted to. Their baby had solidified that, throwing them together in an unbreakable way.

A flash of turquoise blue caught her eye as it passed the window. She stopped wiping down the table and looked up to see her mother walking toward the door.

Romey sighed.

She hadn't spoken to her since the party. She knew she needed to speak to her, but she sure as hell didn't know what to say.

Luna breezed through the door. Her long, gorgeously colored skirt swished around her legs. Every time Romey saw her mother, it was almost like seeing a familiar stranger. A person she recognized but didn't know at all.

"Do you know how difficult it is to get a cab in this town? I had to wait an hour and a half for one to come. I don't know how anyone gets anywhere around here." Her mother dramatically collapsed into a chair as if she had been on a thousand-mile journey.

"Mama, this is Sweetheart Lake, Virginia. We only have one cab, and he spends most of his day taking the elderly to their appointments. Just about everyone else has a car. It hasn't changed much since you lived here."

"Things should change in twenty years! Evolve! There was never enough to do around here. I guess no one would need a cab. Maybe just to get out of here."

"You can go, Mama. Nothing and no one is stopping you. I'm still not sure why you came."

Her mother raised a surprised eyebrow. "I wanted to see you. I wanted to see my grandbaby."

"Why?"

"What do you mean, why? You are my daughter."

"That doesn't answer my question. You stated a fact. I am your daughter. That doesn't explain why you wanted to see me and Lily now."

"I don't know what you want me to say." She crossed her arms over her chest. "They've poisoned you against me, haven't they?"

"Who is *they*, Mama?"

"Gray. His father. Your father. They want you to hate me."

"You're not allowed to talk about Gray anymore."

"Excuse me? I'll talk about whoever I want."

Romey felt her temper spark. "Not in front of me, you won't. You'll be talking to yourself if you try it."

"Romey, what has gotten into you?"

"Nothing. If you really knew me, you would know this is how I am. Gray has been in my life since I was ten years old. He was my first kiss. The first man I was with. The first man who told me he loves me. He's the father of my child. He's extremely important to me. So I'm not going to listen to you say anything bad about him. And as for Daddy . . . you got some nerve saying he poisoned me against you."

"You always were a daddy's girl."

"Don't trivialize this, damn it!" Luna's eyes went wide; Romey's tone had clearly shocked her. "You left him and us. He never said a negative thing about you. He had every right to. We all had every right to."

"You have negative things to say? Now? You haven't said anything in all these years, but now you have something to say? And I'm supposed to believe that no one has gotten in your head?"

"You've gotten in my head! You've been there for years."

"I don't believe this. I saw the way Gray looked at me last night. Like I was trash. You think he won't think of you that way just because you had a baby for him? It's only a matter of time before he acts like his father and decides he wants someone like him to be his wife. Then where will you and your baby be?"

"Get out," Romey said through clenched teeth.

"What?"

"You heard me. I warned you. Now get out!"

Abel came bursting through the kitchen door. His fists clenched. His expression clearly ready for battle.

"Is everything okay?"

"Yes, Abel. I didn't mean to worry you. I'm asking my mother to leave." Romey tossed her rag on the table and began to walk toward the kitchen. There were too many emotions running through her. She felt like she was suffocating. "I need some air. Are you okay here for a few minutes?"

"I'll be fine." Abel folded his massive arms across his chest and looked at Luna. "Ma'am," Romey heard as she walked through the door, "I think you should go now."

Romey stood outside her back door for a few minutes before she sent Callahan a text.

I need you.

Where are you?

At the shop. In the back.

He was there within minutes in his regular clothes. He was never one to take a day off, much less two in a row. She felt incredibly selfish for asking him to come, but she needed him right now. He was the only other person who would understand. Charlie was gone, and in his last couple of years, even Charlie had been so far from the person he used to be that she could barely speak to him anymore.

"What's wrong?" Callahan said, walking up to her.

She rested her head against his shoulder briefly and then looked up at him. "I think I need to fill you in on some things. Abel lives with Daddy now. I live with Gray. I tried to put him in your old bedroom, but the boy can hardly fit in there. I feel kind of bad we made you sleep in a glorified closet all those years."

"What do you mean, Abel lives with Uncle Cy?"

"One aunt moved to Florida. The other put him out. He was homeless for a week and sleeping on the couch in my office. I tried to talk to his aunt and ended up kind of threatening her, so now he lives with Daddy."

"Why the hell didn't you call me before now?"

"I figured you had your own shit you were going through. I handled it."

"Staying with Uncle Cy isn't a long-term solution. You should have called me."

"Daddy is okay with it for now. He's already putting him to work. He told him to meet him at the hardware store this afternoon."

"He did that with me," Callahan said. "I wasn't even out of the detention center for a full day before he put me to work."

"Gray came up with some other solutions. He won't let me adopt an eighteen-year-old, but we're going to make sure Abel is set." She studied his face for a moment, trying to see if it revealed any signs about how he was, but he was so hard to read. "How are you? I've been worried."

"I don't know how I am." He walked to his car and pulled a manila envelope off the passenger seat. "This was sent to me today."

Romey took the envelope from him and looked inside. It was a will. Carey's will. And with it were a dozen photos. Most of them were of a young Carey Norton, but one was of Carey and Callahan. It was from the day he was sworn in as police chief. Carey had his arm wrapped around Callahan, smiling widely. Romey had been there that day. She had been in the room with both of them at the same time more than once. How could she have never seen the resemblance? It was striking.

"Read the back," he told her.

" 'I don't need a test. What happens is up to you.' " She looked at Callahan. "What is going to happen next? Do you think he's your father?"

"I look like him. But that doesn't mean anything for sure." He pulled a picture out of his pocket and showed it to her. It was of their mothers when they were young and still performing. Both of them stunning in their glittery tight red performance costumes. They were with two men, one of them Carey Norton, the other a stranger to them.

"I don't remember my mother ever looking like that. She was beautiful, wasn't she?"

"Gorgeous. They both were." She looked back at the picture. "Carey looks like he's trying to convince you that he is your father. What are you going to do?"

"Try to track down my mother. Other than that, nothing."

"Nothing? Carey Norton might be your father."

"Biologically. He probably is. But Uncle Cy is my father. You know that."

"That means Gray is your brother."

Callahan, seeming slightly uncomfortable, shifted his weight. "How is he feeling about everything?"

"He loves you. Right now he's more concerned about how you're feeling."

"He's been one of my best friends for half my life. What would change?"

"I don't know. Call him. He would like to hear from you."

"What's going on with you?" He looked at her for a long moment. "Your text sounded kind of urgent."

"Gray said I needed to have a conversation with my mother. He thinks I'm not being honest with her."

"He might have a point. You don't let anyone else mistreat you, but when it comes to your mama, you don't have much to say."

"I said something today. In fact, I kicked her out of my shop for talking about Gray. She said that it's only a matter of time before he gets tired of me and wants someone more like him." That had bothered her more than anything else. Gray hadn't done or said anything since he had been home that made her feel like that way. But it had always been a thought in the back of her mind. For years. They had always been a secret. She had always been the one he wouldn't bring home to his mother.

She knew her worth. Her value as a person in this world. She believed he loved her, but long term, was she who he wanted?

"There's certain people who are always going to feel that way about you. About us. It doesn't matter how far we've come—there is always going to be someone who thinks we'll never be good enough. Those are the type of people you have to say fuck you to and keep it moving."

"You're suggesting I curse out my mama?"

"I would never suggest such a thing," he said with a grin. "But you can tell her about herself when she steps out of line. Gray doesn't want anyone else. It had to take him almost never being able to come home to realize that he shouldn't have left."

"What do you mean that he was almost not able to come home?"

Callahan's expression changed briefly to one she couldn't read before it slipped back to neutral. "War-torn country. It was no vacation he was on."

She nodded, knowing that was the truth. Everything Callahan said matched up with what Gray had told her. But she had always thought there was more to his story. The weight loss. The haunted look on his face when he'd first returned. The hardness that had replaced the gentle man he used to be.

The urge to press Callahan for more information was almost overwhelming, but she knew she would get nowhere with him. So she let it go. Right now there were a dozen other things in her life she needed to sort through.

* * *

Gray walked into the little café a few blocks away from Romey's pie shop. Lily was resting her head on his shoulder. She had been a little more clingy than usual today. Her teeth were still bothering her. He had been tempted to leave her with Anna, his father's housekeeper, for a couple of hours while he met with his old friend, but he didn't have the heart to leave her. Especially now that Romey had moved in. He wanted to think it was because she could no longer bear to be without him, but he had the feeling that she wanted to make Lily's home life as stable as possible.

He no longer had to watch them leave him at night. Nights used to be the most torturous part of his twenty-four hours. Nights were when the dreams would come, when he would wake up not knowing where he was, feeling suffocated, remembering back to his time locked away.

The dreams didn't come when Romey was asleep next to him in the bed. As long as he could feel her, smell her, reach over and touch her when he wanted, he felt grounded. He could sleep through the night. It wasn't something he had been able to do in over a year.

He spotted his friend, Dr. Trevor Spencer, sitting at a corner table. Trevor had grown up here as well. He was from Gray's side of the lake. His father was also a doctor. They had known each other in school but weren't close friends. It wasn't until they'd met again as residents that they'd struck up a friendship.

Trevor stood when he saw him. "Gray," he said when he walked closer. "I guess the rumors were true."

Trevor's eyes settled on Lily.

"Rumor makes it sound like it's a dirty little secret. I have a daughter. Her name is Lily." He kissed her forehead. "Lily, can you say hi to my friend Trevor?"

"Hi," she said softly, without lifting her head from his shoulder.

"She's teething," Gray explained. "Won't let me put her down."

"Sit. Let's order something. We've got a lot of catching up to do."

They sat, and Trevor motioned for a waitress to come over. Gray ordered coffee and a fruit-and-cheese plate, while Trevor ordered a glass of bourbon and a BLT.

"It's good to see you, Trevor. I was glad you emailed me. How have you been?"

"A lot less busy than you, it seems like. Much to my mother's chagrin, I'm not married and don't have any children."

"I think every mother is programmed to want to see their child pair off and procreating with someone. Don't rush into anything for your mother's sake. It will never work out."

"Is that what happened with you and Gwen? I hope you don't mind me asking. It's just one moment I was at your engagement party, the next moment I'm hearing you left the country to work for a humanitarian organization."

"I thought it was best to break my engagement when I realized I was in love with someone else."

"Lily's mother?"

"Yeah. Romey Michaels."

"Charlie's sister?" he asked in disbelief. Trevor had grown up here, but he hadn't lived in town since they'd gone away to college. Apparently, no one was keeping him updated on the town's gossip.

"She's owns the Crusty Petal. It's a pie shop. She used to be an executive pastry chef in DC. You have to stop by her shop. Her stuff is incredible."

"The Crusty Petal? Her boxes have roses on them?"

"Yeah. They do."

"I have had her pie before. My parents love that place. In fact, they sent me her Dutch apple caramel pie for my birthday. I didn't even bother with a knife or a plate. I ate the whole thing out of the pan." He shook his head. "I can't believe she's the one who made it. I was picturing some rotund, plain-looking chick. If memory serves me correctly, Charlie's sister looks incredibly hot in a cocktail dress. I'm pretty sure I hit on her at your engagement party."

"How did that go?"

"She ended up having your baby and not mine, so, not well." He looked at Lily for a long moment. "She looks like her mother."

"Everyone says that. I think she looks like me too."

"Charlie's sister." He shook his head. "I can't believe it."

"Why can't you believe it?" he asked, starting to feel annoyed with Trevor's shock.

"She's just the opposite of Gwen. In every way. She's also Charlie Michaels' sister. Their father worked for yours. Their mother was that weird chick that used to be in the circus."

"Their father was there for me more than my own when we were growing up. If I hadn't met him, I couldn't imagine the kind of spoiled pompous asshole I would be now. They are a good family. They are now my family," he said firmly. They would always face this kind of judgment, wouldn't they? Romey would always face this kind of judgment. It didn't matter how much she accomplished on her own, how hard she had worked to be successful; in this town she would be seen as the woman who had gotten pregnant for him. He wasn't anyone special. He just happened to have been born into one of the richest families in the country. It was luck of the draw. It was nothing that deserved respect.

"Did I cross a line?" Trevor gave him a boyish grin. He was handsome, tall, light haired, with model-like bone structure. He looked like the rich-kid villain in every bad teen movie. Gray wouldn't be sitting here talking to him if he weren't a damn good doctor. Trevor worked in one of the roughest hospitals in DC after turning down a cushy job with the federal government. "I'm definitely not judging. I would choose Romey Michaels over Gwen any day. How did you two wind up hooking up, anyway? Gwen must have flipped when she found out."

"I never cheated on Gwen."

"Again, no judgment here if you did. My father regularly slept with his nurses. He likes to think he is some well-respected pilar of the community, but he's trash like everyone else. They all are."

"It started when we were teenagers. It wasn't a hookup. I've been in love with her for years. There was no cheating. Even if I wanted to, Romey would never allow it. In fact, she barely spoke to me after I got serious with Gwen. I missed her. And then I got confused about what I wanted out of life. I had to reevaluate, which is why I took the job overseas. There is no scandal there. You can tell that to whoever is feeding you rumors."

"It's the kid that makes this intriguing for everyone, you know?"

"People think she trapped me. They don't know her. She'd rather cut off her foot than ask me for anything. She doesn't need me. She was fully prepared to raise Lily on her own. She still is."

"All of that is good to know. I'm nosy as hell and am glad you told me all of that, but that's not why I asked you here."

"No?" Gray was surprised. "I thought they elected you to be the one to find out all the dirt."

"My sister was the one who told me you had a kid. She didn't even know the whole story. I hope you don't think I'm in some kind of text chain that spends all our time talking shit about you. You aren't that interesting." He grinned at him again. "I'm here to offer you a job."

"A job?"

"Yeah. I'm opening a low-cost clinic. This area needs it. The amount of people around here without insurance is staggering. I need another doctor, and you don't seem afraid to touch those icky poor folks, so I figured you were the best man to ask."

"I don't know what to say."

"Say yes. The pay is absolute shit, by the way. But you don't need the money. Take the job."

He was surprised by how much the offer immediately tempted him. He hadn't thought about going back to work at all until Trevor brought it up. "I just got home. I'm taking care of my daughter. We're renovating our house."

"The clinic isn't opening till late fall. We still need approval from the town, which is another reason I came to you. I heard you have some pull with the mayor. Maybe you can talk to him?"

"That I will definitely do. I'll talk to him tonight."

"Perfect." Trevor smiled briefly, but it faded as he grew serious. "I really want you to consider taking a job at the clinic, even if it's just a few days a week. We grew up in a protective bubble in this town, not realizing how so many people actually lived. But we both have seen the world, and we can give back. I need someone who will see these patients as people. You are the one who can do that."

"I really will consider it. Thank you for thinking of me."

"Good. Now let's talk about something else. How about you ask me about my love life?"

Gray laughed. He ended up being glad he had come.

CHAPTER TWENTY-ONE

Good things come to those who bake.—Unknown

Romey had been in her pie shop for a little over an hour. She was putting the finishing touches on her extra-dreamy strawberry cream pies with homemade whipped cream. It was her pie of the day, and it sold out within the first hour every week, especially as the summer drew on. Callahan had told her that she needed to raise the prices for her pie of the day; she could get away with it. But as she piped on perfect swirls of the fluffy white cream around the edges of her pies, she disregarded that thought. This was her favorite part of her job, taking ingredients and making them into something beautiful and edible. It was relaxing. It took her mind off everything else. If she hadn't had this shop, she wouldn't have been able to survive the past year and a half. It gave her a purpose. Something that was all hers.

"I'm going to go bring these boxes outside, Miss Romey."

"Okay," she said to Abel as he walked out the back door. They had another half hour till opening. The smell of her savory breakfast pies filled the air. It was almost time to pull them out of the oven. She and Abel would start stocking the display cases in the front of the shop. Alice would be here to start the coffee machine. And soon she would be greeting her regular customers who stopped by almost daily to have breakfast.

Her favorites were a trio of retired elderly men. They had all worked for the town. And each morning they would come in complaining about the cost of cable or medication or their wives. She found them adorable and tried to have their order set aside for them most days before they came in.

They tasted things for her from time to time, and every day, besides their breakfast orders, they would take a piece of pie home for themselves. Most days it was apple. Other days, when they were feeling frisky, they would order something wild, like chocolate peanut butter.

"Miss Romey!" Abel burst through the back door. "You need to come right now."

Romey dropped her piping bag and immediately went to him. "What is it?"

"I . . . you've got to see for yourself." He went back out the back door, and she followed him to see a line of people down the block.

"What is going on?"

Abel pointed. She looked the other way up the block to see that the line started at the front door to her shop. "They are here for you."

"That can't be right. I'm not giving out bushels of cash or eighty-inch TVs. They must have it wrong." Romey walked up the block to the front of the store.

"It's her," she heard someone say.

"Excuse me," she said, addressing the line of people. "Can I ask y'all why you're here?" She didn't recognize anyone in the line. This was all baffling to her.

"We're here for pie," a young woman told her.

"Okay," Romey said, composing herself. "Maybe that was a dumb question. Why are so many of you here for pie? How did you find out about me?"

"Colby Wells."

"Colby Wells?" The name sounded familiar.

"He makes videos about food with his son," Abel told her. "They have over three million subscribers on their channel. Their videos get shared all over the internet."

"He wrote about you too. His articles get published with every major news outlet." The woman handed her phone to Romey, and she saw a picture of herself from a few years ago when she was named executive pastry chef at her last job.

The Crusty Petal is one of those places that every town should have but doesn't. As soon as you walk in, not only are you greeted by the intoxicating smells of butter and sugar, but the owner of the shop warmly smiles at you, making you feel like it's a place you want to settle down and stay in. She took the time out to speak to me about each of her pies, not knowing who I was. She even let me sample a few things she was experimenting with. I found her to be delightful and personable, completely without pretension, despite her background at some of the swankiest restaurants in the country. She is the kind of owner more establishments should have. Dear reader, I cannot begin to describe to you the simple but evolved flavors of the half dozen or so slices I sampled that day. Delicious isn't a strong enough word. I am telling you, if you get the chance to go to Ms. Michaels's shop and try her pies, you will not regret it. It's worth the trip from anywhere.

"You should see the video he posted," the woman whose phone she was holding told her. "He can't say enough good things about you."

"I . . ." Romey was at a loss for words. "You get a free slice," she said to the woman. "I've got pies in the oven!" She ran to the back door of the shop, Abel right at her heels. Luckily, the pies were perfectly cooked when she pulled them out. She put them on the cooling rack and then sat heavily on the stool next to the counter. "What are we going to do? There has to be a hundred people out there."

"I texted Chief," Abel told her. "The crowd . . . we might need some help."

She nodded and then pulled out her cell phone and called Gray. He answered on the first ring. "What's the matter?"

"Can you ask my father to come over and watch Lily? I need you to come down to the shop."

He didn't ask her why. He agreed and was there within ten minutes. Callahan came too, with two of his deputies. They immediately started to monitor the line.

But they weren't the only ones who showed. Everyone who worked for Carey Norton showed up just as it was time for Romey to open.

She looked at Gray as Anna walked through the back door. "I called for reinforcements when I saw the line. It's going to take more than Alice, me, and Abel to get through this."

Romey looked up at Gray, her heart racing, the anxiety about what was ahead twisting in her stomach.

"We'll be fine." He squeezed her shoulder. "Tell us what you need us to do, and we'll do it."

She nodded and took a deep breath before she started issuing orders.

They had completely sold out of everything in a little over two hours. She'd had to limit the number of whole pies she sold to ensure that they could serve as many people as possible. She'd had put Gray on the cash register. She had Alice and Anna on making and serving coffee. She had Kavi and George, Carey's landscaper and maintenance man, counting the customers and letting them into the shop in groups of ten. She and Abel took orders and packed to-go boxes. She had never moved so quickly her entire life.

When everything was gone, she had Callahan make the announcement to the forty or so people still waiting in line. She couldn't believe there were still people there. Callahan reported that they had started turning people away about a half hour into opening. He'd known she would never have enough to sell to everyone. He told her those people said they would be back tomorrow.

She flinched. She had never sold out so fast. All the small to-go boxes were gone. They'd even run out of coffee. She would need to make an emergency trip to the store just to be able to open tomorrow.

She went into her office, closing the door behind her so that she could compose herself for a moment. Everyone who had come to help her was sitting in the front of the shop. She had tried to pay Carey's staff for helping, but they'd refused, looking horrified that she'd offered. "Mr. Norton says we are yours as long as you need us," Anna said, speaking for the rest of them. "We had so much fun today. We'll be back tomorrow."

There was a tap on her office door, and then Gray poked his head in. "Do you mind if I join you?"

"No. Come in."

He shut the door as soon as he stepped in, and she moved toward him and wrapped her arms around him, resting her head against his chest. "You're a champ at the register. If you ever need a job, I'll hire you in a second."

"You're a hit." He rested his lips on her forehead. "I'm so proud of you."

"I'm not sure how I feel about being a hit," she said honestly. "That was never my goal. When I opened this place, I just wanted to make pies and be able to earn enough so I could buy a little house in town to raise my baby in."

"If you keep having a day like you had today, you'll be able to buy your house in a couple of weeks."

She looked up at him. "I don't need to buy a house anymore. Do I?"

"Already filled out the form to put your name on the deed to ours. All you have to do is sign it. My father's assistant will notarize it for us."

She grinned up at him. "Some men buy chocolate and send flowers. You romance me by telling me you filled out some legal paperwork." He didn't need to make promises or fill her head with sweet words. There was that little part of her that wanted to keep her guard up, that wanted not to trust him. But it was harder to keep that wall up around her heart than it was to let him in. Everything he did showed her he was serious about her. "You really know how to seduce a woman."

"I know. Men should take lessons from me."

"Thank you for coming when I needed you. I wouldn't have been able to get through this day without you."

"You didn't need me. You would have figured things out on your own. You always do." She had a feeling that he was talking about more than just today, that his thoughts went so much deeper.

"You're right. Needing you sounds pathetic. Needing you makes it seem like if you left, my whole world would crumble and I would be useless without you. Having someone so weak sounds very unattractive to me. So maybe I don't need you, but I want you. In my life. Choosing to have you as my partner seems like a much bigger thing."

"So I'm your partner now?"

"What do you want me to say? Boyfriend? That sounds so sixteen."

"We're officially together now?"

"Dude, I moved in with you. I washed your underwear yesterday. What more do you need?"

"Nothing." He laughed softly. "I was giving you a hard time. I like to hear you say nice things to me."

She rested her head back on his chest. "I love you, you know. I'm afraid it's terminal."

"You make loving me sound like a bad thing."

"I thought it would go away, but it never did. It got worse over time."

"When are you going to marry me?" he asked, and it surprised her.

"I don't know. When are you going to ask?"

"If I ask you, will you say yes?"

"It depends on when you ask."

"It's too soon, isn't it?"

She nodded. It was. She felt like he wanted things wrapped up in a neat bow. He wanted a wife and a family, to be settled after being away for so long. But as much as she wanted to move on from that, the nearly two years he had been gone stayed with her. The radio silence had hurt her. Eight weeks of him being here didn't change the fact that he had left in the first place.

There was another knock at the door. She didn't bother moving away from Gray before she told whoever it was to come in.

"I made a list of things we're going to need for tomorrow, Miss Romey," Abel said, poking his head in through the door. "Miss Anna said she would take me to the store in her car. Can you look over the list?"

"Of course." She let go of Gray and went over to him. Running her own business was a lot easier than being in love.

* * *

Two days later Romey sat in the front of her empty shop. It was just a little past twelve, and for the third day in a row they had sold out of everything by nine. She had taken Anna on to help with the baking, and even with the three of them, they couldn't produce nearly enough to satisfy the demand. She refused to cut corners to mass-produce pies that lacked the homey flavor she put into everything she made. She had pride in her individual creations.

The hype from the YouTube video and article would die down soon. The crowds would leave. Her regulars would be able to return. Life would return to normal. Or at least to her new version of normal. She thought about Gray and their daughter. About how she was never there to see Lily wake up in the morning. About how Gray had stepped up without her asking or expecting him to. He took care of Lily all day. He made dinner for her every night. He had taken so much off her plate.

She owed him something for that. She owed him time. She was going to close the shop. One day a week for now, maybe two later on. One of her old culinary school friends had contacted her after she saw the video. She'd offered to help Romey set up a system for shipping her pies nationwide.

She knew she was going to have to hire another baker; she couldn't keep Anna with her forever. She hated having to look at résumés and interview people. Callahan had brought her Abel, and she wished he could bring her next employee too.

There was a knock on the window, causing Romey to look up. There were big signs on the doors and windows warning people that the shop had sold out for the day. But it wasn't a customer looking for pie. It was her mother. This time her hair was swept up. Her long, flowy skirt was missing. Instead she wore a pair of jeans, ballet flats, and a simple fitted T-shirt. If it hadn't been for the bold streak of gray through her curls, no one would have been able to tell that she was a woman in her late fifties.

Romey got up and unlocked the door. She was surprised to see her mother there, thinking that she had left town after their last run-in. It was what her mother did. She left. Especially if she didn't get her way. She'd left them when Daddy refused to move them from this town. She'd disappeared from their lives when she couldn't take them to live on a commune. She'd stopped communicating regularly with them when Charlie decided to join the military and Callahan became a police officer and she went to a traditional school. Romey had gotten so used to her leaving. It didn't surprise her anymore.

It was when her mother was there that it was the most surprising.

"Come in." She stepped aside and let her mother pass.

"Hello, Ramona," she said quietly.

"Why did you name me Ramona, anyway? It doesn't seem like a name you would pick."

"Honestly, I wanted to name you Rainbow, but your father wouldn't let me. I liked the Ramona books when I was kid, so we settled on that."

"What about Charlie? How did he get his name?"

"It was my great grandfather's name. Funnily enough, he wasn't a performer. He worked as a ship builder. Why do you want to know?"

She shrugged. "I was curious. It helps me to understand how you think. Also, I'm glad that you didn't name me Rainbow. I would have hated that shit."

"You look like me, but you are very much your father's child."

"You think I'm boring and that there is no romance or adventure in my soul."

"I never said that. You've got a lot of romance in your soul. You've been secretly in love with your brother's best friend for over a decade."

"I never told you that."

"You didn't have to. I may not have been here a lot as you got older, but when I was here, I saw things. The year you graduated from high school, Gray cut his sailing trip short and surprised you at your graduation. Your face lit up when you saw him. Later that day, I saw him pull you behind that big old tree in the backyard and kiss you. I saw how you looked at each other then."

"Then why are you so surprised about us now? The fact that you think he's going to throw me away for someone else like him is insulting. Not to him, but to me. It's like you don't think I'm good enough to for him."

"I think you're too good for him. For the whole family."

"Carey Norton isn't a bad man. He had a fling with Aunt Celesta. I don't believe for one moment he ever made any promises to her or knew that she was pregnant. He wants to acknowledge Callahan as his son. Callahan is the one who's not letting it happen."

She shifted on her feet nervously. "I spoke to her. Her story changed. Not all of it, but some big parts of it."

Romey wasn't surprised. "Where is she? Callahan wants to speak to her."

"She doesn't want to be found. She won't answer his questions anyway. I hate it when she does this."

"If you knew your sister acted this way, then why did you say anything? You can't go around blowing up people's lives without any thought. That little stunt affected not only Callahan's and Carey's lives but all of us around them."

"It wasn't a stunt. Callahan should know who his father is."

"Maybe he should, but you can't tell me that announcing it in front of everyone at my baby's birthday was a well-thought-out idea. You could have told Callahan privately anytime in the last eighteen years."

"I don't know why it came out right then. I was sitting there at a lakefront mansion, thinking about all the unfair labor practices and greed it took to accumulate that much wealth. Patricia Norton liked to throw a charity ball, but let's face it, she was no damn humanitarian. Look into their past. Their family brought the slave trade to Virginia."

"Okay, so we'll kill Gray as a sacrifice."

Her mother's eyes went wide. "I want to believe that people evolve and attitudes change, but if Gray's mother was still alive, there is no way she would be accepting you with open arms into her family. You can't tell me that Gray would have defied his mother's wishes and ended up with you."

"I'm not sure I can give you a good enough answer. His mother is dead, and there are a half dozen other reasons that Gray and I were never together before. But I know that

Gray loves me. I feel it. He loves Lily. He wouldn't let anyone mistreat her or disrespect me. I'm not thinking about what if. I'm thinking about what is."

"You sound so sure of him."

"I'm more sure of him than I am of you, truthfully."

"Me?" She seemed shocked, which made Romey laugh.

"You can't be serious. You are the textbook definition of a dysfunctional parent."

"Are you saying I don't love you?"

"No. Loving someone and being a good parent to them are two different things. You left us. You didn't like it here, so you left your children. More than once. And if you don't know, I'm now going to tell you how incredibly fucked up that was. But I can forgive you for that, because we needed stability and that's what Daddy gave us."

"I came back for you. I tried to take you with me later on."

"Who cares if you came back? You shouldn't have left in the first place. I would die before I left Lily. I get nervous leaving her with her father till three o'clock. You would have to drag me away and lock me up to keep me away from her. You always acted like it was okay. It was never okay. It wasn't okay with me or Charlie. It hurt us. It told us that you cared more for yourself than you did about us."

"I didn't know how to be a mother to two children who didn't want to be mothered. You came to me one day after school and scolded me because I never gave you a bedtime hour or made you take a bath. I was giving you freedom, and you were telling me that everything I did was wrong!"

"It doesn't excuse what you did. It doesn't excuse you for continuing to not be there. I've told you how I feel more these last few days because as much as you drive me insane,

I want to have some kind of relationship with you. I can't hold everything in anymore. You should have been at Charlie's funeral! You should have been there before that when he was discharged from the service. When he was battling an addiction to painkillers. When Daddy was so in denial about what was going on with Charlie that Callahan and I didn't know what to do. You should have come when I asked you to be there for the birth of my baby. You should have met her long before she turned one. You should have tried harder to be a mother. Even if it was difficult for you, you should have tried."

Luna was quiet, her eyes filling with tears. "You had Angela. You've always had Angela. I couldn't have dealt with Charlie. You think I spent twenty-one years in a traveling circus and didn't run into anyone with an addiction? Name an addiction, and I can tell you someone in our family who had one. I'm not normal. I don't know how to behave in those types of situations. Angela was better for you. I resent the hell out of the woman for taking my husband, but I respect the hell out of her too."

"She didn't take your husband," Romey said. Her mother's admission wasn't lost on her. Luna was probably right. She wasn't who Romey had needed in those moments.

"I always thought we would get back together. I adored your father. I still love him. He made me feel safe, but I wasn't the right wife for him. I may not have been the right mother for you, but I would like to be a grandmother. I know I hurt you and I'm sorry I can't be who you need me to be, but I would like a chance to be in your life."

"I want you in my life too. But there needs to be boundaries, and I need to be able to tell you when you are overstepping them."

"I agree to that."

"Good."

"Now give your mama a hug." She rushed forward and wrapped her arms around Romey. "I just spent the last two days telling everyone that my daughter was the famous baker in town. I might need you to make a pie for a gentlemen friend I've been seeing."

Romey sighed and then laughed as she returned her mother's hug. She couldn't expect her to change, but she could meet her where she was.

CHAPTER TWENTY-TWO

Food brings people together on many different levels. It's nourishment of the soul and body; it's truly love. —Giada De Laurentiis

Gray sat across from Romey at their kitchen table. She was still in her pajamas, her hair pulled high on top of her head, and she was sipping coffee out of a mug that said *I bake so I don't punch people in the face.*

"What are you grinning at?" she asked.

"I don't know. I think you're cute."

It had been a few weeks since the story of her shop had gone viral. Three weeks of hundreds of people buying her pies. What people didn't understand about her was that she was a good businesswoman who still wanted to serve the locals who had kept her shop open before the world knew about it.

She'd set up an online system for out-of-towners to not only reserve spots in line but preorder their selections. She'd limited the amount of pie one person could order. She'd also set up a line just for the locals who wanted to enjoy her shop. It was never packed inside, even though the steady stream of customers didn't stop all day. She had made it manageable. They made only what her three-person baking team could handle. Gray's father happily allowed Anna to continue to work for Romey until she found someone she wanted to hire permanently. Gray was pretty sure it would be a while before she did.

"You've got weird taste." She grinned back at him.

"I like having coffee with you on Sundays."

"It makes us seem almost like a normal couple. I still don't know why you get up with me. I've been a baker for ten years. My body won't allow me to sleep past six. You can stay in bed as long as you want."

"What's the point of staying in bed without you?" He had been on her schedule since she moved in a little over a month ago. He actually slept now at night. The entire night through. It had been years since he had been able to do that. Even before he went to Syria, he hadn't. Before Charlie died, he had never managed more than a few hours of sleep. His mind was always racing at nights, occupied with uncomfortable thoughts. Filled with uncertainty about his future. Worrying about his seemingly lost friendship with a longtime friend.

It was as if the world had righted itself. Things felt calm for the first time in too many years. The only thing he wanted was to be able to call Romey his wife, to introduce her to the world that way. Maybe there was no need for marriage. Neither one of them had grown up with examples of long, loving marriages, but it still kind of meant something to him. He wouldn't push her. She knew what he wanted. It was up to her to decide if she wanted the same thing.

"Where do you want to go for dinner tonight?" she asked him. "My treat. Pick anyplace you want. We can go to one of those fancy joints where you have to wear a tie."

"You still have that green cocktail dress?" he asked her.

"Do I still own it? Yes. Can I still fit it? No. I'm almost positive I would blow the back out of that thing if I tried to zip it up. It's all your fault too. If you hadn't gotten me pregnant, I would still be able to fit it."

"You looked damn good in that dress. Buy a new one."

"What made you think of that dress?"

"I thought about that dress a lot. It was the downfall of my engagement. You had no business looking that good around me. Although in all fairness, I find you just as sexy in a nightgown with cats all over it."

"You're just horny."

He laughed at her bluntness. "My friend Trevor actually reminded me of it when we met up a few weeks ago. He said he tried to hit on you at my engagement party."

"Is Trevor the cute blond that looks like a Ken doll?"

"Yeah."

She shrugged. "He seems like the type of guy who'll flirt with a hole in the wall. I didn't pay him much attention."

"He offered me a job at the clinic he's opening up in town. They are converting that old department store on Route 17 to a medical building. If everything goes right with the town and the zoning board, it's set to open in November."

"Why didn't you tell me about this before?"

"I wasn't sure I was interested in taking the job. I've had a few offers since I've been home. One at my former practice. One at the hospital. None of them appealed to me. But this offer is kind of interesting. I can work part-time if I want."

"I knew you would be going back to work eventually. I couldn't expect you to be a stay-at-home dad forever, but it has been very nice."

"I don't have to go back to medicine yet. It depends on what you want. That's why I brought it up. I want your opinion."

"My opinion . . ." She was thoughtful for a moment. "As long as we can still have dinner together every night, I'm good."

"We'd have to put Lily in day care at least a few days a week."

"She'll survive, like millions of other children do."

"We could hire a nanny."

"Nope. Day care. She likes to be with other children."

"What about other children?" he asked seriously. "For us. I was joking about it at the party, but how do you feel about it?"

She was quiet for a long moment. "If we have a boy, I want to name him Charlie. If it's a girl, I would like to name her Charly but spell it with a *y*."

He nodded. "I'm okay with that."

"Give me a year, Gray. Let me be with you for a year. No pregnancy. No big changes. No major upsets. I would like things to be calm for a year."

"You know we can't control outside forces. Sometimes things happen that we would never expect, but I can give you a year. Or longer if you need it. I just want to know where you stand."

She got up, walked around the table, slid her hands up his face, and kissed him. "I guess I'm standing with you."

* * *

Romey walked out of her backyard and into her father's. It was an odd thought—her backyard. Their backyard. She wasn't sure when the shift in her mind had happened. When she'd stopped thinking of the house as Gray's and taken ownership of it too. Her father's home had been her safe place when she was pregnant and terrified of raising a baby alone. But she'd known it wasn't a permanent home.

If someone had told her she would end up living in the ugly green house, she would have called them a liar. But her name was on the deed. Gray had asked her if she wanted to have the house painted a different color. She'd thought it would be one of the first things he did, but he never changed it. He left the decision up to her.

It would stay its ugly green color. So much of the house had changed in the last few months. It was unrecognizable as the one they used to sneak into when they were young. She had a special fondness for the color, for what it symbolized. She didn't give a damn if anyone thought it was ugly. It meant something to her.

She opened the sliding door and walked into the kitchen. Callahan was coming into the kitchen from the other side of the house.

"Hey." He nodded at her.

"Hey, yourself," she said in return.

"Where's my baby?" he asked, referring to Lily.

"Gray took her to see his father. Carey's brother is visiting. He wants them to meet Lily. They're going to look after Lily while Gray and I go out to dinner."

"Oh." Callahan still hadn't gone through with the paternity test. He wasn't acknowledging that Carey possibly and probably was his biological father. He acted as if nothing had happened. It was a very Callahan thing to do. "I've been missing her. Since Gray has been home, I don't get to see her as much anymore."

"You know where the house is. Bring yourself on over anytime you want." Romey had the feeling he was avoiding Gray. They were fine when they had their family dinners once a week, but the two men didn't do more than talk about sports or television. They probably needed to have a conversation, but neither of them was going to make the first step.

Her father walked into the kitchen then. She was struck when she saw him. He didn't look like himself. Or at least the self he had been for the past year since Charlie died. It had been happening little by little, she supposed. He had been working on her and Gray's house, which had filled his time. He was also seeing Carey socially. They had lunch at least once a week. A few nights ago they'd gone on a double date to a movie with a woman Carey had been casually seeing. She was happy her father was starting to live life again. There was a time she'd thought he would never recover. He had never come to terms with how Charlie had died.

She had gone to counseling with a professional who specialized in addictions. Callahan had gone with her, claiming that he didn't want her driving alone at night while she was pregnant. He'd sat in on every one of those sessions, barely saying a word. They'd never spoken of it afterward. But it had helped. Both of them. It had made her realize that they had done everything they could for Charlie.

"I thought I heard your voice," her father said to her.

"Hi, Daddy. You look sharp today."

He looked down at himself. "Angela . . . she made me buy new shirts. She threw out my old ones. She had the nerve to say we couldn't donate them because not even the less fortunate would want them. Can you believe that?"

"I can." Romey stifled a laugh. "She should have made you do that years ago."

"There's nothing wrong with my clothes. Or my furniture."

"Furniture?"

"We're getting a new living room and bedroom set. I think it looks fine, but I've had that stuff since you were kids, so I guess it's time. She wants to paint the living room too."

Romey approved of the idea. A refresh would be good. "It's makeover time for everything."

"She's going to move in here," he told them. "We talked about it. There's no sense in paying bills for two houses."

"That's great news, Uncle Cy," Callahan said. "I'm happy for you." He looked at Romey. He didn't have to say anything. She could read his mind.

Abel.

Her father was so kind to let a stranger stay there, but Abel was her and Callahan's responsibility.

"Is Abel here?" Romey asked.

"Of course he is. If he's not at work, he's home. I had to go tell the boy to take a nap. He kept asking me if there was anything I needed him to do."

"He's a good guy, Daddy. I need to talk to him. Can you call him?"

He stepped out of the kitchen and yelled up the stairs for Abel. Moments later they heard his booming footsteps as he hurried down. "Yes, sir? Hello, Chief. Hello, Miss Romey."

"Romey said she wants to talk to you. Sit down and listen."

He nodded, took a seat at the kitchen table, and looked up at her expectantly. She sat down across from him. "I need to tell you something. It's not up for discussion. I'm just letting you know."

"Okay," he said warily.

"I'm getting a new car tomorrow. I'm giving you my old one. I know you have been saving up to buy one, and my car may not be a girl getter, but it runs good. You're a newly licensed eighteen-year-old male driver. Your insurance is going to be through the roof. You can use the money you saved for the costs."

Abel's mouth dropped opened. "Why are you all doing so much for me?" he asked seriously. "I don't deserve it."

"It's not so much," Romey said. "In this family, we share what we have. Plus, I'm tired of picking you up and dropping you off every day. It's time you got yourself to work." She winked.

He continued to look baffled. "I don't know what to say."

"Say thank you," Cyrus urged. "Ask her when she's dropping off the keys. You need to have more of a social life. This car will help you."

"Thank you so much." He placed his large hand over Romey's. "To all of you. I promise I won't cause you any trouble."

"You've been great, Abel," Callahan told him. "I'm proud of you."

"There's one more thing," Romey started. "My father was so nice to let you stay here with him, but we have to think about where you're going to live next. Gray and I were talking, and we thought you might want to stay with us once our basement is done. Gray's father said he would be more than happy if you came to stay with him. He lives alone in that huge house and would love for it not to be empty. You could also stay in the guest house if you would prefer. Gray used to live there. You would have complete privacy."

"Hold on now," her father said. "Why would Abel be leaving this house?"

She glanced at Callahan, surprised by her father's reaction. "We thought you might like to have a child-free house to enjoy with Angela."

He shook his head firmly. "You thought wrong. I never said anything about wanting an empty house. That's what a house is for. People." He looked down at Abel. "I can't make you stay, because you're eighteen years old and the idea of living on a waterfront estate sounds tempting, but I think you should stay here."

"Yes, sir." He nodded. "I think so too." He looked back to Romey. "If you don't mind, I would like to stay here."

"Of course I don't mind."

"Thank you." He got up from the table. "Thank you, Pop," he said to her father before he walked out.

"What is wrong with you?" her father asked her. "That boy needs to be taken care of. He's been thrown away by everyone in the world. You can't take him out of here."

"I'm sorry. I didn't think. I should have spoken to you first."

"You're right you should have spoken to me first. He's a good boy. He makes me take walks with him after work. He said it's good for me to exercise, but I think he needs to talk. Angela likes him too. He demolishes her food and tells her she's the best cook in the country. He's a kid who needs raising still. He needs guidance. He needs to feel safe. My son was taken from me, but it's like someone put Abel in my path because they knew we needed each other."

"Oh." Romey's eyes filled with tears. "I know how much you miss Charlie, Daddy. We all do."

"He was Abel's age when he left." He looked through the sliding door, his eyes unfocused. "I sent my son off to the military during a goddamn war. He was never the same." He looked back at them. "I blame myself, you know. I couldn't afford to send him to that school he wanted. I should have taken out that loan. Maybe he would have turned out more like Gray. He wanted so badly to be like Gray. But at the time I didn't think that would be possible for him."

"Charlie made his own choices, Uncle Cy." Callahan walked closer to him. "If he had wanted to go to college, he would have. He could have gone locally for a while. He could have worked his way through. He could have busted his ass like Romey did when she was in high school and got scholarships. Charlie wanted Gray's access. The opportunities that Gray's money gave him. But Gray worked hard. He went to one of the best medical schools in the country. Money didn't get Gray there. Charlie wanted the college experience. Charlie didn't want college. If he did, he would have made it happen."

"Instead he chose to stay in the Marines for twelve years. Came back home with metal embedded in him. Shoving pills down this throat every five minutes." Cy banged his fist on the counter. "I didn't want to believe it. Not my son. You both tried to tell me, but I didn't want to listen. He would always pull himself together around me, but I saw the changes in him. I saw that the four of you weren't close as you used to be. I saw him becoming more bitter and angry by the day. I should have said something. I should have stopped him."

"How could you have stopped him?" Romey asked him. "We tried. All three of us tried. Gray offered to send him to rehab. Callahan's second job was to make sure Charlie didn't get into trouble. I begged him to stop. But we had to come to terms with the fact that Charlie had to want to stop in order for him to stop."

"I was his father. I might have been able to help him."

"Do you understand how that medication works?" Callahan asked. "It attaches to receptors in the brain. It literally messes with your mind. Willpower and tough love weren't enough. He needed serious medical intervention. Charlie didn't want it. He thought because his doctor gave it to him, it was okay. None of could have combated that. You cannot blame yourself. You did your job for him. You were a good father to all of us."

Callahan pulled Cyrus into a hug and held on to him tightly. They embraced for a long moment.

"Hey," Romey said after a while. "I want to get in on this hug too."

Her father pulled slightly away from Callahan and smiled at her. "Come on, then."

She was glad they had found Abel. If it weren't for him, they might never have gotten to this healing place.

CHAPTER TWENTY-THREE

Baking is therapy.—Paul Hollywood

Gray pounded on the door of his cell. He screamed so loud that his voice went hoarse. His voice wasn't alone. He could hear the others screaming too. The men he had been captured with. They could all see what was happening. They knew what would happen every time they dragged Rachel away.

She didn't deserve this. She was just like him, a U.S. citizen in a place they weren't wanted. But no one knew his truth. Even when he tried to out himself.

"We checked all of your papers. You have nothing to offer us."

His forged documents had been too good. He was from one of the oldest, wealthiest families in the United States. His father was a DC lawyer who had represented the powerful. Gray would have been much more useful to them than to her. He deserved the brutality she was getting.

He was the one who had betrayed a friend. Who'd left the woman he loved. He was the one who had hurt people with his selfishness. He deserved to be the one who was being dragged away.

"Leave her alone!" he screamed, until his voice gave out.

* * *

"Gray!" He felt himself being shaken, and he opened his eyes to find he wasn't in a tiny damp cell. He was in his house, in his king-sized bed with his expensive sheets. Romey was looking down at him, fear mixed with concern in her eyes.

She pulled the comforter off him. His body was drenched in sweat. He sat up and looked at the clock. It was past seven in the morning. He usually never slept in so late. Especially on Sundays when Romey was home. He always got up with her. But they had been up late last night, watching some dystopian movie. It was fiction, yet it had struck a chord with him. He had been around great suffering and extreme poverty. The movie didn't come close to how hard some people's lives were.

"Why did you let me sleep in?" he asked her as he got out of bed and began to pull off the sheets.

"That's all you have to say to me?" she asked him. "I thought someone was hurting you. You were yelling."

"I'm sorry," he said, not looking at her. "I didn't mean to scare you."

"What were you dreaming about?"

"Nothing." He shook his head. "I don't remember. Just drop it."

"I will not drop it. You kept saying, 'Leave her alone.' Who were you talking about?"

"A woman I met while I was in Syria. She's dead now." He walked into the bathroom. "Please, Romey. I don't want to talk about it."

"But I want to talk about it." She followed him. "You came home skinny, exhausted, and on edge. I know something happened when you were away. You need to tell me what it was. I'm tired of not knowing. You owe me this."

"The American woman that was killed in Syria . . . the one they talked about on the news whose father runs the telecom company? I knew her. She was the girlfriend of one of my colleagues. I was with her when she was captured. I was there the day she died."

Romey sat down hard on the edge of the bathtub. "You were captured with her," she said softly. "For how long?"

"Nine, ten months." He shook his head, trying to shake the effects of the dream out of his brain. "I don't remember the exact number of days. We were released, and then we were sent to France to recover. I spent eight weeks at a medical center, where I attended therapy every day. I was too much of a mess to come home right away. That's why I took the last assignment in Central America." He paused and took a breath. It was still hard for him to say. "I was supposed to fly home the day they took us. Six months. Six months turned into almost two years."

"Why the hell didn't you tell me?"

"What would be the point? It wouldn't have changed anything."

"Are you out of your mind?" she yelled at him. "Of course it would have changed things."

"I didn't want you feeling sorry for me then, and I don't want you feeling sorry for me now. I made my choice. I knew the risks when I volunteered for that assignment. It's my fault I wasn't here."

"You lied to me." Her voice was quiet, as if she was having a revelation.

He was surprised by her accusation. "I didn't lie to you."

"What would you call it? Creative storytelling? Dancing around the truth? An omission? It's all bullshit. You lied to me, and you would have kept lying to me if I didn't pull it out of you."

"I didn't want you to worry about me."

"You never gave a damn if I worried about you. I didn't know what happened to you when you first disappeared. I thought you were dead. You weren't concerned that I was worried then. What difference does it make now? You don't get to pick and choose when you care about how I feel."

"That's not fair! I was so riddled with guilt when Charlie died. I couldn't look at you or your family."

"Charlie died because he overdosed on pills. It had nothing to do with you or me or any of us. He was on a path of self-destruction. I loved my brother, but in the end, I barely knew him."

"You don't know the whole story. I had a bigger role to play in this than you think."

"Then tell me. I have the right to know."

"I betrayed him. The year you turned sixteen was the year I started to realize that I liked you. Charlie noticed too. He got so mad at me, and he forbid me from touching you. He asked me to give him my word, and I did. I broke it a week later when I kissed you for the first time."

"Oh, come on." She rolled her eyes. "We were all kids then."

"But his feelings never changed. He reminded me of my promise for years. He thought we were from two different worlds and that I would just use you for a while until I found someone else who I thought was better. That's really the reason why we kept things so secretive. Charlie never wanted us together."

She looked up at him. He couldn't read her expression.

"That night at the charity ball you all came to, he confronted me about touching you. He accused me of being elitist. He told me again that I was no good for you. By then our friendship had started to deteriorate. But he had been my best friend; if he felt so strongly about it, I thought maybe he was seeing something in me that I didn't. I decided to get serious about Gwen then. It was what my mother wanted anyway. And then you and I stopped being friends, and I missed you. I realized that I loved you. So I broke things off with Gwen and I went to Charlie to tell him that I wanted to be with you. I went there hoping for his blessing and ended up getting a sucker punch to the face. That's why we fought. It was brutal. I left him laying on the floor with bloody face. I cleaned myself up and came to you, but I was sick with guilt then. I had hurt Gwen. I had fought my oldest friend. I was doubting everything in my life when I came to you, and then Charlie died a few days later. He called me that day. I was with you. Even if I wasn't, I wouldn't have picked up. I was furious with him. He died thinking I hated him. It's been years, but I can't help thinking if I had picked up, maybe he would still be alive today."

"I cannot believe that you and Charlie made that kind of decision about my life. Of all the sexist things I've seen him do, this one takes the cake. And the fact that you went along with it . . ."

"He was my best friend. What was I supposed to do?"

"Tell him to fuck off. I would have."

"It wasn't as simple as you make it out to be. Charlie was my first real friend. I wanted to respect his wishes."

"Why didn't you tell me, Gray? How could you have kept this secret from me for so long? I would have spoken to

Charlie if I had known. You both took my choice from me when you decided who I could and could not see."

"I didn't do anything like that."

"Yes, you did. We're a year apart. I wasn't a little girl who needed to be shielded. You should have told him to mind his business and let me decide who I was going to date. I went through years of wondering if my feelings were one-sided. Wondering if you thought I wasn't good enough for you. All of that torture. All of the sneaking around. All of the people we ended relationships with because we were so stuck on each other. All of that because you were too afraid of telling Charlie off. If he was alive, I would knock him on his ass."

"You don't understand. That's a big thing for friends. No guy wants his friend sleeping with his sister!"

"Did Callahan ever care?"

Her question jabbed him. She had him there. "No. He said you could handle yourself."

"He respects me. It's clear you and Charlie didn't."

"That's not true. I love you."

"You loved me so much that you ran away to another continent after you say you betrayed my brother. You left me pregnant when I was grieving. I had to give birth without you. I had to raise Lily without you. I doubted everything I thought I knew about myself because of some stupid promise you made to Charlie. The worst thing about all of this is that you think you have to lie to me to protect me. You lied to me about where you were for all that time. You say you love me, but you can't talk to me about things that really matter. I'm no fragile flower, and the fact that you think that proves you don't love me at all."

She walked away from him then.

"Where are you going?"

"To another continent. I'll have my father notify you that I'm alive."

He thought it best that he not follow her, allow her some time to cool down. But she took Lily, and he didn't see her again at all that day.

* * *

Romey wasn't sure where to go when she left Gray. She was too angry to think. She just knew she had to take her baby and be away from him. She was surprised to find herself at Carey's house. It was the last place Gray would expect her to go. Her father's house was too close, and there were too many memories there. She could picture Charlie and Gray as teenage boys right on the cusp of manhood entering into some kind of weird agreement about who she could and could not date. She could almost understand that it might be something a teenage boy would do, but grown men? It made her blood boil.

She was allowed to enter the property as soon as she announced who she was at the gate. Carey greeted her at the front door, which he opened himself. Not an employee in sight, although she knew that at least one of the caretakers lived there full-time.

"What a pleasant surprise! My two favorite girls." He bent to kiss her cheek, and she handed Lily over to him. "Come in."

"Can we go to your kitchen?"

"Of course." He seemed confused by her request but led the way.

"Would you mind if I stayed here for a little while?"

"Um." He hesitated. "I would love nothing more than to have you here, but can I ask why you need to stay here?"

"I'm very mad at your son. Furious."

She walked into his kitchen, which was any chef's dream. She knew that Anna kept a fully stocked pantry, and she started pulling out flour, eggs, butter, and sugar.

"I would never want to get involved in your relationship, but since you are using my house as a hideout, can I ask you what he did?"

"He lied to me! More than once. Big lies. Huge lies." She pulled out a large bowl and a mixer and started putting together the ingredients to make cookies. She didn't know any other way to channel her anger. When her mother left, Romey had taken over most of the cooking in the house. Her father had worked here for twelve hours a day. Charlie had taken care most of the outdoor chores and some of the cleaning. When she was cooking and baking, she could be alone with her thoughts. It was how she processed things.

Sugar cookies were easy to make. She could make the recipe in her sleep. She could keep her body busy while her anger coursed through her. Rage baking had gotten her through a lot of tough times.

"What did he lie to you about?"

"He never told me about the dumb promise he made to Charlie which completely and totally screwed up the course of our relationship. It made us stay away from each other for years, and when we were together, it forced us to keep everything a secret. I thought all that time that he never wanted to try to make things work with me because he was too afraid of disappointing you and Patricia."

"You know that's not true."

"I do now. Gray never told me that he had gotten into a fistfight with Charlie after he told him about us. He never told me that he felt he had betrayed him or that Charlie had called him the day he died and Gray never picked up. All of that caused him to go into a guilt spiral and flee the country. If he just would have told me, I would have talked him down and made him realize that there was nothing he could have done to save Charlie. He would never have had to leave the country and go to Syria and then get captured by rebel forces and be held prisoner for nine months."

She heard Carey's sharp intake of air. "What did you say?"

Tears spilled down her cheeks. "That American woman who was killed . . . Gray knew her. He was with her when she was captured. That's where he was all the time. That's why you didn't hear from him until he was released. He was going to keep that a secret from me. I never would have found out if he hadn't had that dream. How could you say you love someone and keep such a life-altering set of events from them?"

Carey let out a violent swear. "I apologize." He looked at Lily. "Your granddaddy needs to watch his mouth." He looked up at Romey. "I knew he was hiding something; I just didn't know it was that. I can't believe him! I can't believe that organization! I called the director multiple times. The man lied right to my face and told me there was nothing wrong. He told me that Gray was on assignment in a remote area and he would have him contact me as soon as he was able. I should sue the pants off them."

"You're going to sue the humanitarian organization that provides medical care for the world's poorest people?" She gave a watery laugh.

"Should I sue Gray instead? It's his fault. He deserves a good kick in his behind. I knew something was up. He was different when he came back."

"He could have died, Carey. And all because he wouldn't talk to me. I'm not mad about the stupid promise he made. I'm mad because he didn't feel comfortable enough with me after all these years to tell me about it. Years of pain could have been avoided if he would have just talked to me."

Carey sighed heavily. "It's probably my fault. Gray didn't feel comfortable enough to speak to me either. I thought Cyrus was a good influence on him, and maybe I used that as an excuse to continue to grind so hard and not make enough time for my son. You have every right to be angry with Gray. You stay here as long as you want." He got up. "Me and Lily are going to see about having the guest room set up for you."

CHAPTER TWENTY-FOUR

A good dinner and feasting reconciles everyone.
—Samuel Pepys

The next afternoon Gray knocked on Callahan's door. He couldn't sit at home anymore. He was going stir-crazy in the house alone. The house was meant for a family, for his family, but he had screwed up and was now paying for it. Romey hadn't spoken to him since she'd taken Lily and left. He knew she was safe, though. His father had called and told him.

His father had had a few other choice words for him as well, which made Gray feel worse. He hadn't handled anything right. There was no one else to blame. No excuse. It was his fault, and he took full responsibility for it. He needed to make it right, but he didn't know how.

Callahan opened his door. "You look like shit."

"I know," he said as he stepped inside. "Romey left me."

"Not for good," Callahan said, sounding so sure of himself. "She's just mad."

"Have you spoken to her?" Gray asked hopefully.

"Not about you. I stopped by her shop this morning. She was rage baking in the back. It's when she comes up with her best stuff. Today she made this upside-down apple pecan pie that was damn good. She was working on buttermilk pie when I left. I found her a couple of kids from the school who are helping out with taking orders and packing boxes. Its best for everyone if she stays in the kitchen for a while."

He slumped down on the couch. "She found out about Syria."

Callahan nodded. "I believe I suggested you tell her."

"Don't gloat now. I need advice, not an I-told-you-so."

"What advice can I give? You fucked up. You need to apologize, tuck your tail between your legs, and never keep another thing from her as long as you live. I mean, if you get a hangnail or stub your toe, she'd better be the first one you call."

"I know that now. But how do I get her back? She won't talk to me. She left Lily with my father while she went to work today. I went over there this morning to get her, and my father refused."

"He can't refuse to give you your own child," Callahan said. "Not legally."

"He said he didn't want to make Romey mad and that he wanted to get her permission first. He also told me not to ambush her at work or it would make things worse."

"Carey Norton isn't a stupid man."

Gray looked at Callahan, studying his features. Now that he saw the resemblance to his father, he couldn't unsee it. He had been careful about mentioning it to Callahan before. Callahan seemed perfectly content in pretending it had never happened. But it was a huge thing, one that rippled through every part of their family. It had changed things between Romey and her mother. Maybe for the better.

Luna had apologized to Gray before she left, but he didn't know if she had spoken to Callahan. "You mean our father isn't a stupid man."

Callahan blinked at Gray. "I can't say that. I don't know who my father is."

"It's because you won't take a test or even speak to him. My father has already spoken to me about what his plans are. He believes you are his son. He wants you to be his son."

"Then that means we are brothers."

"Yes. We are brothers," Gray said matter-of-factly. "I'm the cute one."

"How could you be so nonchalant about this? I'm the bastard child of the richest man in town. The mayor. I'm the police chief. The youngest one in the town's history. He was on the committee that hired me for the job. Do you know how it would look if that information got out? It would cause a huge scandal."

"It wouldn't. Neither of you knew about the connection when you were hired for the job. Even if people gossiped about it for a while, nothing would come of it. You are qualified for the job, and there hasn't been a single instance of corruption or impropriety. You cleaned the good ole boys out of the force and ended up hiring one of the most diverse forces in the state. It will be fine."

"You don't know that. I have been the topic of conversation in this town before. You remember what it was like when I first came here and word got out about where I had been? People used to cross the street to avoid me. Fathers would threaten me if I even glanced in their daughter's direction. Everyone treated me like I was a thug. I literally had to become a damn police officer for anyone to respect me."

"That's not true. I always respected you."

Callahan looked at him for a long moment. "You were always my friend," he agreed.

"You really do look like him, Callahan."

"I know. I look at the pictures he sent me. I see my face in his. I had always wondered who my father was. What kind of man he was. I can't believe he was so close to me this entire time."

"Let him acknowledge you."

"I can't. It's better for the both of us. I worked too hard to get where I am to have anyone question it."

"Okay." Gray nodded. "That's fair. But we can't go around pretending like nothing has changed. At least let's acknowledge it in private. I've been an only child my entire life. I really could use a brother."

"Okay, Gray. We're brothers. Now what?" Callahan crossed his arms over his chest.

"Brothers do stuff for each other. Like call Romey and convince her to talk to me."

"Nope." He sat next to Gray on the couch. "She's stubborn as hell. I don't want her mad at me. But I will let you sleep in the spare room if she decides she wants to keep the house and kick you out."

Gray sighed. He knew Callahan was joking, but he wasn't sure if Romey would forgive him. He had hurt her again. He might be out of chances this time.

* * *

Romey had gone back to Carey's house after work. Carey was sitting on the floor of the nursery, across from Lily, playing with an old set of wooden building blocks that had been Gray's when he was her age.

She smiled at the sight of the once-powerful defense attorney looking as gentle as a teddy bear with his grandchild. She was glad that he was a regular part of their lives. Not only was he good for Lily, but Romey knew that having an expanded family was good for him. She hoped Callahan would come around one day and let Carey get to know him a little better. They both could benefit from more love. "It's very surreal for me to see the great Carey Norton sitting on the floor playing with a baby. They showed that trial with the actor you defended on television. I watched you make grown men tremble on the stand. I wonder if you would have been so effective if they saw you with a baby."

"I can still make men tremble with fear, missy." He stood up, groaning as he lifted himself off the floor. "Cross-examining witnesses was my specialty. Being a grandpa is also my specialty. I'm good at a bunch of things."

"I know. You're impressive."

"You going home tonight?" he asked.

"You kicking me out?"

"Of course not. I love having people in the house. You can stay here forever, but I know you won't. Gray came here to see Lily today," he said quietly. "He spent most of the day here."

"I figured he would. He loves his daughter."

"And you. I've never seen a man look so pathetic. You should talk to him."

"I don't know what to say. It all snowballs for me when I think about it."

"Give yourself a little more time. But not too much. Lily misses her father. He wanted to take her home with him today. I told him he couldn't unless he got permission from you."

"Thank you for that, Carey. I half expected Lily to be home already. I wouldn't keep her away from her father. No matter what happens between us, he will always be able to see her."

"Nothing is going to happen to you two. I need more grandkids."

She smiled at him. "I'm going to take Lily and head back to town for a few hours. Do you want me to get you anything from the store? A treat maybe?"

"A treat?" he laughed. "I've got three dozen cookies downstairs that you made last night. If you bring me anything, it had better be a salad."

She picked Lily up and took her to her car. It was the one Gray had gotten for her. She still felt weird about it. She had asked the dealer how much the monthly payments were when they went to pick it up. The dealer frowned and shook his head. "Your husband paid in full."

Gray hadn't been there to witness this exchange. She didn't want him to know that she still had hang-ups about money. They were supposed to be starting a life together. That's what people did. They combined finances. Couples did this kind of thing for each other all the time, didn't they? Romey just wanted to be prepared in case anything happened. She had seen women be completely destitute after failed relationships. She didn't want to be in that position. She wanted to be able to take care of her baby and herself if she had to.

"Da?" Lily asked her as she strapped her into her car seat.

Guilt snaked through her. Gray would never abandon Lily. That was one thing Romey was sure of. Even if Romey had to live without him, Lily never would. He wouldn't allow it. "We'll see Daddy later," she assured her baby.

Romey headed back toward the other side of the lake. Angela's birthday was coming. There was a silk scarf Angela had spotted in the little boutique in town that she had fallen in love with. It was something she would never buy for herself. The people in her family didn't buy those types of things. Romey couldn't remember the last time she'd purchased something for herself that hadn't come off the sale rack.

She walked into the boutique with Lily in her arms, feeling like she didn't belong. This store had been in town since she was a kid. The women who shopped here were the kind who would have shunned her mother. As much as Romey was different from her mother, she shared a lot of the same qualities. She looked very much like her. She proudly wore her hair in ringlets. She refused to dress conservatively, like many of the woman did in these small southern towns. Her body wasn't something that needed to be hidden. She would honor her mother in those small ways.

"Hey, Romey!" she was greeted as she walked in. "Hey, sugar," the woman said to Lily.

"Janell! I haven't seen you in forever. How are you, girl?" She and Janell had been friends in high school. Janell had lived a couple of blocks away from her. They'd lost touch when Romey went away to school.

"Pretty good. My little one has been bugging me to go to your shop. He saw the video. I told him I wasn't waiting in that line. We might have a better chance of seeing you if we showed up at your house."

"I don't keep pie at my house." She walked up to the counter and grabbed a pen and one of the business cards they kept near the register. "Here's my cell number. You can call or text me before you come by the shop. I'll put aside whatever you want. No charge."

"My husband would love that. My son, however, isn't interested in the pies. He wants to see you. He says you're famous. He doesn't know you're the same girl who used to mix chocolate milk, applesauce, and mashed potatoes together and then eat it."

"I only did it as a dare, Janell. I can remember some of the things you did as dares too."

"I was terrible." She laughed. "I was also a good time."

"You were. Don't just call me for pie. Just call me in general. I don't have any mommy friends."

"I will." Janelle smiled brightly. She patted her tummy. "I've got a girl cooking up in here. I might be looking for some hand-me-downs."

"Congratulations! I saved everything. It's at my father's house. Let me know when you need it."

"Can I just tell you how happy I am to find out Gray is your baby's father? I knew he had a thing for you in high school. He made sure he had an excuse to talk to you during lunch every day. Only when your brother wasn't looking, though. I was so glad you decided to go away to college. Charlie scared off every boy in town."

"He didn't, did he?"

"He sure did. Ask my brother Joe. You were untouchable."

She'd had no idea that Charlie had been so overprotective, but a lot of things made sense now that she thought about it. No one had asked her out in high school. She'd thought it was her. That no one found her attractive. But it was deeper than that. They had all heard the names their mother was called. She had been a married woman, but she had performed in their town, in her skimpy, brightly colored costumes. She had been judged for it. Some had even called her a whore.

Small-minded assholes. Charlie had wanted her to escape that fate. She just wished she had been more aware.

"Charlie could be an ass."

"All big brothers are. What can I help you with? You want to pick yourself up something nice?"

"I'm here to get my stepmother a birthday present. You wouldn't happen to have any more of those silk scarves? She really liked the purple one."

"We have them. We got in a bunch more too. We're also having a sale on dresses. You're a famous chef now. You should pick yourself up something fancy."

"I do need a new dress. My baby here is the reason I can't fit into my old clothes."

"You tell your mama you're well worth the extra fifteen pounds," she said to Lily. "Gosh, Romey she looks just like you. My son had the nerve to look like his damn daddy. Ears and all."

Janell showed her to the back where the clothes were and let Romey browse alone. Lily rested her head on Romey's shoulder. Her plan was to pick up the scarf and go, but there was a green satin dress that caught her eye. She looked at the price tag. Even on sale it was well over a hundred dollars.

"You should buy it," she heard a voice say. "You have always looked good in green."

Romey looked up to see Gwen. She was surprised and immediately felt a little guilty in her presence. She hadn't forgotten how hurt Gwen had been when she came to see Gray. If it weren't for Romey, she would have been married to Gray by now.

"Hello, Gwen. How are you?"

"Honestly, I was going to walk out of this shop and hope you didn't see me, but that would be silly. We live in the same town. We work close to each other. We are bound to run in to each other from time to time."

Romey didn't know how to respond to that. "I would have avoided you too. You make me feel guilty, but you need to know that Gray never cheated on you. Not once. I barely spoke to him when you two were together. I really thought he was going to marry you."

"You were the only one. After hearing your conversation with the saleswoman, apparently Gray has been in love with you for much longer than I was ever in the picture. You shouldn't feel guilty. If I blame anyone for the breakup, I blame myself. I should have never accepted his proposal. In hindsight, the signs were all there."

"Don't blame yourself. There's a lot of women who wanted to marry Gray."

"Except you, it seems. I was sure that as soon as the world found out he was the father of your baby, there would be a wedding announcement the next day."

"He did take off to another country shortly after my brother died, leaving me pregnant and grieving. Marriage is not the first thing on my mind."

"Okay. You win," she laughed. "I realize how difficult that must have been for you. You opened up your own business, lost your brother, and had a baby in the same year."

"If we are competing in the hurt-feeling Olympics, I clearly come in first place, but that doesn't negate your pain. It doesn't stop me from telling you how sorry I am."

"You're strong, Romey. That's what he loves about you. He was so impressed with your career. How hard you worked to make a name for yourself. And now you're a success. Even my mother is impressed by your pie shop, and she hated you after she found out about the baby."

"Stop by and I'll give you a piece to take to her."

"You're sweet too. I want to hate you, but I always liked you, even when I suspected my fiancé was in love with you."

"I like you too, Gwen. I always wished I had your grace."

"I always wished I had your body."

"Liar."

"It's true. Everyone wants what they can't have." She shrugged. "He's happy, you know. I saw him from a distance with your little girl and his father. He's visibly happy. He's more relaxed. He's even closer to his father. You did that. I'm glad he has you."

"Now I feel extra guilty. Don't be so nice to me. I'm the other woman."

"No, Romey. *I* was the other woman. All of Gray's girlfriends were. You're the one."

"I don't know what to say."

"Go try on the dress. I'll hold your baby. She's beautiful, by the way."

Romey lifted an eyebrow. "You aren't going to steal her or do anything crazy, are you? Don't forget I am from circus folk. I will mess you up."

Gwen was a good enough sport to laugh. "I wouldn't know what to do with a baby. Plus, I've had a run-in with Callahan in his official capacity. I wouldn't want to be on his bad side either."

Gwen smiled at Lily and held out her hands. Lily smiled back and went to Gwen. Romey took that as a good sign and went to try on her dress.

CHAPTER TWENTY-FIVE

Cooking is like love. It should be entered into with abandon or not at all.—Harriet van Horne

Gray drove back to his father's house after he left Callahan's. He couldn't return to that empty house. It didn't feel like home without his family there. His father opened the door, letting him in.

"You're back."

"I am." He looked around the massive house, wondering where Romey could be.

"She just got in," Carey said, reading his mind. "She's in the guest room on this floor."

"Thank you, Dad. For everything."

"You're welcome. Go make things right."

He nodded and went off to find her. The first-floor guest room was more of a suite, with its own private bathroom and sitting area. There was also a deck that looked out over the lake. It was luxurious by anyone's standards.

He spotted Lily first. She was in a playpen holding on to a little stuffed toy that he didn't recognize. She noticed him immediately.

"Da!"

"Hey, baby girl." He picked her up and kissed both her cheeks. It had been only a few hours since he'd last seen her, but he'd still missed her. She showed him her new doll. "Oh, very pretty. Did Mama buy that for you today?"

"It looks like her," Romey said softly. "I couldn't not buy it."

He looked at her. "You can't keep my kid away from me."

"I'm not. I know you were here today. If you hadn't come, I would have been surprised."

"You can't keep yourself away from me either. I won't let it happen. I was wrong." He kissed Lily one more time and put her back in her playpen before he walked over to Romey. "I was stupid and selfish, and I didn't think. I'm sorry. For not talking to you. For keeping things from you. For missing so much of this past year. I love you! I'm in love with you. You're the only person I have wanted to be with since I was seventeen, and I can't go back to life without you. I want to make it up to you, but I don't know how. I can't buy you anything or take you anywhere. I can't do anything for you that you can't do for yourself, except be there for you. So you have to let me know how I can make it up to you. But you've got to come home. We've been chasing after each other for too damn long, and now it's time to stop."

"You aren't going to chase after me anymore?" she asked him, her eyes going wide. "I think I deserve to be followed to the ends of the earth, but that's just my opinion."

"Don't be cute right now. I'm trying to tell you something. If you aren't coming home tonight, then I am staying here."

"It is really nice here," she said, walking away from him. "Look at this view. You got to live here, and yet you spent more nights at our house than you did here. What was wrong with you?"

"I was in love with my best friend's little sister and would rather sleep on a trundle bed instead of in my own room to be near her."

"I should have known something was wrong with you then."

He was so confused by her reaction. She no longer seemed angry or sad. She was calm. He could handle her anger, but he didn't know how to handle her calmness. "What's happening right now?"

"I was coming home tonight. Unfortunately, your daughter loves you a whole lot. She's going to be a such a daddy's girl."

"The only reason you're coming home is for Lily?"

"I didn't say that. Since you're itching to make things up to me, I have some conditions."

"What are they?"

"I want a pet. Maybe two. There're kittens at the shelter. I stopped by and saw them today. I might want a dog too. I always thought it would be nice to have a dog and a cat. We would need to find the right dog, though. So that can wait for now."

"We'll get a kitten. Tomorrow, if you want. Anything else?"

"I want to be friends with Gwen."

"Excuse me?" He hadn't been expecting that one.

"I ran into her today. She's really nice. You were an asshole for hurting her."

"Should I get her a kitten too? You can be friends with whoever you want."

"I want more friends in general. I want us to be a real part of this community. For years I felt like I was sitting on the outside, looking in. But it's changed since we were kids."

"You are a part of the community. People love you here. Every time I leave the house, people ask me about you. I'm happy to do whatever you want."

"There's one more thing." She turned to face him and went down on her knees in front of him. "I would like for you to marry me. Will you?"

He was stunned silent.

"It would be easy for me to blame you for everything, Gray. But there are two of us in this. We couldn't have been together when we were younger. We were in different parts of the country, working in demanding jobs. My job was so important to me. I wouldn't have given up any of the opportunities I had. I would never have been happy being just some doctor's wife. We both know that. I have been holding back from you. For so many years I have been thinking of myself as a single person, and everything I did had to be for the betterment of myself. But that's not true anymore. If I love you, then I have to stop thinking of myself and think of us. I need to be your partner. I have to trust you enough to believe we can navigate life together. I want to be your wife. I want to be able to call you my husband."

"But . . ."

"What about Charlie?" she asked him. "I think I understand about that. Your relationship with him was complicated. I also need to absolve you of your guilt for being away. You suffered enough. We need to put that behind us if we're going to move forward. So what do you say? Will you marry me?"

"No!" he shouted.

"No?" She frowned at him. "You don't want to marry me?"

"Get up." He grabbed her hands and pulled her to her feet. "Of course I want to marry you! I'm supposed to ask you."

"Don't be ridiculous! Women can ask men to marry them. You're being sexist."

"Call it what you want, but I had a plan. I was going to ask your father for permission."

"I don't need his permission."

"It's not for you. It's for him! I bought a ring. I gave it to my father so you wouldn't find it." He ran to the door and yelled for his father.

"Good lord, what is it, Gray?" He yelled back.

"I need the ring."

"Now?"

"Yes, now!"

"It's in the safe. I'll go get it."

He pulled out his cell phone and dialed Romey's father. "You call Callahan and put him on speaker," Gray told her.

"Are you serious?"

"I'm definitely not joking."

Romey shook her head but looked amused and grabbed her cell phone out of her handbag. She called Callahan. He answered at the same time as Romey's father. "Mr. Michaels?"

"Gray, why are you calling me Mr. Michaels? We're past that at this point."

"Romey, what is going on over there?" Callahan asked.

"Gray told me to call you. I think he wants you hear something."

"Mr. Michaels, I'm calling to ask for your permission to marry your daughter. I would have done it in person, but Romey had to be difficult and mess up all my plans."

Cyrus chuckled. "I appreciate the sentiment, but Romey sure as hell doesn't need my permission. You certainly have my blessing, though."

"Thank you, sir. Callahan? Any objections?"

"Would it matter if I did have any? Romey will be married to you, not me."

"Good."

His father returned with the ring box at that moment. Gray took it from him and went down on his knee in front of Romey. "Romey Michaels. Pain in the ass. Love of my life. Will you marry me?"

She tilted her head to the side and looked down at him. "I'm a little annoyed that you turned down my proposal. I asked you first."

"Romey," he warned.

"Okay." She grinned at him.

"Okay? I need a better answer than that."

"Yes, you dummy. Yes. Yes. Yes!"

"It's about damn time," Carey said. Gray barely heard him. He was too busy kissing his future wife.